Other books by Kat Meads:

Fiction
Not Waving (Livingston Press, 2001)
Stress in America (2001)
Wayward Women (1995)

Non-fiction
Born Southern and Restless (1996)

Poetry
Quizzing the Dead (2002)
Night Bones (2000)
Filming the Everyday (1989)
The Queendom (1998)

SLEEP

A NOVEL

Kat Meads

Livingston Press
at
The University of West Alabama

copyright © 2004 Kat Meads
All rights reserved, including electronic text
ISBN 1-931982-27-9 library binding
ISBN 1-931982-28-7 trade paper
Library of Congress Control Number 2003114280
Printed on acid-free paper
Printed in the United States of America, Livingston, AL
Hardcover binding by: Heckman Bindery
Typesetting and page layout: Jessica Meigs
Proofreading: Margaret Sullivan, Jessica Meigs,
Daphne Moore, Joe Taylor,
Gina Montarsi, Audrey Hamilton
Cover design: Gina Montarsi
Cover art: Philip Rosenthal
This is a work of fiction.
You know the rest: any resemblance
to a person living or dead is coincidental.

Those paraphrased, quoted and misquoted by Repeat (and others): Kathy Acker, Martin Amis, Benedict Arnold, Baptist hymnal circa 1956, Djuna Barnes, Bommi Baumann, Samuel Beckett, John Berger, John Berryman, Alexander Borbély, Elizabeth Bowen, Leo Braudy, Peter Brooks, William Burroughs, Lewis Carroll, Angela Carter, Nicolae Ceausescu, Raymond Chandler, Sidonie-Gabrielle Colette, Samuel Coleridge, Joseph Conrad, Dupont de Nemours, Thomas De Quincey, Fyodor Dostoyevsky, Alan Dugan, The Earl of Rochester via Ezra Pound, T.S. Eliot, Carolyn Forché, E.M. Forester, The Founders, Jonathan Franzen, John Freccero, Patricia Highsmith, Hildegard von Bingen, Karen Horney, Ted Hughes, Henry James, Randall Jarrell, Milan Kundera, Susan Lehman, Vladimir Lenin via Peter Weiss, Malcolm X, John Milton, Lorrie Moore, Vladimir Nabokov, Sergey Nechaev, Howard Nemerov, Friedrich Nietzsche, Eva Peron via V.S. Naipaul, Pierre Proudhon, Aleksandr Pushkin via Andrew Bely, Red Brigades member, John Reed, Laura Riding, Rainer Maria Rilke, Arthur Rimbaud, Phyllis Rose, William Shakespeare, Robert Skidelsky, Lee Smith, St. Benedict, St. Just, Charley Starkweather, Lucy Stone, Malcolm Summers, Tania/a.k.a. Patty Hearst, Gore Vidal, Robert Penn Warren, Edith Wharton, Virginia Woolf, *Worst-Case Scenario Survival Handbook*

Repeat's stories first appeared online in *The Postfeminist Playground* as "Tales from the Revolution."

Special thanks to the mountaineer, Lynne Barrett (q. of p.) and the noble Joe Taylor

Livingston Press is part of The University of West Alabama,
and thereby has non-profit status.
Donations are tax-deductible:
brothers and sisters, we need 'em.

first edition
6 5 4 3 3 2 1

Everybody gets so much information all day long that they lose their common sense
—Gertrude Stein

I

1

No one disturbed them at the lookout—the nods didn't manicure so far afield. Their favorite perch was overgrown, wild with vines, stinky with ragwort. Spying, they crouched on principle, inviting muscle strain, wanting to feel their calves ache.

"Mega," Parish chanted, upping the enhancers' magnification.

"Ultra mega," Luce agreed because even the reg-view of that all-wired, sleepless place mesmerized. Night and day The Valley teased and twinkled through a brown haze.

Parish believed only ancients who couldn't keep pace disliked The Valley; Luce felt less sure. Plenty of Retreat residents gauged younger than 30 cycles—nods, transfers, even her Dream Lab supervisor. Parish's theory might explain why the majority fled, but there were other reasons to exit—had to be.

"Your turn."

Pressing too hard against the enhancers' eye slots, attempting a closer close-in of The Valley and its gridwork, Parish had dented her face, creased her cheeks. All Recovereds yearned for locational specifics, the precise coordinates of where they were found when finally they were. Most of their kind arrived with lacerations, pneumonia, birth addictions; Parish came stenciled, the word "Paris" looping from wrist to elbow. A name too fraught, too suggestive of disruption, according to the *kinder* nods who added the "h," transforming a moniker of chaos into a community comfort tag. Parish loathed the extra letter that made her ID sound like a nod's shush. But at least Parish started with a name, knew her pick-up coordinates—Luce envied those certainties, craved them. On her own finder chart, N/A substituted for every locator fact.

She adjusted the scope, tilting Valley-ward until Parish yanked her sleeve.

"Do me a favor. Describe THIS enhanced."

A huge hand lifted a hunk of hair, exposed a patch of glossy bald. With or without the enhancers, that sleek looked awesome.

"When did you do it?"

"Last night."

"How does it. . ."

"Feel? Altered—but nice. Want to touch it?"

The hairless strip had prickly edges.

"And the nods? What did they voice?"

"What can they voice—even *if* they notice?" Parish grinned. "Hair isn't a rule."

Still, the shave-off was bold. Mega bold.

"I don't intend to be a sleeper for life. *Won't* be," Parish had insisted as far back as *kinder* ward.

Who could imagine being anything or anywhere "for life"? The very phrase threatened, promised, surplus—a Retreat verboten.

Their vibra-belts simultaneously jiggled: Assembly alert. By Founder decree, all Retreat residents, new or veteran, had to wear waist prompts. Old-style timers—clock faces—begot stress, needlessly complicating the process of rest and revival. Bylaw number five.

"Snot!" Parish cursed.

In the late afternoon sun, The Valley's smog bank shone

almost golden, impossible to resist, difficult to leave.

They fell in among a line of residents funneling back toward East Gate, skirting clipped lichen and panic grass, blackberry vines and hemlock, meditation benches, reflecting ponds, white, eyeless statuary. Fans of the Cistercians, The Founders modeled The Retreat on an abbey sketch resurrected via PRIME. A few residents called the cafeteria the *frater*, the dorms, *dorters*, but Severe Sleep Deficit (SSD), a more recent plague, lacked monastic equivalent. Everyone called the sleep labs sleep labs.

The gray-robed nod on greeter duty handed out chew sticks of Shut-Down, shivered on their behalf.

"Time to switch to wool, girls," she encouraged, glancing at their brown, baggy, cotton pulls—equally brown and baggy in wool. They'd be encouraged to switch shoes too: from straw to leather slip-ons.

Inside the compound, winter, summer, all days and nights in between, the temperature never varied. 78 (old style) drowse-inducing degrees, The Founders' preference.

"Like we need *warmer* in this joint," Parish complained, sounding like Connie, tucked and snug in Deprivation, supposedly already asleep and dreaming. An important qualifier: supposedly. With Connie, you couldn't presume total obedience. In any situation. Ever.

From the shadows, a monitor nod stepped forward, pushed downward on air with both hands, finger-tapped her lips.

They slowed their gait, ceased conversation. Speed walking counted as a minor infraction, yelling a far worse pre- or post-Assembly offence. Yelling startled residents, awake or asleep. Yelling derailed dreams.

The Assembly Hall's nave and transepts, clerestories,

mullions and lancet arches drew attention God-ward in the Cistercians' case, PRIME recorded. But those same architectural features served The Founders' purpose too, the bylaws revealed. Staring upward, straining upward, eyes eventually grew tired, longed to close, did.

She and Parish disposed of their Shut-Down, selected overstuffed chairs side by side, settled in. Other residents chose recliners or cushioned rockers, but Recovereds, as a rule, avoided rockers, tempted by the impulse to pump.

Ahead and behind, snack nods stooped to listen to whispered requests.

"And for you, dear?"

"Nothing. Gratitude."

Mint tea, hot milk, therma-wraps, cuddle toys, rock rose sniffers. From experience, Luce knew none of those would lure her to immediate dream. It was too early. She wasn't sleepy. Beyond the clerestory, the sky remained blue, fluffy with clouds. Less-than-sleepy Transfers and new recruits were allowed—max—a single glass of brandy at Assembly. Excess interfered with the chemical-out process. In tandem with their ABCs, Recovereds were taught that too much alcohol, like too many downers, disrupted and endangered REM. In The Valley, citizens who boozed and popped to ensure a good night's sleep found themselves wide awake and dry-mouthed midnocturnal, robbed of the very thing they most craved.

—Or so The Founders claimed.

"But notice," Parish pointed out. "Lots of Transfers transfer back, as soon as they stock up on Z's."

Luce had noticed. So how awful could The Valley actually be?

A nod further dimmed the lights. To Luce's right, a Recovered with a milk mustache curled into a ball, sucked her thumb. On her left, Parish craned toward the door, stroking her secret.

A few bald or near-bald new recruits darted in just prior to final latch, required, as part of their orientation regimen, to attend Assembly. They spent the rest of their hours camped out at E-screens, consuming whatever Automatic spit forth, interfacing with Founder-modified PRIME. The weaning process was lengthy, convoluted, Founder logs insisted, and the nods agreed. Adjustment took time, couldn't be rushed, moderation/self-regulation the ultimate goal. "We are not anti-information," emphasized The Retreat's mission statement. "We are anti-*glut*."

But for herself, Parish, Connie—for all Recovereds, "glut" was less than likely. Since rescue, they'd been rigorously shielded from overload and burnout. In 14+ cycles, Luce hadn't once felt truly exhausted.

The evening's moderator carefully wheeled Founder Phineas, the last of the original Founders, toward the podium and parked him alongside. The skin on his face and hands looked as grooved as tree bark. With assistance, he finger-drew a line across his chest—The Founders' secret signal, back in The Valley. The nods said the evenness of the swipe translated no upset/no frenzy/bliss. To Luce, it looked feeble, like Founder Phineas himself.

As a mock, Parish had invented a contrary signal she dubbed "tribute to turbulence." Raise hand, chop air.

The moderator closed her eyes, breathed deeply. Nods assumed their sideline positions, canvassing. Whenever anyone drifted off, a nod crept to his or her side and escorted the sleeper to bed, eliminating the need to return to full consciousness.

"Welcome," the moderator warbled eventually, melodically.

When Founder Phineas nodded, the Bedtime Script began.

Once upon a time The Founders lived and unhappily worked in The Valley. Little by little their disgruntlement grew. A core of five began to meet and plot a better life, far from the blip and blare of ceaseless stimuli, hallmarks of a sinister, wakeful age. Their goal was the antithesis of overdrive, a colony where the human mind had the leisure to sort the trivial from the crucial, the opportunity to heal. Assimilation. Contemplation. The opportunity to achieve a natural balance between intake and understanding, availability and comprehension.

But—where?

Not in The Valley. So great and worthy an experiment couldn't survive in The Valley.

Somewhere else, somewhere apart.

After The Founders laid the first cornerstone among the mountain's wood fern, phlox and bleeding heart, in celebration they rested. Under spring stars, they experienced the sweet release of deep sleep, that great chemical replenisher, that fortifier of immune systems under siege.

Stage 1, eyes close. Stage 2, lids quieten. Stage 3, muscles unclench. Stage 4, pulse slows, breathing slows, body temperature drops, blood pressure drops, dropping the sleeper into the land of gargantuan Delta waves, prelude to magical REM.

Without REM sleep, rats could eat like lions and die of starvation.

Without REM, humans behaved like frantic boar.

The nods grew busy. The Recovered with the milk mustache was carried off, still sucking her thumb. Even Parish's eyes had glazed.

Luce rested her head on her arms, trying to coax surrender. But every time she exhaled, the hairs on her arms tickled and waved.

Because the moderator's hush had stretched too long, she raised her head. A cassandra had wandered in. As the walker blindly steered toward the podium, her wrists wobbled. She pursed and un-pursed her lips. The recording scribe who trailed behind motioned to a nod to activate the floor recorders—a precaution to offset human error.

In The Valley, walkers were drugged with diazepam, regulated and restrained, the nods reported. But at The Retreat, cassandras were revered as mobile dreamers, always afforded the right of way and right of speech. In accordance with protocol, the moderator had fallen silent because nothing rivaled the importance of a cassandra utterance, should a cassandra choose to speak.

Kinder nods spent hours reassuring Recovereds that cassandras weren't ghosts, that they meant no harm, shouldn't be feared. But for Luce, a single hallway encounter negated that benign rep. Pre-five-cycle Recovereds weren't supposed to make a flusher trip unattended, but one night her bladder couldn't wait for escort. She journeyed alone. Eyes gluey with sleep, she hadn't noticed the cassandra until she bounced off her. When she screamed, the cassandra reached out, grabbing what would have been Luce if the recording scribe hadn't shoved her, the obstruction, offside.

The cassandra nearing the podium this evening moaned twice, bumped into an empty rocker, she and it briefly swaying in sync. After a moment's stillness, she reversed directions and departed as jerkily as she'd arrived.

The moderator resumed, reciting a susurrus list of sleep facts and fables. A king named Louis reigned from his bed, the fictitious Oblomov conversed from nowhere else. In a car travelling seventy miles per hour, old rate, drivers dozed without mishap for twenty consecutive minutes, proving: sleep had a mind of its own.

Was everyone else in dream or merely faking?

Luce stretched, scrunched, resettled, striving to concentrate on the moderator's voice, its progression up and down the scales. She tried to extend her breathing, deepen it, but the more she tried to dictate, the more her lungs sent out ragged, shallow gusts, an ode to anti-rhythm. When the moderator's voice unexpectedly fled the Assembly Hall, she surprised herself by following it, through the iron gates of East Gate, past the meditation benches and statues, into a meadow of white mustaches toward shadow-black woods. To keep up, keep contact, with the voice, she had to hurry. Branches slashed at her knees, her ears began to ring. Rushing as fast as she could, she fell farther and farther behind. "*WAIT! PLEASE WAIT!*" she called, stranded in air darker than a nod's robe. "*COME BACK!*" she begged. And then she began to scream.

"There, there," a nod soothed. "There, there."

2

"Farting winter," Lieutenant Maud said, stirring a skimpy fire of kindling at a campsite near the eastern pass.

Looking up toward a flank of ridge, she half expected to see a membrane of hoarfrost, a frozen copse of rhododendron, white as far as the eye could see. Instead the distant view replicated the near: sapped and shriveling leaves, lumps and bumps of gray dolomite. Autumn still horsing around, having its fun, fooling the natives with a pre-blizzard tease. Once started, the snow wouldn't quit till spring.

"Farting winter. I can already feel it gearing up."

"And you in perfect fall fashion," jived Deserter Four.

Yellow cap, red sweatshirt, orange overalls, grimy gloves and duster blue with painted birds—her current and future wardrobe until those glad rags rotted away, requiring a Valley run.

"Look who's mocking."

Four's outfit was no less garish. Purple Zip-Alls embedded with thistles, a green roll-cap that, in a pinch, doubled as mask. A purple tool belt that dangled frayed rope, slingshots and makeshift truncheons.

Cook, Repeat, Seven—all Deserters dressed like ragamuffins or some mutant form of old-style orphans, garish being a Valley lesson they'd failed to trash. Garish stimulated the retina, kept the brain awake. It also made them easy pickings on a winter mountain—*if* the PROs or any Corporate mercenary still scoped a bunch of failed saboteurs—a very unlikely scenario, in Lieutenant Maud's opinion. Surely the PROs hunted fresher delinquents than a tribe of Terminateds turned Deserters fifteen long and brutal winters ago.

But a commander's opinion invariably aced a lieutenant's.

"PROs have obsessions too," Rosa argued. "It only takes one PRO, on a retro kick, determined to track the remnants..."

And remnants the Deserters most definitely were—on that commander and lieutenant fully agreed. Huddled in a circle small enough to spit across, their never multitudinous forces had dwindled to a measly, bedraggled eight—scarcely worth the trouble of organized capture. Truly clever, as clever as their reputation, the PROs would sit back and cede the massacre to winter. Let the hellhound snow finish off what started Valley.

Red-eyed, on a jag, Repeat shuffled by, flapping his plaid muffler.

"'I am well aware that we form, all together, one monster. But I refuse to giggle, and I refuse to be frightened.'"

"Oh goody. A crash and burn file," Four got out before a coughing fit bent him double.

"'The revolutionary is a doomed man. He has no interests of his own, no affairs, no feelings, no attachments, no belongings, not even a name. The revolutionary is a dedicated man. Between him and society there exists, declared or undeclared, an unceasing and irreconcilable war of life and death. I am bound for the Promised La—aa—nd, I am bound for the Promised Land. O who will come and go with me? The true plot will be the most deviant.'"

"Ease off, Repeat," Cook pleaded. "We've got a long night ahead."

"'Terrorism is not being conscious. Terrorism can be fun,'" Repeat reminded, then cupped his hands to bay at the darkening treetops: "'Shall we burn down the Barrio Norte? Shall

I give you fire?'"

No chance of that particular fantasy coming to fruition, given their puny flamer stock, Lieutenant Maud surmised. They'd used one flamer to start tonight's pitiful lick of a campfire—start, not sustain. As soon as the kindling lit, she'd extinguished the igniter, saving the bulk of it for later use. They couldn't afford to waste flamers on merely chilly nights. Not until supplies got replenished.

"'The white men have landed! Now we must get dressed, go to work. You're on the elevator, cable snaps. What to do? Lie flat, distribute the impact.'"

"Re-sort, Repeat," she demanded, losing patience.

Back in The Valley, way ahead of the curve, Repeat neé the stutterer Sebastian had recognized the futility of original expression, the vanity of adding to the glut of already/better said. To back-up that belief, he'd memorized whole databases of PRIME, thereafter ready with a pithy, piercing quote, skimmed from centuries of the tried and true, for any and every occasion. As Repeat, he never stuttered, only majestically declaimed. But lately his talent had begun to spasm; tonight he talked as circularly as he walked, mixing and matching files, riffing on himself and his storehouse of aphorisms, a wunderkind in logorrhea mode.

"'Remove socks, remove shoes, attach heart monitor, strap into metal chair. Drop two cheesecloth packets of sodium cyanide crystals into mixing bowl, watch lethal gas rise. Don't you know he's one of those Corsicans? They're all on the make.'"

For lack of a better plan, she grabbed him on the fly-by.

"Comrade Repeat, a reference tally, if you please. Which do the poets favor: 'winter' or 'cold'?"

"Mother of PRIME!" Four cried. "He'll be scanning till

dawn."

"Cold is good. Cold keeps you awake."

Four leapt up, wisely skittered elsewhere. Pretending to gather nonexistent kindling, he at least escaped their commander's hectoring.

"Don't you agree, Lieutenant Maud? Cold is essential to the Deserters' cause."

"Absolutely."

"Absolutely," Rosa parroted, swaying with fatigue.

The commander sounded as if her vocal cords had been slashed. Even so, she sounded better than she looked. If the birds on Maud's duster had a human equivalent, it was Rosa: all leg and neck, reedy in every department, sharp nose, sharp teeth, sharp eyes, perennially bloodshot, black hair hacked off in clumps, all that scrawniness, that birdyness, accentuated by her Deserter garb: silver tunic, torn leggings, ear muffs that didn't quite fit her birdy head.

A woman too intense in the best of circumstances, Commander Rosa's actions were beyond predicting after three days of self-imposed sentry duty. She might scream, she might bite, she might try, until she collapsed, to execute jumping jacks.

"Sit," Maud invited.

"Not tired," Rosa countered. A ludicrous denial. She seeped exhaustion. They all slept too little—in The Valley, hooked on and into PRIME; here, in mountain exile. But Rosa slept least of all, on permanent full alert, fighting every eyelid flutter.

Part of their commander/lieutenant quarrel—but only part.

"Even if the PROs still cared enough to want us dead, they wouldn't kill us outright. The hackers would have a field day, spreading the news."

"An eye for an eye," Rosa rebutted.

"The PROs can't afford the negative publicity."

"So maybe it's never 'official.' Maybe it's just a wager, down on the streets: *Finish off a Deserter, profit.*"

"That's nonsense."

"Brilliant nonsense."

Rosa's mad stubbornness on the point made her lieutenant feel more than a little mad herself. But then again, they must all be insane, mustn't they, to go on like this?

"If anything happens, if anyone *else* dies, I'm responsible, Maudie. Me."

Thus far, she had refrained from stating the obvious: they were all dying, Rosa and her exalted sense of responsibility faster than anyone.

The barrel of the commander's assault rifle smacked the ground, jolting its carrier out of her trance.

"You need to *sit*."

Instead Rosa used her VZ 58 V to prop herself upright.

The last of the batch, that old-style weapon—ordered and operated in a sentimental gesture of solidarity with rebels of yore. But irony of ironies, it was those retro-works that, in the end, saved their collective ass. Everything else in their arsenal—sighters, fusers, x-plos—malfunctioned in that bloody Corporate corridor, convincing Rosa she should have stuck with her initial instinct: *only* attack new with old. But by then they were already on the lam, in no position to collect on warranties.

"'Voluntary consumption is a kind of alibi. History develops, art stands still.'"

Rosa twitched. "Hear that?"

"Repeat?"

"The other."

"What other? It's nothing."

"It's not nothing. It's never nothing."

"Then let me check," she offered, but Rosa pushed her aside and staggered off, forgoing what passed as supper: 1/8th share of wood rat, crushed acorns and sour berries.

"Only one rat? For all of us? *Again?*"

"You got something else to fry, hand it over," Cook said.

"So you can burn that too?"

Comrade Seven. She was sicker of Comrade Seven than wood rat.

"You think you can do a better job?" Cook growled. "Be my guest!"

A half-plucked, half-roasted corpse sailed in Seven's direction. She lunged, caught it, mid-arc. Sure as schiss, Seven would have dropped it or, worse, watched it wing by to avoid sticky-ing his fingers. "Comrade Pretty Boy," she called him to his back and to his face. Appropriated the one and only slicer every morning to shape his goatee. Stripped down to his crack and scrubbed himself with snow. Coming upon that spectacle last winter, she'd yelled. "Hey, Pretty Boy, who's dumber: a clean dead man or a dead clean man?" In answer, he'd grabbed his prick, shook it at her—as if she'd be impressed by that voodoo.

"Enough!" she ordered, sore tempted to suck her fingers for rat residue.

As second in command, she monitored the bitching, noted who bitched to bitch, who bitched to incite. Within days of his arrival, Seven ranked high on the inciter list. He wasn't an original Deserter, no one who'd shared the bloody corridor. After-the-fact he'd showed up at North Camp, exile cycle 2, presenting, at first, more goofy than snide. A "Valley casualty," he called himself before pulling out an alto harmonica and performing peace-preachy tunes for an audience of Antis. From the start he rode Rosa's heels, mawkishly devoted, his romantic pursuit a resounding plug for E-courting, given the awkward, painful, in-your-face mortification of the alternative played out for all to see. In those days, even she felt a little sorry for Seven and his well-scrubbed equipment. But that was when she still ranked Seven a dope, not a bucko. Occasionally, he and his sulky hormones slunk off, stayed off, a day or two, but before she could adequately celebrate, he'd always slink back, phonily contrite and "re-committed" to their inactive cause. "Just ban the self-indulgent bastard," she'd howled at Rosa a hundred times, amusing the rarely amused commander.

"A reject policy, Maudie? For the Deserters? You're either here or you aren't. There is no other requirement."

"How's this for an idea?" the bucko proposed tonight, chumming up to the grub-man he'd just insulted. "Lieutenant Maud forgoes her feeding, and we divvy up her share."

It was a favorite camp snicker: wide of hand, thick of neck, short, squat Lieutenant Maud could starve for years (and basically had) and still look disgustingly well fed. Some suspected she kept a secret stash of chocs. When their food situation was only tight, not dire, she attributed her bulk to an over-ingestion of Valley techno-vitamins. This cool evening, she tried a different tack.

"If you need my share, Seven, have it."

In contrast to that blandly reasonable offer, a kicker wind swept through camp, smacking the trees.

Did Seven have the gonads to accuse her of choc hoarding outright? She suspected not, suspected correct. A sullen pull on his goatee was the extent of his counter-putsch.

"What about the commander's share?" Cook asked.

A legitimate question. Rosa ate less than she slept. But a certain sense of protocol had to be observed, even if the commander went missing.

"Save it," she ordered.

Cook tore off his bit of wood rat, passed that lump of charred gristle.

Unlike the usual torpor that descended with nightfall, this evening's mood was tense and edgy, inspired by Seven's sniping example. Without some other kind of diversion, they'd fall to throwing punches. She couldn't let that happen. To survive, the Deserters had to conserve energy, not waste it on slaphappy brawls.

"How about a story, Repeat?" she pressed. "A little treat for the troops?"

At once Repeat rose from his cross-legged position, inhaled as if suckling breath at the teat of the universe, expelled that nutrition in one great hoo-ha.

Of the Deserters, only Maud and Four had heard every rendition of every Repeat tale. Rosa and the rest were privy to the streamlined versions of a repertoire shaped and perfected in the bowels of a tube station, the earliest performances staged for a handful of disconnects, a breed then still too transitional to be labeled what they would become: the first class of Terminateds, homeless, jobless wanderers, cut off from PRIME and PRIME access, stripped of their vital user codes. In that underground hole, while supply trains hurtled overhead, Repeat paced among the shadows, a shadow himself, familiarizing his audience with a roster of rebel saints, crooning tributes that moved from oppression to vengeance to victory before doubling back on despair, its overall message shunning uplift. No matter. Few paid attention to content or theme or the meaning of the words, individually or as a cluster. It was Repeat's hypnotic, stutter-free voice that soothed.

"The same story we've heard a hundred times? What kind of entertainment is that?"

Seven again.

"The best you're going to get. So zip and listen," Four croaked.

Instead the whiner stomped off into the darkness.

Glory, glory! she thought, canvassing. None of the smudged faces, minimally lit by firelight, expressed concern for the outcast; none took up Seven's cause in his absence. No one made a peep.

"Floor's yours, comrade," she said to Repeat.

A fire branch popped, shot sparks. Cook added the last of the bundled twigs. If stars shone, a canopy of fir blocked their glow from the Deserters, struggling to find more comfortable seats on the unaccommodating ground.

Repeat cocked his head, clapped twice.

"*The Tale of Saint Simone.*"

—An unfortunate choice. Too much cold, too much hunger in the tale of anorectic Simone, the niceties of revolution taking second place to self-denied, abundant food.

"*The aching head of Simone. A busy head on a shrinking body. No wonder it hurts.*"

And on it went.*

No great blaze to begin with, the fire cooled, then flattened to ash. It was Rosa's job to organize the night circle, but in the commander's absence, those duties fell to her lieutenant.

"Are we ready then?" she asked, pushing up from her ground seat.

---

* The Tale of Comrade Saint Simone, p. 257

The others clambered up also, linked arms. If anyone nodded off, the fall jerked them all awake.

"'We are divided between liking to feel the past strange and liking to feel it familiar. Much about Rome was a pity—leave it at that. Those who make a revolution by halves, dig their own graves.'"

"Spare us the grave quotes," Four advised.

Just spare us, she thought as if in prayer, peering into the darkness, sifting it for Rosa jitters.

3

Roaming, Rosa felt safer. The circle trick no longer staved off sleep. If she remained motionless too long, vertical or horizontal, her mind dozed. Horses slept standing, yes? Why not a commander? At least if she fell dreaming upon briars, she'd suffer the scars of thorns.

At every dark thicket, she sensed the presence of something crouched, something with a grudge.

"Identify!" she yelled. "Identify!"

No one real or imaginary dared.

Spineless cowards, the bunch.

Some nights the moon served as a giant beamer, whitelighting her route. Other nights on her rambles she had to bushwhack her way clear. Some evenings she saw the sap running through the tree veins; others she went slumming with darkness, hid herself from herself, a blankness, a nothing, shoulder to toe. Tonight she seemed to be making good time, proceeding, progressing, at a valiant clip. But was she? A vindictive vine grabbed at her foot, wrapped and entrapped it. When it wouldn't scare off, she dragged it—weed, pistil, stalk, root—forcing it to honor the great god movement, the last of the mighty faiths. In the mountains, in The Valley, in that blood-flecked Corporate corridor, a thing started continued. A beginning begot its end.

Break it down, Rosa. Keep it simple.

She could defeat the body's conspiracy to close-up shop; she could.

"'Sleep is moronic,'" Repeat liked to say/re-say. Corporate believed the same.

Why are you here?

She stopped, twirled, vised her temples. When the earth groaned and the stars sang and the trees danced a tango, when leaves pissed and boulders belched, the skew stayed exterior. Preferable, far preferable to nights when every act started and ended inside: memory come alive to taunt.

Where are your guardians? Where do you live?

She was five, maybe six full cycles. During a routine late-night sweep, the Saver brigade found her, huddled in a stairwell, waiting for her parents to come home. For hours she'd been true to that pose, squatting, waiting, suspecting she was the reason they refused to return, trying to do penance via discomfort. The night before she'd been a brat, interrupted their work, monopolized their time, forced their attention with a self-inflicted wound, her finger pressed against the sharp edge of her mother's desk until the skin tore and bled. To turn that slit bigger, bloodier, more worthy of sympathy and solace, she sucked before she howled. Cursing, her mother dragged her to the apartment's medical dock, bent close to clean the cut. Hardly realizing what she did, she reached to touch the asymmetrical mole on her mother's cheek, the only imperfection of that face, causing her mother to draw back, slap that inquiring hand, scream the daughter annoyance elsewhere and retire to her bed with a cool compress. The next afternoon, back from instruction, she'd searched for her father first, mother second, neither hunched as usual in his or her work cube. Clothes still hung in the closet—but not quite as many as the day before. Food in the chiller—but not in its usual abundance. Clues she fought to misinterpret. She had chosen the stairwell because when they returned, if they returned, she wanted to greet them, touch them, instantly. But instead of her parents, the Savers materialized. She recognized their insignia, tried to squirm away, but there were too many of them, their reach too wide to evade.

Who are you? How long have you been here?

With visceral certainty, she knew not to answer Saver questions, however innocuously phrased. When people want something that badly, when they come at you that aggressively—withhold. It wasn't a child's lesson, but she'd already learned it regardless.

Don't you have a name? Can't you talk?

Could, but refused. For weeks in hold/care, the Savers cajoled and bribed. How proud she'd felt of her own resistance. Then one night a Saver making the rounds noticed her wide open eyes past midnight.

Not sleepy, eh? How about a stroll?

They hadn't strolled far. Squeezing her hand too hard, the Saver pulled her into a nearby cube and pointed at an E-screen.

Do you recognize these people?

The enlargement stunned her. She wasn't prepared to refute the outsized mole on her mother's cheek or her father's cleft chin. She should have shaken her head, stayed mute; instead she squalled her denial. "You can go back to bed now," the Saver dismissed, taking a seat at the keyboard, typing addendums to the image. She'd betrayed her parents, but she couldn't bear to leave the repro. Not flesh and blood, not real, not the best construct of her parents' features, but somehow she sensed that flawed composite would be the last of them she'd ever see.

"Where are they?" she'd whispered, hating the weakness that made her ask.

"Your guess is as good as ours," the Saver said, not quite

convincingly.

"Are they dead?" she'd probed, then held her breath.

"As far as you're concerned, yes. Once a child is abandoned, Corporate decides where he or she resides."

As an officially stigmatized genetic contaminate, she stayed, on Corporate orders, put. To please her Saver/keepers, little Rosa J had to learn fast, perform fast—and did, gifted with the one attribute no one could teach: she required little sleep. Too short for the standard seat, at eight cycles she used an elevated to reach the E-screen. By nine she knew PRIME at coder-level. By fifteen she was assigned her own cubicle, endowed with every Valleyite's inalienable right: ALL ACCESS/ALL THE TIME, a perk she used to parent-search.

Theoretically, they should have been trackable. Everyone who lived or had lived in The Valley was cross-ID-ed. The truth finally penetrated one late night as she retrieved and negotiated yet another junked database. SHE hadn't changed her name. SHE wasn't hard to find. Her PRIME file was totally current—and accurate, down to the plus/minus-age photo. Listed in the Savers' log, the intern log, the Corporate file, the residentials file, Rosa J was thoroughly accessible, but quite obviously no one cared to gain access.

Promoted to glitch scanner, she never met her boss, and he never met her, content to monitor her work rate on a second-by-second basis. She, and an army of others like her, located and flagged linguistic and format errors. Tagged and flattered as a rising star, she worked, initially, at impressive speeds. Even so, for every file she cleared, another five downloaded, maxing her incoming. She couldn't keep ahead of the backup; she could only try not to fall further behind via stay-awakes. For a while, drug-hopped, she still appeared, comparatively, to be a prodigy. But each promotion required reasserting her endurance at a higher level. At level four, she slept three hours a night, occasionally less, in no way the exception in that arena. Half the E-screens of her live/work complex flickered blue when nature went dark.

Her eyes began to water continuously; her ears rang—and still she stayed inside her cubicle, brain sucked into PRIME and vice versa. Eventually, when she could have slept, she stayed plugged in, flipping through random menus, confusing entertainment and obsession. At the comedian site, serviced by an on-call crew, the troupe had two seconds, three, tops, to snag the interest of an audience with a collective attention span reduced to the infinitesimal. Punch lines were whittled to a bark and a screech, pratfalls done without setup. Even without virtual engaged, you could taste their panic. She never laughed at the comedians' jokes, but she guffawed scanning the "Defunct Careers" file. Predictably, her favorite docu-enactment featured the scanner's predecessor, the librarian. From the moment that throwback appeared onscreen, wearing goggle glasses and a crisp white blouse, her flat, twisted hair soldered to her neck, the gags multiplied. In a vault lined with bound paper texts, none of them equipped with IQ modifications or interactive options, the librarian silently labored. "Patrons" browsed, shuffled to the left and right, craned their necks, reached above their heads or below their knees for texts, thumbed dozens of pages subsequently rejected or hand-carried to a desk for checkout. An enormous number of operations, a staggering waste of time, a preposterous spectacle. And yet, while she hooted, she also envied—she, a glitch scanner with shaved head, 20/15 eye implants and non-wrinkle Zip-Alls, a certified PRIME operator with anytime access to the past and ongoing world. Here's why: her predecessor checked out come sundown, off the job, outta that bunker. If a scanner went offline for five minutes without clearance, a red warner flashed. Five minutes later, the flash beeped. At the fifteen-minute mark, a supervisor reactivated the screen to investigate the lapse. One too many lapses and you lost not only access but your cubicle and a 24-hour Rx for stay-awakes.

And up here in the drugless land of hoot owls? How to cope? She walked. Marched. Mock-patroled. Jabbed, pinched, mauled, mutilated her carcass—whatever it took to outfox the enemy sleep, to straddle that doze/no doze divide—because to close her eyes was to dream of bloody corridors or worse: a child's wail echoing off stone walls.

Better to live with bats, flee bats.

Near the tail end of a 36-hour E-screen stretch, operator piss breaks only, she'd made the acquaintance of those red-eyed uglies, experienced the first installment of their clever torment. From the blue edges of her blue screen, they swooped toward her keyboard before shooting up to dive-bomb her retinas. To escape that wing halo she ran, swatting, out into the streets, zinging past lines of shufflers. Only later did she understand why those proto-Terminateds hadn't been perturbed in the least by her frenzy: they too had been stalked by bats, beetles, scorpions, cobras or dog-eared rats. Biting animals of one sort or other persecuted every E-screen zealot. Her case wasn't extraordinary; it was mainline norm.

For a very little while, sex helped fend off the bats. Virtual sex, voyeur sex, or, if the itch of horniness coincided with a delivery boy's arrival, the flesh-on-flesh kind. The louder the bats squealed, the less she bothered with the tease and tickle phase, fusing randomly with the other walking crazed in doorways, in alleyways, between tube stations, in plain view of Corporate surveillance cams, in the glare-bright light that was The Valley all-time/anytime, not a corner or cubbyhole left to its shadows.

Haphazard couplings with strangers who weren't exaggerated or toned down by techno tricks.

Sticks that, pulling out, dripped genuine seed.

More and more she gravitated toward her near-kind: The Valley castaways. Underground, on tube platforms, deprived E-screen junkies bunched around anything that flashed: transit maps, PRO warnings. They looked insane, and yet, she knew, they looked exactly like her.

Designed primarily as food and drug coaches, the tube trains began to crowd with users other than delivery personnel. Terminateds, seeking no particular destination, climbed on for the perpetual ride and streaming message boards. As long as they stayed clear of the cargo pouches, the PROs generally looked the other way. She wasn't a PRO target then because she still looked marginally legit. Appearance-wise, she didn't yet fit the disconnect profile: head still shaved, Zip-Alls not yet tattered. Nonetheless, she constantly skirted discovery and with discovery disaster. Eventually someone would investigate the phonied-up work reprieves, countercheck her productivity scale.

A hefty woman in the adjoining tube seat, scalp tufted with red fuzz, fingers topped with spiky nails, interrupted one such reverie.

"Three weeks in a row," the stranger said, holding up three of those spikes. "Same line, same hour. Why's that?"

"Are you speaking to me?"

"Are you listening?"

Unflappable, Terminated Maud.

As they whooshed through a tunnel, her new bud leaned close. "If you're curious, process this: there are more of us than you could ever guess, but there can never be enough."

Exiting, Maud dropped a slip of paper, not unlike the PRIME-simulated library card, on the seat her broad ass had occupied. To reach it, the tempted had to shoo aside the swarming bats, but reach it she did, instinctively covering that warm contraband with her palm. The smudgy words weren't unreadable, just odd, as any penciled words were odd in the era of PRIME.

Odd and titillating.

At the appointed time, as instructed, she waited on the platform of another tube station. Passing by, Maud said nothing, only gestured toward a barricaded stairway at the far side of the tracks. Beyond the stairway, they ducked beneath a crossbar and entered a jagged, narrow hellhole. Trying to keep pace with the amazingly nimble fat gal, she banged her head, gouged her knees. She could have turned back, the route itself excuse enough, but didn't. Whatever lay at the core of that tunnel, she wanted to see it. The "it" turned out to be a circle of folks, illuminated by flickering flamer light, and at their center a slight, wiry man who looked like a scarecrow but spoke like a seraph. A dirty seraph with blistered feet.

Her surprise surprised her escort.

"Where else would discards commune?" Maud asked sharply, motioning her closer to a cadre of lost souls that seemed to be multiplying faster than the colonizing rats of that underground lair.

"Marat's head in exchange for two hundred thousand others," declares Charlotte of the timbered manor house, of the minor Norman gentry.

*It seems a fair exchange.***

**The Tale of Comrade Saint Charlotte, p. 259

Even sleep-challenged, her brain remembered every syllable and pause of the Charlotte tale, the Joan tale,*** the Emma march **** —all of that agitprop.

When they were also dead and gone would a Repeat Deux broadcast the Deserters' story? The tale of benumbed Terminateds who tried and predictably failed to recode The Behemoth Valley?

Hardly.

To count as a celebrated enemy of the state, one had to prove minimally effective, rate at least a partial blip on the scanner.

Karl, Mao, Malcolm, Ivan, asthmatic Che—PRIME had supplied why and how bios on every certified blip-maker since the Big Bang, a readymade rebel's kit for anyone who cared to peruse the database, including hero/heroine index, weapons inventory, a catalog of save/rule the universe schemes and symbolic accoutrements (Zapata's sorrel, Meinhof's Alfa Romeo), inspiration via locale (Fidel's sugar fields), resistance via guile (those hard-to-kill Romanov kids with their jewel-lined corsets). There for the imitating: plots, counter-plots, contingency plots, a vast plentitude of conspiracy options. When she joined the Terminateds' coven, still fueled by NicSticks and stay-awakes, still with PRIME access, despite a pooching stomach, she could plot and conspire all night. Doggedness—that had been her one true talent, her primary skill. Doggedly she schemed an attack on Valley politics. Trained to activate PRIME, not deactivate it, she and her comrades forwent the thrill of destroying techno with techno, voting, at her shrill insistence, to snatch a Corporate info titan. A suit.

***The Tale of Comrade Saint Joan, p. 261

****The Vladimir/Emma march, p. 264

Even the memory made her wince.

From second one, nothing and no one cooperated. Rather than PRIME center, in error, they stormed a minor terminal, bursting in on worker bees who blithered in surprise, then terror. She'd tossed an x-plo to send the innocent scurrying, but those who scurried hardest were her and her addled comrades, trying in that maze of cubicles to locate the correct office, decoyed on PRIME. Two wrong time/wrong place Corporate drones appeared out of nowhere, and the invaders didn't think, didn't discuss; they reacted, pointed, fired and watched two bodies drop dead where a second before they'd stood, breathing. As killers then, their rebel band blundered on, down another corridor, hunting blind. Only a fluke of bladder politics delivered the victim they sought into their shaky hands. When he exited the gents, by chance, he stepped directly into their swerving path.

Maud crushed his body alarm, activated by a wildly pounding pulse. In a clump they ran with him, while he squalled:

"Why are you doing this? What could you possibly want in here that you don't already have access to out there?"

To cut off that incessant, maddening commentary, she bashed him hard across the mouth. Miraculously they regained the streets and their bearings, located a vacant apartment, broke in. In the room farthest from the entrance, they stashed their questionable prize, bound his hands and feet, and fought like cheetahs over ransom demands. And while they fought, the info titan, human despite his informatted soul, curled in a ball and fouled himself from fear.

"Do something!" she had screeched at her collaborators when that stench reached her nose—flying, just flying, on nerves.

Four performed diaper duty, cleaning up the multi-billion-dollar shit that stank precisely like the piss-poor kind. In that fetid sewage, she already smelled the end, their end, but as in nightmare they remained at the mercy of playout.

"You think I'm important, but I'm not," the shit-smeared, puffy-lipped info titan said. "No one of us is."

"Gag him!" she ordered and Maud complied.

"We're doing this for your own good. For The Valley's good. The workers need a break, a holiday!" she screamed, bizarrely compelled to explain.

The info titan gaped. Maud gaped too at that inane, ludicrous explanation. A farting holiday—was that their ultimate goal? Their core motivation? The desire that led them to murder strangers, torture a suit?

Listen, his eyes pleaded. *I'm a workhorse too. I've invested my time, my emotions, my spirit, into an E-screen. Just like you. Just like you.*

Throughout that fiendishly long night, they took turns standing guard. First Maud, then Repeat, then her, then Four, and so on, a theoretically error-proof tag team. But in the murky light of dawn, too late, she woke to discover, in every direction, comrades sprawled, dreaming, drooling, snoring. And in the back room, instead of a snoring info titan, a terribly neat pile of chewed-through, shredded ties. The exec had outwitted his captors, just as Corporate—then, now, always and forever—outwitted its slaves. If for a second she doubted that conclusion, a glance downward verified. For there The Valley glowed in reminder and rebuke: unchanged, unscathed, as awake as a roaming Deserter commander.

"Looks like a farting question mark, doesn't it?"

She started, spun, stepped hard on nothing and would have plunged headlong back into that glittery enigma if Maud hadn't grabbed and held.

Bats loudly disputed the wisdom and ethics of that last-second save.

"This can't go on," Maud bullied, still clutching. "You know it. I know it. Skimping's one thing. Zero snooze another thing entirely."

She snatched free, wobbled, tried her best to sneer.

"When I want a lecture, lieutenant, I'll request it. Until then . . . until then . . ."

Her brain froze; her tongue locked; the bats flapped for joy.

4

It was one of her worst nightmares recast as real. Rosa on the prowl, addled with sleeplessness, catapulting off a cliff's edge, half by accident, half by design. Tonight, she'd grabbed in time to save the body, but tomorrow the commander's luck might improve, hers diminish.

Almost ten cycles ago, they'd been straddling a similar edge-patch of moss when Rosa announced: "I'm tired of it, Maudie. I've had enough."

"Enough of what? Waiting, watching, marching? Feasts of grass and ground squirrel?"

A diversion. No Deserter could afford the indulgence of self-pity, commander included.

"So you're saying you could . . . continue? That you want to?"

To argue automatically was not necessarily to argue deceitfully. For all the hardships of exile, it had its perks. Would Lieutenant Maud exchange mountain asylum for an E-screen ghetto?

"Here at least we're Cook and Four, Rosa and Maud, with quirks, not codes, to prove it."

"The thrill of camaraderie? That's the plus you're hawking?" Rosa smirked. "Ole Maudie. Ever the trooper."

"You don't fool me, Rosa," she'd challenged, desperate to dilute the fatalism. "You're trooping right alongside me."

Since that conversation, to keep Rosa trooping, she'd often pushed for Valley raids not only to restock supplies but to give the commander something to fix on, orchestrate. Tonight, however, pacification took second place to necessity. For the evening "meal," Cook had seared the final wood rat putrefying in his sack; they'd reached the last of the last of dregs of their perpetually meager food supply. Someone *had* to risk a foray. Soon.

A commander/lieutenant co-raid wasn't sound policy—never had been—but when Rosa made the trip, she went along, primarily because she didn't trust anyone else with full-scale Rosa protection. Should the commander collapse from exhaustion en route—more likely than not—she was the only Deserter capable of slinging that body load across her shoulder and continuing upward. This round, she'd prefer they both pass on the adventure, leave the grab and flee operations to Four and Cook, or to Seven, for that matter. Whatever she thought of Seven the comrade, he'd proved himself a shrewd and artful Valley thief. It was Seven who'd found the trash bin of a theatre troupe that specialized in old-style happenings and scavenged the first round of surprisingly durable clown and dandy costumes. A follow-up raid had netted the orange overalls that still covered her butt without a single burst seam. Unfortunately, those drama mavens had since closed up shop. Whether their demise came by way of infighting or a PRO shutdown, the Deserters never heard. Either way, they lost a tailor.

Food was a trickier loot than clothing simply because the competition was fiercer. Looking like hell didn't kill you; starvation did. A good haul for the Deserters meant a sizable snatch of discarded jerky, fruit packs and stale bread. Once she'd managed to cart off her weight in fresh grub because a rube driver left his delivery transport unattended and deactivated—a miracle thus far without sequel. Even if a similar opportunity presented itself, getting such rich booty up the mountain would be a trial. The first wave of Terminateds had morphed into a sea of sharks. Anyone carting red meat would definitely have to fight her way through Valley streets.

Last raid, broad daylight, she'd been slugged in the back of the head—hard, just not hard enough to knock her out. Which meant her attacker lost his advantage and his chance to avoid payback pain.

Flipping his ass, she'd squalled: "Data check! I'm one of you."

His excuse when she'd lifted her foot off his throat?

"Human error. You don't smell like Valley."

"Yeah, well, living in the mountains, you stink of dirt not cube," she'd informed.

At that clarification, he hadn't even blinked.

Heading back to camp with too light a load, she and Rosa had come across two Terminateds in hill brush, grappling over a strip of spoiled meat.

"Stop it! Stop this!" the commander ordered, inserting herself between them, succeeding only in redirecting their rage. As a unit, they pummeled the interloper, would have kept at it if a fat lieutenant hadn't beaten off those frothing dogs.

Scratched and bleeding, Rosa scrambled to the top of the first ridge without looking back, but there she stopped and turned to stare at Valley shimmer.

"It's worse down there than it was."

Useless to debate the point, then or now. But whereas Rosa took on the blame, the guilt, of that deterioration, Lieutenant Maud did not. The Valley was what it was. To honor the commander's knee-jerk moratorium on Valley raids spared no one and helped no one, least of all hungry Deserters. Her toes might go numb from frostbite, her cunt might freeze shut before spring, but she would not, on principle, starve. Tomorrow, the day after, a raid must occur. She said as much. Again.

Rosa scowled, but stayed upright.

"You know the rules."

"Some rules require breaking."

"Are you DEFYING me?"

"We have to stock up," she insisted, was prepared to insist, until Rosa agreed. "Winter's all but here."

The commander pivoted unsteadily, swiped at air, staggered off—not precisely in the direction of camp.

In the sweep of sky above The Valley's perpetual cloudbank, constellations burned and reconfigured. The longer she stared, the more clearly she perceived a floating bed and, beside its cushiony comfort, a table piled high with a luscious midnight feast.

"Star gazing are we, Lieutenant Maud?"

"Are *you*?"

Seven snorted. "Gazing is worthless. Raiding, on the other hand..."

He stepped closer; she, sideways, a healthy distance from the drop-off but still within hooking distance. If he planned a "mishap," he'd best prepare to plummet alongside her.

"You and I could start now. Be there by first light."

She despised agreeing with Seven on anything. Despised it.

"You're suggesting we just sneak off? Behind the commander's back?"

"Behind her back, in front of her face, she won't register the difference."

Too true, the prick.

"We raid when the commander says we raid. Not before. Not until."

"Your commander is hallucinating. I just saw her shooting vines."

"*My* commander?"

"Your commander, my commander, the woman keen to kill us all."

"Nobody's going to die," she disputed through clenched teeth.

"Lieutenant Maud declares—that's what you're offering as insurance? Duck-walk to oblivion if you want. I didn't sign up to expire."

"I wasn't aware you'd 'signed' anything," she said and evoked a gratifying twitch.

"You know what I mean. We suck our thumbs and wait for orders that may never come. You, me, somebody has to act. NOW."

Yes, but coming from the mouth of Deserter Seven that sentiment sounded vile. Worse, it sounded like mutiny.

5

Luce exited the Assembly Hall with the last of the nods. "Would you like a bed escort, dear?" several asked at once.

"Gratitude, no."

"Sweet dreams, then."

"Sweet dreams to you too," she replied.

In the sleep wing, the hallway lights had been switched to night cycle; she followed the floor's diffused white glow. Three cycles from now, she could transfer to a co-ed section if she cared to. Both Parish and Connie counted the days. Her feelings were less clear-cut. She'd been sleeping in the same room since graduating from *kinder*, since proving herself capable of unsupervised sleep. If she left those familiar quarters, she feared she'd miss them, sleep worse.

The ward nod had turned down her covers, laid out softer resting pulls, a pair of foot warmers. Despite those welcomers, if she climbed into bed straight away, she'd never dream. Her brain was still too alert; it needed more lulling. In such cases, a late soak was permitted. In the communal washroom, she passed the reflector, then returned to it. Parish spent her reflector time zapping pimples. "The poxies," she called those puss-filled eruptions. So far, for Luce: no poxies, just one blemish, permanent but tiny, dotting her left cheek. It was her face that stared back from the reflector. She owned it—but who else shared those features? A Recovered's question.

Side by side, reflector image or real, Parish and she and Connie appeared sliding scale, big to medium to small. Parish the tallest and most solid, sprinkled with freckles. Connie the tiniest, blue-eyed and fair. Luce neither short nor tall, leveling off somewhere in between, brown-eyed, brown-haired, only her nose certifiably distinctive: long, thin and "hawkish," according to the nods. Her lips were thin too. Smiling stretched them thinner.

Smiles, as well as pouts, were controlled by muscles directed by the seventh cranial nerve, PRIME reported. Behind the skin of her face, any face: fourteen kinds of bones: nasal, lacrimal, zygomatic, maxillae, palatine, vomer, mandible.... Just before Connie relocated to Deprivation, the bones of her face seemed determined to break surface, the half-moons beneath her eyes bruise-blue. Valleyites invariably arrived with the whites of their eyes streaked red. Both conditions temporary, the nods assured. Both correctable.

In the bath basin, she tried to float her legs and toes; pressed her wrist, felt her pulse. The heart was also a muscle, PRIME divulged: a muscle the size of a clenched fist. What you heard, ear pressed to another's chest, was not precisely a heartbeat; rather, the bump of valves closing. A baby's heart in its mother's womb stayed open. Only after birth did it clamp shut.

A nod knocked on the partition. "Time to finish up, dear."

"Gratitude," she answered.

At the washroom doorway, another nod waited. What could she do to assist? Would Luce prefer a hot water bottle, heat sheet, sound machine, wind chimes, a dollop of honey? Night light? Cuddle toy? In the adult sleep wards, residents chose from a wider facilitator selection: vibrators, vintage television, blue movies, low-dose relaxants, stay-overs. The Founders had no objection to actual, consensual sex. Sex promoted sleep.

"Gratitude, no. I'm now inclined."

"Assistance with your night cap?"

She shook her head once more.

The nod crept away.

In bed, night cap in place, she switched on the monitor, punched in her dreamer code. Physiological data streamed directly to the sleep labs but to contribute to dream research, residents transcribed old-style, using a Morpheus pad and pen. New recruits invariably protested. Why not mobile pads? Voice-activated recorders at the very least? But the bylaws were very specific: pen and paper only. The laborious nature of handwriting contributed to the culling process. Lost details were meant to be lost. "We are here to forget all but the essential," The Founders declared.

Eyes closed, she imagined she heard music—a brain tease. The wall pad blocked any sound other than sounds she activated. Parish preferred breaking waves. Connie, a tuba medley. Usually an open window and year-round airflow eased her to dream.

Confined to Deprivation, surely Connie was sleeping now. She was supposed to sleep continuously until she re-balanced. Working in Archives had tipped her. Recovereds were rarely permitted Archival access. "Those without histories crave history; those without stories of their own, appropriate," The Founders said. A supposedly unhealthy mix: Recovereds and Archives. Regardless, Connie managed to bamboozle a supervisor, swore she wouldn't overdo—very persuasive, very convincing, Connie could be when she chose to charm. For a half dozen sessions, she kept to the posted assignments, stayed within approved search and browse boundaries, but couldn't, finally, resist the temptation to rifle through larger chunks of the chaotic past. Everyone noticed the change: the nods, everyone. Perpetually excited, wired to the point of zoomy, she started skipping early meal, then mid-meal, then early, mid- and final. Every session she fixated on a new topic: erotomania, witch trials, a preacher and Kool-Aid, a spiteful daughter with a hatchet.

"Picture desperation," Connie chattered. "Picture dust. A black car, forever on the way to somewhere else. 167 bullets fired. Boom, boom, boom. One big smear of bones, veins and cartilage. One big mush of brains and no more Bonnie and Clyde."

Scandals, murders and murderers, fiction or fact, thrilled her. "'But dad i'm not sorry for what i did cause for the first time me and caril had more fun,'" she trilled, skipping down the hallway. Caught at the E-screen after curfew, she claimed to be doing her job: investigating executions, but the nod wasn't fooled. After a week or more of all-nighters, Connie was barely lucid, spraying saliva, wound tighter than tight, jabbering on about a tart who'd killed her swanky lover, mid-century, last century.

"So, honest-true, I *was* a little skewed," the new addition to Deprivation confessed, the first time friends were permitted to visit. "When the nod came after me, I thought she intended to execute ME."

Hearing that revelation, Luce had shivered with discomfort. "No you didn't," she'd contradicted, trying to blot out the image.

"Did too," the patient insisted, eyes still not entirely focused.

But lately, Connie did seem improved. Her face looked rounder, less drawn. She didn't jabber, although she remained obsessed.

"And get this: when they flipped the switch, she filled her pants. Filled her pants! And they took PICTURES!"

"Maybe we shouldn't discuss Mrs. Ellis, Con," she'd urged, glancing over her shoulder.

"Wait, it gets better. Before they fried her, you know, when she was already sentenced and everything, waiting it out in prison, she wrote a letter to the guy's mother! The guy she shot! HIS MOTHER," Connie reemphasized—unnecessarily.

It was the kind of detail any Recovered would remember and savor. After that rushed paragraph, a technician tapped Luce's shoulder.

"That's enough visiting for today."

Led off to bed, Connie alternately grimaced and waved.

She missed Connie. Especially at night. With Connie in bed down the hallway, in the regular sleep wing, she knew someone nearby was having trouble sleeping too. A comforting thought despite its restless content.

"Connie will feel much better when she returns. Calmer, more relaxed," the nods assured the Recovereds and maybe the spoken of too.

In the sanctuary of her non-Deprivation quarters, Luce flexed her wrists and ankles, trying for calm, trying to achieve relaxed. But Connie's thoughts weren't the least bit relaxing.

"Wrote his mother! His mother! Can you believe it?"

To the count of fifty, she massaged her forehead beneath the night cap, rolled to the side, stuffed her hands beneath her cheek, listened as her lashes scraped pillow. The night cap pinched on one side; she readjusted. Forced her breathing deeper.

And then a sound channeled through her open window: the faintest rustling of leaves. Instantly she sat up, that fist-sized muscle, her heart, beating fast.

"Mother?" she whisper-called into the darkness. "Mother? Is that you?"

6

When Maud returned to camp, she found what she expected, her comrades collapsed onto leaves, the night circle now a ground wreath of overlapping legs and arms. No Seven in sight, no Rosa either—the reason the commander's army chanced sleep on the spongy liverworts of Spider's Ridge.

As lieutenant, she was under obligation to wake them. Instead she dropped ass herself, forcing her witless brain to strategize. Before first light or Rosa interfered, she needed to concoct at least a rudimentary plan to get her comrades through another depriving winter.

This late in the season, they'd get no Decorative relief. True to form those parlor rebels hadn't paid the Deserters a clandestine visit since the leaves started shedding. Mountains in hibernation held no allure for weekend Antis. Cold wasn't glamorous; it wasn't contraband; it was plain and simple nasty. Better to stay put, forgo that strenuous trek in cushion boots, pass on the opportunity to test out their heat/cool pads in open air. A wise if wimpy choice on their part with results dire for their occasional hosts. Along about yesterday, the Deserters could have used an infusion of gourmet gear and grub.

The very memory of Decorative fare sprung loose the floodgates of saliva. The last of those welcomed feeds had been forcibly liberated from a pair who'd finished the climb near nightfall. Near Brush Fork, she and Rosa had heard falling rock, plus this peevish exchange.

Him first:

"If you can't carry it, just say so!"

"I can carry it. I just need a break. It's steep here."

"You said you practiced!"

"I did practice! Ten simuls a day."

"Then you should have practiced twenty."

But baby doll got in the final jab.

"I'm carrying the food AND therma units on my back. You're carrying—what? A glow map?"

Giddy with anticipation, she and Rosa had grinned like birthday baboons awaiting the pop-up of those bickering heads.

"Got business around here, chums?"

Strictly for effect: the brusqueness and gun pointing. Even to a Deserter's jaded eye, that pair of Decoratives came across young as sunrise, trusting as puppies. And loaded, farting loaded, with food treats. Bread, cheese, meat packs, wine— enough for a bacchanalian feast.

Tummies taut with food, an extravagant number of flamers stoking the fire, chocs and NicSticks for desert, the Deserters settled down to fun with Dick and Jane.

"How many words in a Dick and Jane reader, Repeat?" Rosa queried, in rare high spirits.

"Look Oh Jane See Dick Funny Sally Puff Jump Run Spot Come Time Up Go Down And."

"Seventeen, by my count," Four calculated.

"'You'd be marvelous company slightly stunned,'" Repeat interjected.

"Seventeen words, then. You've got 17 words to state your case," Rosa informed.

"Well, we, we just wanted . . ."

"*Well-we-we-just-wanted.* Five words and counting," Rosa warned. "Better skip the intro."

"We just admire you so much. I mean, what we've *heard*..."

"'Fame consists of four elements: a person, an accomplishment, his immediate publicity and what posterity has thought about him since.'"

Rosa made a buzzer noise.

"Time's up, comrades. I regret to say you failed the State Your Case test."

"But we totally support your CAUSE!" Dick protested.

"Ah! THE CAUSE! THE CAUSE!" Cook yipped.

"And what cause might that be?" Rosa taunted, sarcasm itself.

"The end of technological tyranny," Jane supplied, enthusiastically bobbing her meticulously shaved head.

Rosa slapped her cheeks, her thighs. "Oh THAT cause! Then, by all means, stay the night!"

A craven bunch, Decoratives. Absurdly eager to please, absurdly easy to mock. Even tenderhearted Repeat felt free to taunt Decoratives, reaching deep into his grab bag of sanctimonious, nihilistic quotes and roaring them nonstop.

"'You think it's absurd that I should go out and shoot a man just because I'm ordered to? That's your bourgeois mentality. Revolution is bloody, revolution is hostile, revolution destroys everything in its way. What troubled me most in dealing with him was not his monstrosity but his banality. I find the passion for justice boring. Neither life nor nature cares if justice is done.'"

—And similar rehashes, many of them rolling off a Decorative's thin skin while cutting a little close to a Deserter's brittle bones.

During that evening's reveries, Rosa's cheeks had turned pink from fire and wine; she had looked almost, almost at peace. Cook danced, singing his own accompaniment, until

Four challenged him to a pissing contest. Repeat, inspired, cleared his throat, whinnied and launched into a tribute to the other Rosa.***** Even Seven sat back, blew smoke rings, content as cream.

Was there any sensation more pleasing than a full stomach? None that Lieutenant Maud could summon—except, maybe, the release belch that followed. In The Valley, she had belched nonstop, engorged with food and drink. Crumbs continuously rained onto and into her keyboard, eventually crusting up the works. But keyboards were easy to replace. As long as she met her quotas, her boss supplied new keyboards. Chocs and Vita-liq too.

"'The best possible play is one in which there are no actors, only the text. I'm trying to write one,'" Repeat had confided to Dick and Jane, who took him at his word.

"Go ahead," Dick urged Jane. "Ask him if he started it."

Four's head shot up along with her own.

"Started what?" Rosa asked, reaching for her gun.

"The legacy virus," Dick and Jane simultaneously voiced.

"And which legacy virus would that be?" the commander followed up, face fierce as thorns, query pure bluff.

None of them knew squat about legacy viruses.

"It's systemic and random. Cycles pass between incidents. But when it hits, whole networks of E-screens blank out."

"And what makes you suppose Repeat is the genius responsible?" Four wheedled.

"The messages that appear right after the blank-outs," Jane said. "They read just like he talks."

Cook nearly choked on laughter. Repeat looked beatific; Rosa, wary.

*****The Tale of Comrade Saint Rosa, p. 267

"A slogan-spouting virus Corporate can't eradicate?" she clarified, and Dick and Jane confirmed.

"Is that TRUE, Repeat? You masterminded that?" Seven sputtered.

"'I have chosen to stay and fight,'" Repeat demurred.

She had assumed, hoped, she was blotto drunk, and drunk, misunderstood. Because if Repeat actually possessed the wherewithal to virus the system, their disastrous Corporate raid was rendered doubly foolish, doubly tragic. No one had to die. No one even had to desert. They could have rigged a revolt from within and stayed within—as long as the mastermind evaded discovery. Regarding that crucial loophole, she didn't kid herself: Corporate would quicker condone violence than pardon a virus.

Dawn crept in gray as a vole, but a cold-blooded one. When the sun edged a bit higher, maybe Cook would capture one of its edible cousins. In memory at least, vole tasted better than ground squirrel: juicier, less gamy. But maybe everything tasted better in memory.

When she stood, her knees cracked, none of her joints quite limbered up before the specter Rosa came hurtling through brush and thistle, excoriating her derelict troops. One after another of those languishing piles, she kicked. Viciously.

"Easy, commander. You want them awake, not wounded."

"Bunch of cows," Rosa hissed.

"Not cows, Rosa. You'd be happy with cows. Three hours a day and they're chipper. Bats, on the other hand. . ."

"Don't message me about bats! Just get them up and moving."

Before Lieutenant Maud could obey, another prodigal rejoined their merry band—maybe smirking, maybe grinning, that line too fine a call when dealing with Comrade Seven.

His rawhide jacket looked bulkier than usual, however. A sweetness emanated from his pockets.

"Apples," he announced.

"And where exactly did our comrade find those apples?" Rosa inquired of her lieutenant, ignoring the bearer of fruits.

"*Food for thought*," Repeat wheezed, revving up.

"Save your farting food for thought! This is gut food!"

Once again, to Maud's supreme irritation, she and Seven agreed. Besides which, she disliked the Angeline saga. It sounded too much like a Biblicals' tract. It also sounded like what it was: the end of leisure time chronicled.

"*Saint Angeline's rotten apples. Rotten to the core. 'Reject those rotten apples, however golden they appear,' instructs Saint Angeline and the women of The Valley agree.*"

"Do you *see* these? Are you processing *this*?" Seven bellowed, bobbing two impressive specimens in Repeat's face.

Regardless, Angeline's tale proceeded.******

As inconspicuously as possible, Maud licked her lips, ventured a justification.

"How's this, commander? Apple eating as an act of solidarity."

"Apples from *where*?" Rosa demanded, of Seven this time.

Would he be smart enough, brave enough, to lie to the commander?

Stupid stick.

"From the sleepers' orchard—where else?"

Rosa went dangerously still.

"And there's plenty more for the taking," Seven elaborated. "Plenty."

Maybe from nerves, maybe to illustrate his plenty assess-

******The Tale of Comrade Saint Angeline, p. 269

ment, he took a bite, smeared his goatee with apple pulp, threw the rest of that succulent to the ground.

At any moment, Maud expected the rest of the Deserters to jump the discard, fight and squeal over it in the manner of pigs.

"Sleeper apples," Rosa said, "From a sleeper orchard. Filched during a sleeper raid."

"Why not? They're there—and asleep!"

"Exactly. They're there, and we're HERE," Rosa said, massaging her gun.

Angeline's mishaps concluded, Repeat focused on Deserter Seven's dilemma.

"'Burn a leech, it will regurgitate, causing infection.'"

"You know the policy, Seven," Four parroted less than enthusiastically, his leer reserved for apples.

"I've heard *no*," Seven persisted. "I've never heard *why*."

"And that oversight, you imagine, entitles you to challenge *policy*?" Rosa taunted, aligning eye to eye with the challenger.

When the rifle grazed his temple, Seven flinched but stayed put.

"Crazy bitch."

"Crazy and getting crazier," Rosa said, and fired past the fringe of his rawhide sleeve.

"'The first shot came from the Schoolbook Depository, and then when the second shot came, I couldn't tell who all was shooting,'" reported Repeat.

Crowding an armed woman whose grip on reality waxed and waned—beyond stupid.

"Bye, bye, comrade. See you in hell but not a second sooner."

"Don't sit there like dumbers! Speak up! You know I'm

right! The sleepers are overstocked. What do they care?"

"'Courage is a strange thing,'" Repeat declared. "'One can never be quite sure of it.'"

Once more, Rosa gun-nudged her target.

"Move along, Seven. Time's a-wastin'."

"Are you going to keep listening to HER? The mighty Rosa?"

"I'd reconsider that line of persuasion if I were you."

"And you, her farting mouthpiece!" Seven charged. "Head dumber: Lieutenant Maud."

"Catchy title. I'm impressed. Aren't you impressed, commander?"

But Rosa was beyond diverting. Even with sarcasm.

"'When the smoke cleared it became obvious this had happened too often before. . .'" Repeat started.

"'. . .and would happen too often in future,'" Rosa finished.

"Recitations from the lit freaks. That'll feed us."

Not a new objection. Seven had been dissing the Repeat channel since inhabiting its broadcast area. Somewhere in the lost past, in response to that same gripe, Rosa had egged a substitute:

"Let's hear it, Comrade Seven. Ode to the mega chip, part one."

"It works," Seven had snorted. "And nothing can destroy it."

"You seem proud of that fact," Rosa baited. "Are you *proud*?"

But today's pride whammy was lobbed at the Deserters, at their woefully incompetent leaders, to be precise.

"Neither of your so-called officers could find the major terminal. They couldn't hex PRIME. They couldn't even keep a suit kidnapped. He got away on his own two feet!"

With that brash insult, all suspense ended. The runt had sealed his fate.

Rosa removed the last inch of distance between herself and sometimes stick.

"Help me out, Repeat," she called, breathing on the doomed. "How does that gem of a quote go? 'You are a little confused by the Revolution in action. . .'"

"'. . .because you have dealt with it only in theory. You'll get over it.'"

"Adios, Comrade Seven," Rosa said, stepping back just far enough to accommodate a metal sighting. "Take care at sudden drop offs. Wouldn't want you to suffer a laming accident on your way down." Twice she clicked her tongue against her teeth. A passable imitation of trigger cock.

"Crazy farting bitch!" Seven sputtered, his curses as shopworn as Repeat's. Attempting to run backward, he showed little grace. "I'll remember this," he shouted before his fruit- and spit-soaked goatee vanished, by all indications, permanently this time.

As much as Lieutenant Maud longed to applaud with vigor Comrade Seven's departure, the apple booty strewn at her feet prevented glee. Even inept lieutenants looked to the future. And in banishing an inciter, Commander Rosa had also banished a first-class raider, winter storming in.

II

1

Sometimes waking up felt marvelous, sometimes spooky. Accordingly to PRIME, there were sects that believed the soul left the body during sleep to roam the world—a belief The Founders acknowledged, but stopped short of endorsing. And yet the concept made perfect sense. Luce's body often felt alien when she woke, as if part of it had spent the night elsewhere. She and it had to become reacquainted; she had to get used to the fit all over again.

Fingers—Elbows—Knees. This is me.
These are my proportions.
This is what other people recognize as Luce.

Gingerly, she removed the night cap. The hair on one side of her head felt plastered, the other side electrified. Without leaving bed, she reached for the Morpheus pad and pen. In their zeal to write down every dream detail, new recruits developed writers' knots, a pre-chip ailment. Veterans understood a blow-by-blow account wasn't necessary. A few words or quick sketch would do. This morning she drew a door and labeled it "closet," then a stick figure of herself lifting the latch.

A search dream. Her dreams were always search dreams.

Her gaze strayed toward the window. As long as she didn't actually check, she could imagine, believe in, telltale tracks, a message half-hidden in soggy leaves. While she lingered in that hopeful trance, her vibra-belt jiggled at half-speed, the first alert for early meal. Welsh on early meal, the largest feed of the day, and by mid-meal you were ravenous, by final, faint. New recruits, used to starting with caffeine and building, had trouble adjusting to the descending menu. Recovereds did too. Parish often cadged for extra food, but as a rule Retreat dietitians refused to serve on demand. The Founders opposed overfeeding the body as well as overfeeding the brain.

Running late, she grabbed for the nearest wool pulls, belting while she dashed, and in the hallway, fell in among a tour group under nod escort. The daytrippers, by ordinance, didn't attempt to speak to her nor she to them, but she did, as much as she dared, sideways-stare—her one and only opportunity to view Valleyites who still classified as pure Valleyites, to inhale their specific antiseptic. Today's predominately male group all exhibited worried mouths and frown divots, talked too loudly among themselves, displayed zero patience. Frustrated by the nods' slow pace, they constantly heeled the person walking ahead, herself included. Connie once claimed she'd seen a daytripper shove aside a cassandra. But Connie liked to seize on a possibility, inflate it. You could never be 100-behind Connie's stories.

At the cafeteria, Luce and the daytrippers parted ways. Visitors weren't fed or housed overnight—another Founder decree.

From a foldout table near the back of the room, Parish signaled, her hand 3-D-ing the *kinder* art taped to the walls. The sketches on display had been accomplished with paper and crayons, not computer dials, but they imaged the usual *kinder* landscapes: yawning houses, sleepy-eyed suns, blue birds flying south. At each food station, the server measured out a portion, added it to Luce's tray. Parish waved faster, frantically, for fun.

"I'd almost given up on you!"

"Apologies. I was a laze this morning."

"Tired out from all that dream drafting?"

Luce scrunched her nose. "No. Things in the lab are serene. What about Disorders?"

"The same. Dully serene."

To work Disorders, you had to be at least fifteen with no priors in insomnia, narcolepsy, apnea and such. Technically, Parish's night terrors should have disqualified her for the job, but her file remained flag-free because no nod had ever discovered her out of bed, kicking the wall, disoriented and screaming.

"Care to Valley gaze this afternoon?"

"Unless the lab is dreamer-packed."

Parish bulged her eyes, threw her voice high and squeaky. "'I can't remember everything, just snatches. I was in a classroom, and, and, the teacher handed out a test, and, and, I realize I hadn't studied . . .'"

Jokes weren't allowed in Disorders, so Parish had to do her kidding elsewhere. Gut laughs triggered attacks among the narcos. One minute they're giggling, the next they've collapsed to the floor, out cold for half an hour. The Founders revered sleep, yes, but narcos had to be protected.

"Five DON'T KNOW MY LESSON dreams by mid-meal—that's my guess."

"Only five?" Luce spoofed, playing along. Mostly she heard descriptions of E-screen morphings. Or dream scripts that starred rodents. Rodents that danced, rodents that sang.

In adios, Parish lifted the hair flap, mooned her with bald.

No one rested in the Dream Lab's waiting room—she wasn't actually tardy, just later than usual. On pass-through, she checked the walls, counted frames. It was part of her job to report all borrowings. Frequently, during the night, new, restless recruits appropriated the dream posters, particularly the script-only version that declared: "Dreams: 135 million years and counting." They also liked to cart off the Oneiric Wing's display, an old-style polysomnograph, complete with dangling silver-chloride cups. But keeping tabs on retro sleep monitors wasn't her responsibility; she only catalogued and reported tampering with the Dream Lab set. If there'd been no overnight high jinks, she proceeded directly to her workstation, took a seat and logged on a Founder-modified PRIME.

Drafting dreams wasn't strenuous, mentally or physically. She merely had to stay awake, listen and record. Unlike the Viennese icon, The Founders believed dreams were stunningly direct communiqués—not masterworks of devious indirection. To benefit, dreamers simply had to pay attention to the messaging. In the Dream Lab, residents used their Morpheus pads as crib sheets, recited those messages and, in finale, for research purposes, she or another drafter keyed in a theme: escape, estrangement, rescue and so forth, forbidden to ask follow-up questions or delve deeper into scenarios of muddle and chaos. Further investigation/interpretation was considered a private matter, left to the individual's discretion.

And yet Luce found that Founder-imposed passivity very difficult to maintain. Invariably she longed for more intricate details, a thorough accounting of each and every plot twist, full-blown descriptions of all characters, vermin included. What kind of tune did the rodent sing? What color costume did the rodent wear? Exactly *how* sharp those rodent teeth? Try as she might to resist filling in the gaps and ambiguities, sometimes she couldn't help it, in her head she elaborated, inventing a fuller narrative.

"There was a bomb in the cube," a resident reported last week.

A blue bomb, she supplied. *With sparklers.*

Sleep

"And it was rolling toward my unit, us. Like a bowling ball in slow-mo."

She had no idea what a bowling ball looked like or how it rolled, but in her accompaniment, that circular zigzagged.

Only dream hogs effectively quashed her fill-in impulse by leaving her no room to maneuver. They overplayed, overexplained, overanalyzed every sequence; reviewed, regretted, and incessantly revised; argued categorization, resisted closure.

"But it wasn't *exclusively* a rescue dream," they'd shadowbox. "There were elements of estrangement and transfiguration. Rescue by itself is totally misleading."

For research purposes, the rules were clear: one dream, one category. She followed her supervisor's instructions. "Don't upset them," he advised, "but don't clutter the database."

In their presence, and at their insistence, she typed or voiced multiple categories. After they left, she deleted all but one.

Once, during an excruciatingly endless session with a dream hog, she actually dozed off. Horrified by that lapse in conduct, she immediately reported herself to her supervisor. Instead of dismissing her on the spot, he'd laughed his gulpy laugh.

So what if she'd snoozed through a couple of the standards? No harm done, he said. "We have a million plus database. One blank-out won't warp the findings, I guarantee."

An amazing reaction. Parish thought so too.

"You're lucky," she said enviously. "The supers in Disorders are serious as saints. Around them, smiling is a sin."

This morning the supervisor's gulpy chuckle preceded him. Luce heard it a full three beats before he appeared at her station, cheeks shaved smooth for now. By afternoon, his beard always re-sprouted.

"Fresh out of dreamers—or did you scare them all away?" he asked, winking.

"None so far," she admitted without too much sheepishness. Gradually she was adjusting to his humor, less afraid it hid a stinging reprimand.

"Bum-it while we can, eh? A month from now, we'll be swimming in dreamers."

—Definitely. Winter meant extra sleep and extra sleep meant extra dreams. Once the early night/late dawn cycle started, the lightest to the deepest sleepers logged additional hours and lengthier dream plots. During winter, all the drafters got backed up. In a pinch, the nods, even the supervisors, drafted.

Bum-it. She liked that term. A Valley phrase no doubt, a leftover her supervisor had forgotten to purge. She should do an origin check. Although grid maps were strictly off-limits, Recovereds could legitimately access the bulk of Valley vocabulary via PRIME. Within certain boundaries, the database answered the asked. Parish logged countless queries.

What do people eat in The Valley?
(Anything they want to eat.)
Where do workers work?
(At E-screens, as many of you do.)
Does everyone wear Zip-Alls?
(Not everyone. But Zip-Alls are a favorite. They're comfortable, practical and attractive.)
<u>Would YOU live anywhere else?</u> Parish once typed.

The curser pulsed—the sum of its reply. That query verged too close to a Valley/Retreat comparison. Not allowed.

"Take a cruise-around, if you'd like. No sense staying

cooped up here with zilch to do."

Zilch. That must be another Valley throwback. Regardless, she bolted.

From courtyard vantage, the sky looked motionless, stymied, one big blob of gray. But across it, clouds raced. The wind raced too, through her pulls, through the orchard, shaking off, scattering leaves. Outside West Gate, the gardening nods raked and raked but seemed to make no headway against the leaf downpour. Farther along, in the Resting Grove, another nod brigade cleaned headstones. As they bent over the blocks of granite, their gray robes looked like droopy, sooty angels' wings. Four of the five Founders were buried there, Founder Phineas's burial plot awaiting its occupant. Already scripted, like all Founders' markers, Founder Phineas's epitaph connected sleep to death, death to peace: "A long dream of sleep itself."

But others in the cemetery rested beneath snider farewells. Her personal favorite: "Go, Go. Humankind cannot bear very much reality."

Residents often reported death dreams—but none sounded the least bit peaceful. Last month, a new recruit, glum, chinless and still mostly bald, described his cramped and crooked dream coffin. In it, he couldn't get comfortable. A dilemma. To illustrate, he drew its shape. The letter L.

"I didn't mind my relatives setting fire to the coffin," he confessed, agitated but not unduly so. "What I minded was the crookedness. Does that make sense?"

Few dreams made waking "sense," The Founders warned. If they did, of what benefit would they be?

Response protocols were complicated, convoluted and frequently confusing. During her first term, she'd been a procedurals pest, constantly running to her supervisor for advice and clarification.

"When residents ask my opinion, what should I say? What should I do?"

Staying mute seemed unnatural—and terribly rude.

"Quote bylaw 43," the supervisor advised, chuckling his gulpy chuckle. "Or just smile and nod."

She probably frowned at that answer; inside, she fretted.

"Lax. You're responding correctly," he assured. "If not, I'll let you know. That's MY job."

And dream drafting hers. She wanted to be better than "adequate" at it; she wanted to excel.

When she returned, a little girl sat on the floor of the waiting room.

"Apologies. Have you been waiting long?"

The dreamer shook her head no, but her slip-ons were off; crayons littered the floor.

When she scanned the arrival's palm, the database ID-ed Norma, six cycles young. She wasn't a Recovered; she'd been born at The Retreat.

"Would you like a beaker of milk before we start?"

"No. Gratitude," Norma whispered, looking at her toes.

"Do you remember what we do in here?"

A half-swallowed "yes."

If Norma elected to toe-stare all morning, Luce was obligated to sit patiently with her. No bullying or prodding allowed. On the inside seam of Norma's miniature pulls: a damp patch. Long nights were tough on *kinders*' bladders. As a *kinder*, Connie's timetable had been repeatedly outfoxed by extended darkness, the too-lengthy stretch between doze and dawn. Very often Connie soaked her cot. The nods replaced the soppy sheets matter-of-factly, without reprimand, assuming the cot-wetting phase would pass, which it did. But Connie didn't immediately stop wetting herself. For another unadjusted stretch, she kicked off the sheets, climbed free of the cot and, half-asleep, sprayed the floor.

"Difficult dream?"

"Bad" and "dream" were never linked at The Retreat.

Norma nodded, reluctantly shared her sketch. A creature unrecognizable to the drafter's eye.

"It came during the dark," Norma explained, "and hid in the corner."

Since "it" didn't pounce, bite, turn into an orangutan or disappear, only "sat there, looking ugly," it probably counted as a non-REM beast.

"Am I finished?"

"If you choose to leave."

In person and on E-file, Norma's image came across incomplete, prone to further flux. As they grew, some children's appearances underwent enormous change, the nods said. "But not you, Luce. You've looked like Luce since cycle 2. "

Was that a positive or a negative?—a question she'd yearned to ask the nods but never had.

Currently Norma's hair was blonde—like Connie's, her mouth similarly bow-shaped.

"Until again," she meekly murmured in departure. A resemblance buster. Connie, young or older, shunned meek.

Connie on the brain, during the dreamer break, Luce roamed the Deprivation menu.

Deprivation, General; Deprivation, Historical; Deprivation, Anecdotes; Deprivation, Symptoms: fatigue, irritability, mood swings, overeating, undereating, hallucinations, disorientation, death.

In Connie's case, before irreparable harm occurred, the nods had intervened, scotched her goal to beat a broadcaster's on-air record of 110 old-style hours of gab before he ran shrieking from the studio, an irresistible dare for someone who adored talk, despised sleep. As a nod-trainee, Connie hadn't adapted well to judicious silence or the nod-glide. In the sleep wards, in the labs, in the corridors and courtyard, she chattered and she scampered, frequently tripping on the hem of her voluminous gray robe. New recruits complained, residents complained, supervisors complained. Not nod material, Connie. Not adept at soothing grace.

A buzz at her waist. Another, more prolonged. Then the E-screen went blank. An auto shutdown.

Drilled in emergency procedure, she walked slowly, not rapidly, through the waiting room to the corridor, assumed position flush against the wall, palms out, to accommodate a scanner check. Her supervisor and his chief assistant lined up nearby. Light, both natural and artificial, flooded the hallway. The nearest monitor emitted no visuals, only the soundtrack of a prerecorded speaker's voice, meant to calm.

"'Oh sleep! It is a gentle thing, beloved from pole to pole.'"

Two nods, one for either side of the hall, passed through with portable I-dents.

"Please remain where you are until final clearance."

In the event of a security breach, certain response actions were mandatory; rooms and laboratories had to be thoroughly searched and re-secured.

"'Just as food causes the flesh to grow, marrow, thinned and weakened by the waking state, regenerates itself during sleep,'" the audio assured.

"Drug break-in, had to be," her supervisor declared.

"But what kind of idiot assumes we stock stay-awakes?" the chief assistant mocked.

"A recent transfer. Who else?"

"The nods aren't doing their job."

"The nods are overextended," her supervisor sharply corrected. "We can only re-clock so many at once."

Neither whispered. They must have forgotten she stood so close, all ears.

2

Like the vibra-belts strapped around residents' waists, The Retreat pulsated with rumors. Everyone had a theory.

"Too bad Connie's quarantined," Parish lamented. "She loves this kind of stuff. Then again, maybe it was Connie." She smiled wickedly. "The first-ever Deprivation breakout."

"Did your supervisor share her theory?" Luce asked for comparison sake.

"Not the supervisor. But one of the narcos claimed he'd witnessed the incident: a nod went psycho."

You couldn't put much credence in a narco tale, but still: both Luce and Parish hoped for an outlandish explanation, the more outlandish the better; both hoped a wily usurper still circulated, evading discovery.

"How about the dream docs? What's their explanation?"

Luce hesitated, but only for a blink. If she didn't trust Parish, whom did she trust?

"Drug snatch."

"Because the snatchers were too pumped or too laxed?"

A nod approached; they attempted solemn, exceedingly concerned.

"Special assembly, girls. Please report to the Assembly Hall."

"Assemble. That's original," Parish scoffed, a pro at not-quite-audible backchat.

Without pause the nod continued on her way.

At the Assembly Hall entrance, in addition to passing hands over the I-dent, each resident recited his or her dreamer code. There were clots of nods stationed everywhere.

Mega-thrilled, Luce and Parish squeezed each other's pulls.

"What excess! This might be WORTH missing a Valley gaze after all."

The murmurs that surged and eddied around the room were uncommonly anxious. Tension fed off tension. Veteran residents hummed with apprehension; Recovereds, with excitement. Only the supervisor contingent seemed uniformly irked. Scarcely resembling his easygoing self, Luce's supervisor, arms entwined, glared toward the podium.

With seats at an all-time premium, she and Parish flopped onto the floor. A moderator approached the podium with the usual measured steps, but Luce noticed a deviation; Parish, too. The speaker delegate held to the podium, leaned against it as if to steady herself before she began to speak.

"Apologies for the suddenness of this assembly and its disruption. We will be as brief as possible."

Oh, don't be brief! Anything but brief! Luce wanted to squeal.

"Late this morning, in response to a security breach, PRIME shut down, residents were verified, and all units, labs and common rooms extensively searched. There is absolutely no cause for distress. The Retreat is absolutely safe. No resident is in danger from anyone or anything."

Danger, Parish mouthed, cheeks splotched between freckles.

Luce felt her own cheeks heating to a burn. The suspense was totally thrilling.

"The problem originated in Transitional suite," the moderator continued. "We miscalculated the extent of a recent transfer's dependency. A pharmaceutical drawer was jimmied."

Parish groaned with disappointment, but a near-unanimous sigh of relief rose up from the rest of the crowd. Over on supervisor's row, Luce's supervisor fronted an expression that mixed irritation with vindication: he smiled thinly but kept his arms crossed, his jaw line faintly shadowed.

"What a gyp," Parish groused in the hallway.

Luce agreed. There they were: gathered up, revved up, and for what? To hear a moderator blandly assure all was well.

"A little less soothing, a little more chaos," she said longingly.

"Exactly." Parish pouted. "Is that too much to dream?"

A nod in passing patted each in turn.

3

After the drug snatch, security tightened. Now, when Luce arrived at Dream Lab, she had to palm the I-dent, submit to a face scan and recite her dream code. It was a nuisance, the triple check, but necessary, the nods said, because of a recent overabundance of transfers, a temporary imbalance between new and old.

The first dreamer of the day was a regular, well-versed in recitation. As soon as he took a seat across from her, he consulted his Morpheus pad, closed his eyes, started in.

"Panic," he said. "An overwhelming rush of extraordinary panic."

Parish's head popped in the room. She had shaved bald another patch of her skull directly above her neck, but no one except Luce had seen it. Inside The Retreat, she continuously wore a bandana. A bandana wasn't off-list; a headscarf wasn't forbidden.

Behind the dreamer's back, Parish mouthed: *Connie—definitely—out—tomorrow.*

REALLY? Luce mouthed back.

"But then I realized I didn't have to remain inside the panic. I could separate off and watch." When the door closed, the dreamer opened his eyes, frowned. "Are we alone?"

"Yes, " she said, dumping her grin. "We're alone."

When she returned to her room, Parish was already there, waiting.

"Isn't it mega?"

"Mega to the nth."

"Think she'll be the same old Con?"

Luce opened her mouth, closed it, too uncertain to hazard a guess. Since Connie's visiting privileges had been revoked, none of Connie's friends had seen her. No one really knew how she'd act or react, sprung from her long-term nap. More to the point, her supporters weren't exactly sure what to root for. If Connie resembled her old self too much, she'd be sent back to Deprivation by midnight. But if she'd transformed into the polar opposite, rested and lethargic and indifferent to, say, regicide, how would anyone recognize her?

"Maybe not QUITE the same," she ventured, hoped.

"Connie has to learn to agree to sleep when her body telegraphs the need," the nods said—again and again and again and again."

"But what if she's dull and boring and whipped?" Parish brooded.

"She's just been sleeping; she hasn't switched brains," Luce argued, sounding far more confident than she felt.

"Regardless, we ought to celebrate. She IS getting out of Deprivation, after all."

"A gather, you mean?"

"I'd like a gather, wouldn't you?"

"Will the nods permit it?"

"If we schedule it for the afternoon. Then everyone will have plenty of wind-down time."

"We could have it here, in my room. Invite all the Recovereds."

"But just our-age Recovereds," Parish qualified.

"If we pooled our Morpheus pads, we'd probably have enough scratch for a 'welcome back' banner."

Parish frowned. "I don't know about 'welcome back.' Technically, Connie never left."

"No," she admitted, embarrassed. Sometimes in her head she pictured Connie on a grand adventure, not merely sleeping in the next wing.

Begged and badgered, the nods did finally give permission for a gather—with several provisos: "The door stays closed, the sound proofing stays on and no one over-stimulates Connie."

"Exactly our plan!" Parish enthused—which went a little far, even in a please-the-nods context.

Their banner simply read: C-O-N-N-I-E!

—Which confused the majority of their guests, who didn't understand the reference, clueless about Connie's retro zeal.

"Like an old-style cheer," Luce felt compelled to explain. Continuously.

For the gather, the nods upped the thermostat, closed the window she preferred open—snow or no snow—and brought in extra floor cushions. The dietitians provided juice and squares, sugar-halved. One of the insomniacs in Disorders contributed tissue flowers, each petal painstakingly separated, and Parish had strung them into a crown.

"For Her Royal Highness Connie."

Altered or not, Connie would absolutely adore a crown.

Her nod escort agreed in advance to maneuver the guest of honor toward Luce's room without mentioning the gather inside.

The partiers waited in a clump, trying not to giggle. Footsteps. Two sets. The latch clicked. The door gaped. And then . . . the surprise they'd planned ricocheted. The person beside the nod looked less like Connie than Connie's mother, if Connie had a mother. Her new cheeks were chipmunk round, her entire face a puff.

"Parish! Luce! How lovely!" (Connie never said "how

lovely.") "Is all this for *moi*?"

After sweeping in, the honoree greeted the rest of the Recovered clan, cooing and mooing like someone—but not Connie. Even her voice sounded strange.

"I'm thinking the squares were a mistake," Parish said. "Low sugar or not."

Luce couldn't speak for staring. Connie carried the flower crown on her wrist as if it were an old-style purse.

Another nod knocked, entered. "Experiencing joy?"

"Enormous joy," Connie declared. "Do join us."

Connie? Inviting a nod to join?

"This is too skewed," Parish muttered.

"It is . . . skewed. But we can't *act* like it's skewed. Connie will think we disapprove."

"I do disapprove!" Parish grumped. "She's not Connie. She's a Connie inflate."

"Maybe that's what happens if all you do is eat and sleep."

"It's not *supposed* to happen," Parish vetoed. "You know the policy on overload."

"Lucy!" Connie exclaimed, waddling over. "Was this your idea? This little crunch and munch?"

"Not only mine," she defended, smiling too wide. "Parish's too. We wanted to celebrate, you know, seeing you."

Sharing the blame didn't exactly help. The gather was a disaster. A nod consumed most of the squares; the C-O-N-N-I-E banner sagged.

"To celebrate seeing me," Connie repeated, then paused. "Well? Seen an eyeful?"

Was that a wink? Luce looked to Parish for corroboration. With so much puff encircling Connie's pupils, any signal originating there was particularly hard to decipher. After executing a series of twirls, the celebrated announced her "tuckeredness" to the room at large and begged forgiveness for cutting the gather short.

There were disappointed groans, but no one absolutely refused to leave.

Since it was her room, Luce didn't leave. When Parish tried, Connie stuck out an arm. With a few too many flourishes, the guest of honor "graciously" donated the rest of the squares to the appreciative nods, closed the door, checked the sound-proofing bar, spun around and bark-laughed at her hosts. The bark-laugh both friends recognized, but surprised once too often in the last hour, neither immediately laxed.

"Finally. We've lost the losers. Do me a favor: no more Recovered soirees. It's like being in the bottom of a well fighting for airspace."

That barbed churlishness also sounded like the old Connie, but—

"Stop looking so quaked! I haven't *really* turned into Miss Congeniality."

"But you are . . . different," Luce ventured.

"You can say it: fat. Swelled up like a toad."

Parish grimaced. "That's not the worst part. You called someone 'dear.'"

Connie shrugged, plopped on the bed. "Since I look like someone else, I thought I'd try out a new personality too."

"So it's a gag?"

"Good enough to fool you two—apparently."

"But is it a permanent gag?" Parish pressed, dissatisfied with the brush-off.

"Who knows? As long as it's fun, as long as I'm fat."

Connie fell back on the bed cloth, extended her arms toward the ceiling. "You have no idea how ELEVATED I am to be here!"

They joined her on the bed, one on either side of her new girth.

Parish tried once more: "So Deprivation WAS awful?"

"Twenty-four-hour nourishment, twenty-four-hour doze. If I never sleep or eat again, I'm stockpiled, buds."

In a moment she bounced back up. "Turn around," she directed Parish, who obeyed. "Am I seeing what I think I'm seeing? Is that a true patch of non???"

4

Farting fall.

What a coy bastard it had been. A few damp mornings, crusty with frost. The occasional sprinkle of rain. No thunder-scored, lightning-lit storms blown in over the ridge; milquetoast temperatures, day and night. A model, mild prelude that gave no inkling to the sadistic brutality of the season ahead.

Within hours of its arrival, winter ruled the world, sealing ground, trees, rocks, stones, worms and lice in sparkling ice, trapping the Deserters in a white nightmare that swirled.

In The Valley, snow counted as a special effect, something to peer at behind therma-glass on the way to and from the flusher, something municipals carted elsewhere as soon as it licked pavement. Lieutenant Maud had to become a Deserter to feel a flake on her cheek, taste it on her tongue, but the charm of that intimacy also dissolved quickly. At her core, she was convinced: it wouldn't be hunger, filth, boredom or a vigilante PRO that finished off the Deserters. It would be the demon snow.

Safety in numbers, safer in a pack.

Silently she chanted that mantra, hiking in a blizzard, following Rosa and the erratic course their commander set. From her end-of-the-line position, she incessantly counted the heads that weaved and wagged ahead of her, spirits in a theatre of white, trying to dodge snow darts.

Cook pitched forward, knocking against Four, taking his comrade down with him as he toppled. She got to both, got them on their feet, but during the assist lost sight of the commander.

"Rosa, stop!"

No shadows churned in the blur ahead.

"They've left us!" Cook howled as Four slumped sideways, coughing until he spit red.

"Commander! Circle back!"

For one horridly extended moment that petition produced no response the abandoned could see, hear or imagine. They faced whiteout, pure whiteout, terrifyingly alone before a familiar face parted the snow scrim.

"The cave at Brush Fork," Rosa ordered, the last to emerge, ghostly but seemingly lucid.

Prior to stumbling toward other drifts, Maud insisted on linkage: one comrade holding to the duster or tool belt ahead.

"*Don't* release. Whatever you do, don't release."

The low and muddy cave blocked the snow and the worst of the wind. By cramming in and squeezing close, they shared what body heat their near-frozen limbs could generate, and still she pushed and shoved their pack closer, determined to jam them tighter than a keyboard's keys.

"No space between you!" she insisted, jostling legs and arms and unfeeling feet. "Four, take the far end. I'll cover the front."

She spread frayed therma rugs over their laps and tucked. No one spoke or resisted her arrangements. But soon not even the roaring wind could counter the exhaustion and keep them conscious. One by one they nodded off, Rosa included, sleeping if sleep it could be called, every muscle in contraction. Twice more she counted off bodies, a lieutenant's responsibility, then she too closed her eyes. In her anxious dream, the cave groaned and rumbled like a two-ton bear, threatening at any moment to fall upon them, smother, consume.

Neither crashing cave nor equivalent noise woke her from that fretful sojourn—what woke her was the quiet. Profound, ominous, unnatural silence, invading her dream space. Quietness on the march, fanning out in all directions. Soundlessness reconfigured as powerful, palpable threat.

Without disturbing the others, she edged toward the cave's opening to preview the revelations of a pale dawn. Like the Deserters, the blizzard had taken a breather, leaving piles of itself as a token gift. Behind her, Rosa stirred and pushed to her feet, cursing her stiff limbs. At the sight of the snoozers around her, she cursed louder and started down the line, poking and prodding them awake, ordering them up and out.

Uttering amazing: that no one bit at those jabbing fingers or lunged for that sniping throat. Miraculous: that weary beyond weary, the others still obeyed their commander, struggling to queue up, single file, in knee-deep snow.

One, two, three, four, five. One, two, three, four, five, six—Maud counted. But she only counted six when she included herself.

"Where's Four?"

Like confused children, her comrades turned and twisted in place, blinking at the faces left and right.

"Where's Four? We're missing Four. Have you seen him, Repeat? Did he transfer in the middle of the night?"

"'We lived like normal citizens. It's incredible what you accuse us of.'"

"I'm not accusing, I'm asking," she bleated, but her gut had gone queer.

Squalling about the hold-up, about insubordination so early in the day, Rosa kicked a white tunnel toward the caucus and demanded an explanation.

"It's Four. He's not here."

Back at the mouth of the cave, the commander dropped to her haunches and snarled: "Four? You still in there, you farting slacker?"

"He was next to you, Cook. Do you remember when he left? Focus!"

"I remember him next to me when we went in," Cook answered hazily.

But what about now? What about <u>now</u>?

Rosa's head, then feet, disappeared and she followed. Inside the cave Four's name reverberated.

"We're too far from the opening! There's no light," Rosa carped, voice hoarse with annoyance, but the flamer revealed terrified eyes.

"Four, you virus, we had to light a flamer!" the commander ribbed. "You're really on the crap list now."

Fear in the guise of snide.

Deeper than it appeared from the opening, the cave narrowed quickly.

"He's hiding," Rosa grunted. Louder, she charged: "You think you can hide from me? You think a commander won't find you? You'd better be dreaming up one bitch of an excuse, comrade!"

Hindered by girth, she had a tougher time navigating, but the padding also helped. Rosa had shredded her palms on the rough floor. The path Maud followed was speckled with commander blood.

"Take my gloves. Take them!"

Rosa refused, continuing to shout insults, continuing forward until, with sickening abruptness, that progress halted. By the time Maud caught up, Rosa had folded into herself and begun to moan. Low, inconsolable moans.

To reach the body ahead, Maud had to keep crawling, up to and over the commander obstruction. Stretching, she finally made contact, found Four's wrist, pressed that fragile joint of bone and sinew, searching for the beat of a pulse and searching in vain. Curled into a tighter ball than Rosa, knees at his gut, the Four they had known had departed. When the flamer illuminated the eyes staring from his green mask, those glazed, unblinking orbs told everything. Four possessed an unassailable excuse for shirking orders; the dead cannot obey.

"Lieutenant? Commander?" Anxiety intensified by echo, the cave's entry all but blocked by peering heads.

"We're coming. Stay back," she shouted and that instruction echoed too.

Pummeling her thighs with her fists, mouth clamped shut, Rosa moaned internally now, but Maud heard that wailing as clearly as she heard the thudding fists. Four had been with them, a trusted comrade, from the beginning. Now he lay contorted by cold and exile, victim of a Deserter's fate. Never large, he had finished his term at bantam weight, as wrinkled as an ancient, a skeleton wrapped in tissue.

"Rosa," she said, grabbing hold of those beating fists, deflecting another self-inflicted blow. "We've got to take him out."

Rosa pulled away and bit into her bloody thumb. "My fault—"

"Stop it!"

" . . . if I'd stayed awake—"

"Stop it! We've got to get him out. We've got to deal with the others."

Rosa sobbed once, then jerked her chin, assenting. She grabbed hold of Four's useless legs; Maud swiveled his shoulders and hooked his arms. Between them, they bumped him toward light. An awkward, undignified ride.

"'All art is temporal. All art is lost. Go to Egypt. Go look at the Sphinx. It's falling apart,'" Repeat keened as soon as the three emerged.

The rest circled round.

"Is Four sick?"

"Did he hurt himself?"

"Can't he walk?"

But once the carriers released their hold and Four remained balled, the questions ceased. Distraught and desperate, the survivors shunned the dead to fixate exclusively on their commander, to emulate her example. But Rosa inspired no one. Still on her knees at the mouth of the cave, she plucked wordlessly at Four's sleeve.

"We have lost a dedicated comrade," Maud said, in Rosa's stead, to the hollow-eyed in a field of snow. "But as Deserters, we must continue."

To communalize the personal, abstract the specific, one resorted to, relied on, the language of revolution.

Communal and abstract debilitated less.

She removed Four's tool belt from his waist, fastened it around Repeat's. With Cook's help, she maneuvered her duster under Four. Via that carry-all, the dead was hoisted into air. Rosa still hadn't moved; now she plucked snow.

"Repeat, make sure Rosa follows us."

A reversal of the usual order, but there it was. At all costs, especially now, Rosa must be shielded, guarded, prevented from going completely mad.

"'When you look into the abyss, the abyss looks into you.'"

"Repeat? Do you process? Assist Rosa. Keep her in sight."

"'Let me stand for a while in front of the transient: not accusing, but admiring, marveling.'"

"Repeat! Do as I say!"

The makeshift cortege headed downhill, eastward, on the hunt for a piece of less than solid ice, a plot of frozen earth they could get at, dig into, dislodge by dent of labor, their grim procession moving slowly but in accord, Repeat trailing Rosa, both canting, both wailing.

"Mourn all ye groves in darker shades be seen. Let groans be heard where gentle winds have been, melancholy flowers— once men.'"

Near Dodger Spur, they came upon a small, flatish clearing where fir trees had taken the brunt of the blowing drifts; inside that circle the snow was half as deep as elsewhere. If Rosa registered how close they had veered toward sleeper territory, she gave no indication. Working in teams, all but Rosa used Four's collection of salvaged tools to dig his grave. Rosa dug barehanded. But when the commander began to dig with her teeth, heedless of rank, Maud snatched her from that deepening pit and forced her on the sidelines. Mourning could be assimilated; mania further traumatized.

They didn't dig a six-by-six-by-two-foot hole. They didn't need to. In his near-fetal position, Four, what remained of him, was scarcely larger than a young boy. Using fir needles, Cook tied together the slits of the green cap—to spare the dead eyes beneath the insulting bombardment of soil. She couldn't bury the duster without condemning herself to Four's fate, but gladly donated her yellow cap for his grave pillow. In unison they reshifted the crusty dirt, none prepared to perform that hideous act in solo. As their comrade disappeared, she tried to recall some prayer of religion, not revolution, but the phrase that surfaced was as harsh a fact as the corpse: "'In deep sadness there is no place for sentimentality. It is as final as the mountains: a fact. There it is.'"

She devised a marker of sorts: a crooked 4 made of twigs, encircled by fir branches. Once the hole was no longer a hole but a mounded shape, Cook and the others edged it with rocks. With solemn deliberation Repeat assumed speaker position, and all but Rosa bowed their heads.

"'Peace to the bearded corpse. He saw in the forest something coming grim, but did not change his purpose. Honest and cruel, peace now to his soul. A wrinkled peace to this good man.'"

"Peace, peace," those left echoed.

"'Do not deny, do not deny, thing out of thing. Do not deny in the new vanity the old, original dust.'"

A lone turkey vulture swooped low over the disturbed and their disturbance. Cook more neatly arranged the fir tribute. She knelt and shifted a muddy, vagrant clod. Rosa pulled steadily at her blackened fingers.

"I here begin and end my narrative—melancholy my story be.'"

A sudden wind blew through, toppled the 4, scattered the greenery.

"'It was the conclusion reached by some students of the supernatural: you could speak to the dead, but they had nothing to say,'" Repeat informed.

And then, in silence, they turned as one and walked away.

5

"Fail-proof, I'm telling you!" Connie insisted.

Whenever the nods looked elsewhere, she scraped another section of food off her tray into a bag conveniently lodged between her knees.

Released from Deprivation less than a week, already angling to break another rule.

"During my enforced rest, I worked out all the kinks," she swore, bobbing up and down on the cafeteria bench. "After lights out, a sneak-about. Just me, you and fun, fun, fun."

Risky fun: Connie's favorite kind.

"Are you with me? Yea or nay?"

Luce considered, reconsidered and considered some more. She'd heard fail-proof Connie schemes before.

"What about our night caps?"

"There's a way to jimmy the works. Trust me, I know all about tricking sleep monitors."

"But what if they catch us?"

"They won't catch us! They haven't even caught me ditching food. Nods are a non-factor."

"You don't know that."

Connie dropped her voice. "They took me on as a trainee. How smart can they be? Besides which, the smartest nod would have to be in exactly the right place at exactly the right time. What are the chances of that?"

"What were the chances they'd catch you in Archives after hours?"

Connie stiffened. "So they got lucky. Once."

"They didn't get lucky. They *knew*."

"Knew/schmoo. We can be out and back before anyone realizes we're gone. If you're spooked, we can try a trial run."

"Just as risky," Luce stalled.

"Come on," Connie goaded between food dumps. "Whaddaya got to lose? A few measly hours of sleep? The moon will be mega-watt tonight. We won't even need to snitch beamers."

"But how are we going to get out?"

"Lower from your window. The nods expect that window to stay open. Am I right or am I right?"

"I hope I don't regret this."

"Will you lax? We're leaving the compound, not kidnapping a nod." Connie giggled. "THAT treat we'll save for another night."

She didn't bother to protest; not even Connie would concoct a nod snatch.

Before dark, as prep, they dangled an experimental bed cloth. It didn't reach the ground.

"Two is still good," Connie revised. "We'll use both of yours."

"But we can't *shred* them."

"Twist and tie," Connie said, as if no solution could be more obvious.

"But what if we can't climb back in?"

"But, but, but. Is that your contribution?"

She scowled. "Sometimes it's better to review in advance, Con. We can't fly back in."

"All right, all right. Let me drift a moment."

Once more they cased the angle.

"Forget climbing cloths. See those jutting stones? They're as good as handholds, maybe better." Connie clapped. "For

Sleep

once, fake-monasterial works in our favor."

Next, they synchronized alibis.

"And remember," Connie advised, "make the bed look lumpy, but human."

"Like anyone would mistake rolled pulls for a body."

"For your *information*, I happen to have scanned every pre-chip prison flick in Archives. Want to guess how many plots depended on a stuffed blanket flubbing the guards? Just every single one."

"We're not breaking out of prison."

"Spoken like someone who's never been confined to Deprivation," Connie replied with no trace of her trademark grin.

"And why do *you two* look so smug?" Parish suspiciously inquired at final meal.

"'Cause it's a smug day," Connie zinged.

Luce concentrated solely on her tray and a bland blob of milk pudding. Unappetizing, that stomach settler, but she forced down several spoonfuls. Her stomach definitely needed settling.

Parish continued to stare. "Something's in process. What?"

Luce had warned Connie: Parish sensed secrets, honed in on skewed behavior of any sort.

"So don't act skewed," Connie dismissed.

But Parish's probe had jangled Connie—*Luce* could sense that. Too quickly Connie manufactured a burp, wiped her mouth and declared: "That does it for me."

"But you haven't eaten anything," Parish said.

Connie yawned. "Too crashed to eat. Need to sleep."

Luce also picked up her tray.

"You're leaving too?"

"Bumper dream day."

Not a whole lie—a partial.

"Until again."

To their backs, Parish called: "I almost forgot. Disorders is sending over a dreamer tomorrow."

Disorders never sent dreamers to the lab. Luce swiveled.

"Yeah, well, we're too pooped to voice about dreamers now," Connie said, steering for the door.

"Says who?" Parish bristled. "The energy patrol?"

"Go ahead, Con. I'll catch up."

Connie halted, tapped her foot. "No," she sniped churlishly. "I'll wait until *you're* ready."

"So who is this dreamer? A new arrival?"

But Parish had refocused on Connie.

"Are you jagging?"

"No."

"Are you *sure*? Because the nods aren't blinkered. Eventually they'll notice you don't sleep."

"If you want to worry about something, worry about the nods confiscating that shaver of yours!"

"It's a de-maner. Nobody calls them shavers anymore."

"*Parish*! Is the dreamer a new arrival?"

"Better," Parish confided, still glaring at Connie. "The oldest Recovered on record. As old as Founder Phineas. Maybe older. A nod found her on the grounds yesterday, half starved, half frozen."

"So why is Disorders sending her to the Dream Lab?"

"Because the head super doesn't think she's hallucinating. He's convinced she's reciting dreams. White hair, cataracts. Mega spooky looking, crazy too."

"Then she'll love it here," Connie said. "Crazies always do."

Two of the three exchanged glances.

No, Connie wasn't the same old Con, but now wasn't the hour to check out all the bells and whistles of her latest operating system. The moon beamed.

"Caution," Parish said.

"Gratitude," Luce acknowledged before realizing neither she nor Connie had confessed to undertaking anything dangerous.

And yet she did feel daring, extremely daring, out of bed past lights-dim, crouched at the window, dressed warmly and clutching two bed cloths.

"Perfect!" Connie enthused, stroking the fake Luce lump in bed. The night cap tinkering was also an unqualified success; if the monitor wasn't fooled, it pretended to be. Only the bed cloth proved difficult. No matter how energetically they twisted, they couldn't crimp the fabric small enough to tie in a knot that held.

"I feared that."

"No fear talk," Connie outlawed. "We'll use a single."

"And then what: *jump*?"

"It's not that far."

It wasn't close, either. The battery-bright moon disclosed as much.

"We have two choices: stay here all night twisting cloth or jump part way."

Connie went first. "Since I'm still a cow, you might need to double loop."

Holding tight, Luce watched her partner clamber over the sill and disappear. The cloth jerked in her hand. "Snot!" she heard, then a softer whisper-warning:

"Expect to roll."

Taller than Connie, at the end of the sheet, she dangled closer to impact.

"No nods, no broken bones. Mission accomplished!"

They travelled the gully between walls and snow banks. From the outside in, The Retreat look big and boxy but not luminous. Even the courtyard lights were dark.

At East Gate, Connie assured: "Don't fret. I hacked the code," and went to work.

Beyond that iron divider, the mischief makers didn't stop to celebrate or congratulate; they ran willy-nilly, swerving left at the trailhead, pushing through branches that rebounded snow, giggling loud and louder. Destination didn't remotely matter. What mattered was the race itself, bodies doing what bodies did if permitted: spinning, leaping, squealing, no nods to enforce a calm down.

"Time out," Connie panted and fell against a tree trunk for a breath boost. "I'm not quite back to petite."

Then off again they went, weaving in and out of rhododendron thickets, baying at the moon, pelting each other with snowballs. In the center of a ring of fir trees, they aped the stiff-legged gait of cassandras, invented prophecies to shriek at each other and the silent night.

"Beware of earthworms."

"Beware of wood rot."

"The world will end tomorrow."

"You will meet a tall, dark, mysterious stranger."

"I will? When?"

Imitating a log, Connie snow-rolled as far as her new bulk would carry her. When Luce did the same, she came to a stop beneath Connie's raised finger, pointing across moon.

"Over there. Share what you see."

"Fir branches?" she guessed, struggling up, beating snow off her bottom.

"Again."

"A root?"

"It's not a root. It's some kind of . . . marker."

Stripped of the comfort of mutual silliness, she suddenly felt very, very exposed.

"Leave it alone, Con."

But Connie had already started inching back.

For the first time since leaping out the window, she registered the brutal cold and their vulnerability within it. The moony night no longer seemed so benign. When she looked around now she saw a landscape laced with menace, an unsettling mirage of the unknown and indistinct.

"Connie! Leave it."

But Connie had already hunkered down, reached.

On her own she started to run before Connie grabbed hold of her elbow, propelling them both faster, their second snow sprint a caricature of frantic dream rush. Every element in the universe seemed to conspire against their progress, collude to impede their escape. Even the air felt leagues thick, motion-proof.

At the farthest rung of statues, but not until, Connie doubled over, gasping.

"A . . . grave."

The blood pounded so loudly in Luce's ears she thought she'd misheard.

"But we were nowhere near West Gate."

"Not—a—resident's—grave."

"But if it wasn't a resident's grave . . ."

"Ex-act-ly."

She had never heard Connie's voice crack before—from exertion or fright.

That novelty terrified too.

6

What the others always assumed was Maud's secret stash of sweets was in reality a stash of carbo chips. After counting out Rosa's share, she handed the remainder to Repeat.

"Get the troops to the cave at Spider's Ridge, then distribute these. The commander and I will join you in the morning."

Whatever the necessary persuasion—fistfight or half nelson—Rosa would sleep tonight. Sheer grief might land her in the grit beside Four, but it was a lieutenant's responsibility to prevent that force from coupling with fatigue.

"'Disappointment is the lot of woman,'" Repeat warbled, cradling the chips. "'The business of my life is to deepen the disappointment until my sisters no longer bow to its burden.'"

"Is that supposed to be a pep talk? Go!"

Rosa had wandered off from the gravesite on her own, but in her condition neither could nor would get far fast. A single set of footprints headed north. If the snow didn't start again before midnight, if the lull stayed a lull, one puny respite before the next deluge . . . *if, if, if,* Maud thought, crunching through territory that denied the possibility of spring.

By the second switchback, she'd caught sight of Rosa, a dozen yards ahead, stumbling, listing, the curio in this winterscape. Although the silver tunic blended nicely with the scenery, the commander's spasmodic movements blended with nothing. Lurching to the right, rebounding to the left, Rosa staggered like a drunk. Would that she were drunk. Drunk her lieutenant could handle. Drunk she could cure. But

Rosa's addiction was exhaustion, exhaustion complicated by new loss, new guilt.

When Rosa finally toppled, Maud was close enough to save the commander's nose if not her knees the damage of sharp ice.

"It's Lieutenant Maud. Maudie," she identified—in the unlikely event Rosa's brain still distinguished one apparition from another.

Her superior gave no sign of caring where she sprawled or with whom. Pulled to her feet, blank-eyed, Rosa took one step into another march, collapsed backward into the unfurled therma rug. With a bit of a tug that rug wrap circled twice.

Between boulders, semi-sheltered from the wind, she deposited the bundle, prepared an extravagant flamer fire, unwilling to risk ranging for combustibles. Even swaddled in therma rug, Rosa might try to flee.

Jump-started, the scanty pile of saplings lit quickly; Rosa's cheeks took longer to flush. Occasionally she fisted the restraining wrapper, mumbling nonsense, but that kind of resistance was easy enough to override. Getting chips down a recalcitrant throat and keeping them down proved tougher. Rosa fought off nourishment as ferociously as she fought off warmth, hissing and batting at any morsel that approached her mouth. Twice defeated by a clamped jaw, her feeder dispensed with the niceties. With one hand Maud grabbed Rosa's hair, forced her head back and kept it back; with the other, she pried open the commander's lips and one by one shoved chips past those clenched teeth. Whatever Rosa spat out got licked clean and shoved back in. Even after the Rosa's fists gave up the battle to shadow-punch, her eyelids fought the good fight, fluttering up and down, up and down, trying to flap off drowsiness.

"Give it up, Rosa," her lieutenant crooned, a makeshift lullaby for a frigid afternoon.

With excruciating slowness, the day dimmed, blacked out. The slope blocked the moon. The light that scored Rosa's slack face was firelight, and only that.

Judging by the number of flamers left, as best Maud could calculate, neither of them would freeze before sunrise, but they wouldn't sweet-dream of roasting in hell either.

"'The people in hell say nothing but WHAT?'" Repeat was fond, a tad too fond, of reminding. Regardless, after a lifetime of rhetorical babble, that single, tetchy syllable sounded almost swell—an ideal war cry. Only one catch, esteemed comrades: you gotta be dead to utter it.

In the Biblicals' version, hell streamed: here today, not gone tomorrow. Before the Deserters deserted, a few of that persuasion still hawked God at Valley intersections, scattering when the PROs arrived. But Biblicals never actually posed a legitimate threat to techno-order precisely because they didn't believe in rebelling against hell, major or minor. Their sect fully expected earthly existence to stink, waiting for their deity to snatch them up and away, into the glorious blue yonder.

And what were the Deserters waiting for?

"'There is no entrance fee, but quitting is impossible—the only way out is through the cemetery.'"

Another of Repeat's favorite quips, but one he kindly suppressed standing over Comrade Four, the first of the last to go.

In fifteen cycles, they'd never buried one of their own. People got fed up, disappeared or, like Seven, got booted out by Rosa. Politics, or what passed for politics, depleted their ranks, not death.

Until today.

Today the turkey vultures got wind of a new taste treat: Deserter carrion. Deserter guts. Deserter gristle.

Asleep and agitated, Rosa heaved and mewed. A thin line of drool snaked down her chin. As gently as possibly, her lieutenant-cum-keeper dabbed it off. Out of flamer range that saliva trickle would turn into an icicle. Out of flamer range, they'd both expire. But for what exactly were they staying alive? A Corporate reprieve? Even if Corporate miraculously pardoned their crimes of murder, kidnapping and a conspiracy to overthrow, as registered Antis, reformed or otherwise, they'd be denied PRIME access. In The Valley, without a PRIME connect, you might as well be dead. Down in the maze, PRIME *was* life, the only life.

A good comrade was supposed to embrace the bitter end, revel in it. A good comrade was supposed to relish adversity, excel at sacrifice, exalt in her own demise—not mourn a fallen comrade.

So she made a lousy comrade. So farting what. She loved Four, wanted him back: miserably alive, not heroically dead. To preserve the Deserter remainder was her new cause, her only cause, now.

Deep into dream, Rosa thrashed, trying to run, trying to flee.

As if Maud dreamed it herself, she knew every twist and turn of that nightmare. Before its conversion to sleep story, she and Rosa had lived its plot, run that race in tandem.

To spare the commander, she'd offered to make the delivery herself, in solo, but Rosa wouldn't countenance the sparing, wouldn't accept that small relief.

"I have to do this, Maud," she insisted. "This much, at least, I have to do."

That the baby ever breathed was more than half a miracle, a testament to nature's genius. Nothing was sterile and—among Deserters—less than nothing known about giving birth, emotional or procedural. When labor started, Rosa squatted over a patch of bluets and touch-me-nots until something slick and slippery as an eel slid out. As lieutenant, she had crouched alongside, holding a rag between Rosa and petals in case the mother's bloody grip gave way.

"It's a girl," she'd announced—to the birth-giver, to the indifferent mountains all around. Rosa's baby girl. An infant who'd survived the womb plunge but rejected the breast, refused to swallow pulped nuts and berries. To save her, Rosa had to give her away: to the sleepers or Valley charity—which meant: no choice.

To serve as lookout, she'd accompanied them as far as a shimmering pond guarded by statues, foolishly obeyed Rosa's request to wait there while the two of them ventured deeper into the sleeper zone, diminished, then obliterated, by swollen green.

Since the baby had slept throughout the hike, there was no reason to suspect it would wake, deposited at the sleepers' door. But vehement squalls had vibrated the air long before Rosa's panicked flight vibrated ground. As soon as the commander's anguished face became visible, Maud ran too, instinctively toward Rosa, then with her, holding on to her hand as schoolgirls do, fleeing a misdemeanor.

But Rosa's deed hadn't been wrong, just difficult.

"You did what was best," she said as they ran, and again when Rosa woke from the first instance of memory restaged. "For the kid. For all of us."

What tiny comfort Rosa might have drawn from that cliché had abraded with the years and the countless repetitions of a dream that harped on failure, charged her with abandonment. Against that tide of accusation, Rosa jogged in place and wept, slapping at her ears, struggling to block out what she never could: her child's cry.

Maud took the tortured dreamer into her lap, rocked back and forth, cuddled the upset without hope of lessening it. As she did, a single flake floated down, brushed her eyelash, followed by another that grazed her lip. White dots in a dark sky, on white ground, dousing yellow flamer fire.

She would not relinquish another Deserter to that whiteness. *She would not.*

7

The next morning Connie missed early meal, but Luce stood first in line, delighted by daylight, eager for the company of cheerful nods, soothed by the toasty safety of a Retreat cafeteria. Last night, back from their sneak-about, she hadn't once closed her eyes, afraid what dream would make of her and Connie goofing next to a grave.

If there had been a grave.

Maybe it was just a pit.

"You look tired, dear," a ladling nod observed.

"Do I?" She strove to sound perky.

"Did you have a restless night?"

"Restless?" she repeated nervously.

The nod smiled. "Lots of busy dreams?"

"Busy—yes," she agreed, lifting her tray.

"You look like dung," Parish said. "What about Connie? Why isn't she here, looking the same?"

"Maybe she's sleeping. She's supposed to be on B schedule."

"Supposed to be," Parish said.

After that, Luce lost track of the conversation. Her head hurt; her eyes felt bruised and swollen. She wanted to talk to Connie and wanted never to see her again because seeing her would evoke a flashback of moon and suggestive shadows, a mound of scraped dirt where snow should have been.

"You'll be there, won't you?" she heard, directed her way.

"Where?"

"What are you practicing, auto-dream? The old lady? Will

you be at the lab when she arrives?"

"I think so."

"Because I need to hear from a reliable source whether it's dream fugue or fact spew."

"Why do you care so much?"

"You'll see."

Not instantly. When she reached the Dream Lab, no old woman with cloudy eyes waited with a nod escort. Settled in the drafter's chair, she kept remembering, seeing and remembering the clearing, watching a mind-cam film of her and Connie running scared.

The dreamer balefully stared.

"Apologies. You had a question?"

"No. I'm finished."

But which category to check? Exhibition? Transfiguration? Estrangement? She hadn't been listening; she had no idea.

"Which classification do you think best represents your dream?"

The resident dithered. "I'm not sure."

"Take your time," she said, shocked by her own brazenness. Is this what happened when you started breaking rules? You just kept breaking them, one after another? Is this what The Founders meant, linking deficit with ethical blips? One night's loss and already she was glibly lying, shirking her obligations, flubbing her job? The resident left, pouting. "Estrangement" it was.

The en route special dreamer—fortunately—wasn't her responsibility, but as part of her supervisor's team, she'd been invited to attend the interview.

"Who knows?" He chuckled. "We might all learn a thing or two."

When the nods had found the woman, her hair was clotted with thistles and dirt, Parish reported. Today it fluffed around the visitor's face like a cotton ball, whiter than the bandage across her nose. Her skin was striated with age, purple in patches; her gnarled hands hooked inward. A cataract clouded her left eye, making the laser glare sent out by the other all the more unnerving. Despite Parish's prep report, face to face, the woman looked much older than Founder Phineas. Even her weariness seemed mega-ancient.

"Soothing to meet you," the supervisor greeted and cleared a chair for their guest.

The nod escort eased her charge into the seat provided. The good eye cased the room. Briefly the supervisor consulted a chart, then launched in, using his standard chipper voice.

Unwilling to stand directly in front of either the sighted or unsighted eye, Luce gravitated toward the corner.

Post-intros, the supervisor politely, correctly, paused to allow response. But the woman made no response.

"We understand you have some . . . interesting stories."

Still she didn't speak or move. The supervisor leaned back on his stool.

"Don't be afraid," the nod escort encouraged. "You can voice freely here."

Tilting her head slightly to the left, the woman replied: "Why would I be afraid? I've known real danger."

Her voice sounded phlegmy but uncowed.

"Tell us about the danger," the supervisor coaxed.

The good eye jerked. "I've already told."

"Humor us. We'd like to listen again."

The old woman raised a claw-y hand and spun it round her head.

"As long as you can work, you're fine. After that, as long as you can run—fine. There is no after that after that."

"Running from . . . whom?" the supervisor pried.

The attending nod frowned sternly in rebuke. Not even a top-ranking supervisor had permission to contour a revelation.

In any case, the woman seemed to have lost the inclination to accommodate. Minutes passed; she sucked on her lips. The supervisor rose from his stool, thumping his clipboard, clearly on the verge of terminating the session when the woman pitched forward, gushing words.

"There was an old woman who lived in The Valley. She had so many children she didn't know what to do. "

"Nursery rhymes," the chief assistant harrumphed. "She's reciting old-style nursery rhymes."

The supervisor signaled quiet.

The longer she spoke, the more the old woman's face and hands contorted. The matter-of-fact monotone completely disappeared. She gurgled and she shrieked.

"In The Valley, when the sun disappears, children disappear too. You can make them disappear. It's not so hard. Turn your back, they're gone. I turned my back, my children flew into the moon. 'Climb up. Rescue us,' they taunted. 'A mother ought to be able to rescue her children. A mother ought to save what she has so carelessly thrown away.'"

Inexplicably light-headed, Luce felt herself leaning harder and harder against the solid wall.

"I started at dawn, climbing on sidewalks; at noon I climbed on rocks, and when the sun went down and the moon came up, my children jeered from its shine. 'She's not going to make it. Too old, too weak, too late. Maybe we never had a mother,' they said. 'Maybe we were always moon.' 'No, no,' I corrected. 'I am your mother. I will reach you. I will. I'm younger than I look, stronger than I seem.' And I tried, I did so try!"

The claw-y hands bounced up and down. The good eye

leaked tears. "I tried, I tried, I tried."

Luce felt her own arms pimple; she could not fold herself tiny enough.

One last flurry, and the thrashing ceased. Silence filled the gap, and then, as if the audio had rewound, the monotone resumed.

"There was an old woman who lived in The Valley. She had so many children she didn't know what to do."

"Interesting diversion," her supervisor mused in the aftermath of that scene.

"Interesting as in potential or as in deranged?" quizzed the chief assistant.

Luce's knees shook, but she forced herself to relinquish the wall brace.

"I was wondering . . . would it be possible . . . since we're not too backed up . . ."

"A nap unit? Of course. You're due a few."

"I'm just really, really tired," she sputtered, making excuses her supervisor didn't care to hear.

"No justification required," he replied, shooing her along.

Once in her room she crawled into bed without removing her slip-ons or vibra-belt. She must have slept because she dreamed children's faces had replaced the moon, but when she opened her eyes it was Connie's moon face that hovered, shouted.

"Wake up! Wake up! Wake up!"

"Is it morning?" she asked groggily. But it couldn't be—not yet. Could it?

"Just rise, will you? We should be in Archives already!"

Confused, she stroked her temple; her mouth tasted unbelievably foul. "But you're not supposed to be in Archives," she slurred. "You're restricted."

"Do you or don't you want to know whose grave we tripped over?"

She rolled on her side, burrowed beneath bed cloths that Connie instantly stripped away.

"How could you not want to know? It's a mystery! It's better than a mystery! Someone could have been *wiped* right next to us!"

"Dead doesn't necessarily mean killed."

"Not necessarily, but *possibly*."

Connie was much too revved. Never a good omen when Connie got this revved.

"Isn't it after curfew?"

"So what? You'll double as lookout."

At the half-opened door, Connie peeked into the hallway.

"*Hurry*! We won't have a clear shot forever."

"A clear *shot*?"

"Just follow. I'll explain reference-prompt later."

Far too expertly, Connie negotiated corridors Luce didn't recognize. Months in Deprivation hadn't blanked the back way to Archives or the procedural intricacies of tricking the I-dent.

"This isn't smart, Connie."

"Lax, will you? I've done this a gagillion times."

At the E-screen partially blocked by a partition, Connie keyed on because, she said:

"PRIME's finicky about voice commands for Archives. Sometimes it won't register whisper."

Since Luce had never had occasion to whisper at PRIME, she had no basis for comparison. Which meant she had to rely solely on Connie's judgment. But could Connie's judgment be relied on? In regard to anything?

"I've already scanned Crime/Generic. Now I'm scanning

Assassins."

Before Luce could balk, the screen filled with enough data to titillate even the most extreme retro junkie.

Victims of: Caesar, Dutschke, Gandhi, Nero . . . *See*: **"I had a dream . . ."** *See*: **"Give peace a chance."**

"Whoa! Are you reading this? The Avengers, The Cell, Fatah, Front Line, IMRO, Red Brigades, Red Guards, Tupamaros."

Speculative causes of terrorism: poverty, boredom, youthful aggression. . . . *See also*: **Fright Decade, Prague Spring, Citizens to the Rescue . . .**

"Did you know assassins prefer Makarov pistols?"

"In what *century*? This is a *recent* grave! Why even *scan* the terrorist file?"

"Hunch," Connie said, typing in the refinement: 21st c. "Check the hallway again."

"Check yourself. I'm going back to dream."

"I wouldn't. Not until you read this."

The E-screen spun in her direction.

Deserters: Valley splinter group. Organized: ?? Classification: Anti. Status: At large. Proclaimed leaders: Rosa J, Maud D. Kidnapped: CEO Louis F, 11.03.62 A.M.C.

"Standard Valley dating," Connie informed. "Post-chip numerics."

Charged in absentia: Raul S, Lithia P murders. Last verified sighting: 10.04.77 A.M.C., Burnt Mountains, Wind Range. Coordinates . . .

"Snot! Did you hear that?" Connie hit "clear screen" and dove behind the partition. "Cover for me."

"Luce?"

"Yes, salutations, it's Luce." Absurdly she waved at the nod, not ten feet distant.

"It's after curfew, dear."

"I know. I had a long nap this afternoon. It threw me off schedule."

"It's not good to go off schedule."

"I know," she parroted again. "That's why I'm here. Archives always eases me to sleep."

The nod moved closer. "You're a Recovered. It's not wise to linger in Archives."

"I won't over-stay," she swore. "Already I'm fading." To demonstrate, she yawned extra wide.

"You recall what happened to your friend Connie?"

In case the referred to spit or hissed, her coconspirator faked a diversionary sneeze.

"Catching cold?" the nod inquired.

"Must be a reaction to Archive dust."

The nod didn't smile. "Don't tarry."

"I won't. Honor."

"'Don't tarry,'" Connie viciously mimicked, springing to her feet.

"That was tight."

"Too," Connie conceded. "As much as I hate to admit it, we'd better cease for now. She'll be back for another inspection, guaranteed."

"I'll exit by the front entrance, since she knows I'm here."

Connie consented, but neither stepped away from the E-screen. Its restored revelations included location coordinates.

"Can you believe it? Actual terrorists. Close enough to finger!"

"It could be totally unrelated to . . . the other," she countered, trying to be sensible, trying not to assume they'd discovered a terrorist's grave—simply because it jazzed.

"Oh sure," Connie grandly scoffed. "And the moon could be made of cheese."

8

She must have dozed off.

The last time Lieutenant Maud punched through the blockade of snow at the mouth of the cave, afraid of suffocating as well as freezing, she'd been greeted by the sight of more white. From miles up that color started, hit without a bang.

Get up, get up. Time again to check. Time again to hunt for air pockets, heartbeats.

Eyelids heavy as her limbs. Heavy as Valley Maud in her fattest phase.

She blinked, blinked again at her comrades, clinging to each other, needy and terrified, even in sleep. They looked like aged members of Take Care.

Remember Take Care? some part of her brain boomeranged.

Parents dropping off children, children collapsing to the floor, screaming, weeping, fondling the scent strips left with them. By five cycles, Maud had become an old hand at Take Care, her screaming/weeping days long over. With the keepers, she circulated among the distressed, dispensing toys and comfort. One nondescript afternoon, during pick-up, a keeper complimented: "Such an administrator, your little Maud!" A keeper's highest praise. But her father reacted as if he'd been insulted. Without responding, he grabbed her arm and jerked them homeward in tight-lipped silence. From bed, later that night, she overheard her parents bickering on her behalf, her father still fuming, her mother seemingly resigned.

"They're sucking her in, Eliza. She's already eager to follow their lead."

"If her instincts run that way, all the better," her mother reiterated. "Let it be."

Let it be, her brain regurgitated. *Let it be. Give up, give in. Why not? Why struggle? Why resist?*

Woozily she pushed off from the cave's wall, bumped across a carpet of bodies to get to a body named/re-named Repeat. His beard had turned into a frozen bush. The plaid scarf at his neck looked more like a noose than a band against the cold. Reaching under it, she jiggled his shoulder and jiggled again.

"'Stay in the corner, be modest and most of all do not be conspicuous,'" he blurted without opening his eyes.

"Repeat, wake up. We're raiding the sleepers. Tonight. You and me."

"'Revolutionaries who cannot move slowly and patiently are bad revolutionaries.'"

"We're out of options, comrade. Raid or die."

Alongside them, Rosa suddenly stirred in her sleep, brandishing the stick she mistook for her missing rifle, fencing with an enemy only she could see.

"The commander stays here. Just you and me. As soon as night falls."

Eventually he nodded.

"'While life is life is long.'"

If we're lucky, she thought, *only if we're lucky*, a brain prompt she could have done without since never once had luck been a Deserter's chum, much less a down and dirty comrade.

9

Connie had the basics wired, she said. "Down pat. Down cold. Wrapped and tied. First a plot, then a counterplot. A Deserter breaks rank, gets caught, then snuffed, then dumped in a shallow grave. Because Antis *always* kill off defectors. Remember that quote? In the first file?"

First, second, fifth, twentieth. Every terrorist file had been littered with cold-blooded quotes.

"Luce! That one about 'stifling all consideration of kinship and love'? A revolutionary must do this, a revolutionary must do that. Remember now? The one that says they're *obligated* to kill friends, family—anyone—who trashes the cause???"

Obsessed again, fixated on Anti files, Connie neglected to be careful. Twice more she'd sneaked back to Archives on her own and would again if a pal didn't intercede. For days, the nods had been ultra-vigilant, casing Connie for hyper, checking for bloodshot eyes. Discovered in Archives again, she'd lose every solitary/solitude privilege and rebound yet again to Deprivation.

Returning to Archives, Luce would also run a risk—not quite Connie-level, but still substantial.

"You're a *Recovered*," the nod had warned, relatively friendly on first offense. Good will that wouldn't—couldn't—last.

To keep them both off nod radar, what they needed was another way in: access that didn't require Archival clearance. Between dream reports, more on Connie's behalf than her own, Luce diddled, trying out various search and retrieve options.

Finally PRIME beeped but didn't cut her off.

V-A-L-L-E-Y S-E-C-U-R-I-T-Y, she typed, waited.

Retreat PRIME was not only modified, it was fiendishly slow, the bane of recent transfers.

"I could flip through scratch faster than this!" many, many complained.

D-E-S-E-R-T-E-R-S, she typed.

Valley splinter group . . . At large . . . Charged in absentia . . . Last verified sighting . . .

The same info logged in Archives, down to the commas.

Surprised, she typed faster, tried a bolder, wilder query.

P-E-R-S-O-N-N-E-L R-O-S-T-E-R.

THE FOLLOWING IN ALL PROBABILITY ILLEGALLY OBTAINED. CANNOT GUARANTEE ACCURACY. BIAS INDICATED.

A-C-K-N-O-W-L-E-D-G-E-D, she typed.

The E-screen hummed, cleared, refilled.

Rosa J, Born: ?.?.42 A.M.C., North Sector. Employed: Data Center. Level 4, 23 months. Disciplinary actions: 7. Abuses: Inadequate hours, coding errors. Dismissal pending when disappeared 11.03.62 A.M.C.

V-I-S-U-A-L, she hesitantly typed.

Visuals took longer than text to appear. Someone was sure to enter the waiting room before the pixels congealed into anything recognizable. A dreamer might already be there with Morpheus pad, falling prey to dream amnesia. She left the chair to check the waiting room, the adjoining hallway and to consult with the chief assistant, all to reconfirm her assessment of a dreamer lull. She had just returned to her seat when PRIME again beeped.

IMAGE COMPLETE.

A neck, a chin, a mouth, a mole, two eyes and the eyebrows above them, the clean curve of a perfectly bald skull.

With great care she adjusted screen brightness, tilted the monitor to achieve a better viewing angle, but the fingers managing those maneuvers had begun to tremble. For a split second, she blamed fatigue—fatigue playing tricks. But she wasn't that tired. She wasn't that addled. Again she touched the monitor to remind herself she interfaced with a machine—a machine without emotions or interest in waging vendettas, incapable of devising an elaborate, vindictive, torturing con.

The only mismatch between herself and the screen was hair. Her thatch.

Grabbing a fistful, she yanked—hard.

Trying to break the spell.

Trying to prove she couldn't possibly be seeing what she saw, that what she saw couldn't possibly be authentic.

The shaking made her clumsy, her typing inept. Attempting to call up her own file, she repeatedly misspelled her name.

"Voice!" she shouted in frustration, temporarily abandoning the keyboard.

Recovered: Luce. Six pounds, 3 ounces. Unmixed Caucasian. Arrival date: 5-7-21 (old style). Location: N/A.

A hundred times before she'd read that description and logged off, assuming her file contained no other specifics. Now she imitated Connie, pushing for further facts. Over the N/A grid, back in keyboard mode, she typed E-X-P-L-A-I-N.

No Valley pick-up, PRIME revealed.

E-X-P-L-A-I-N, she typed again.

Found on premises.

E-X-P-L-A-I-N.

East Gate Entrance.

—A once ordinary, now extraordinary, portal, flanked by uneven stones; the entranceway she'd passed through yesterday and days and days before as the nod-named Luce.

Her chair tipped backward, clattered; the waiting room door slammed behind her, but the volume of neither of those clangs and bangs compared to the volume of the voices nattering inside her head as she ran heedless of nods or reprimands backward from now to then, toward the initial site of contact and castoff, her personal coordinates of recovery and loss.

A revolutionary stifles kinship and love.
A mother ought to rescue.
A mother ought to save what she so carelessly gave away.
A MOTHER OUGHT! A MOTHER OUGHT!

10

They walked side by side when they could, one mini-flamer between them.

"Another who died to save us. Rushing about, organizing. Crowds, plots, schemes, save, serve," Repeat howled at intervals.

The other Rosa's tale—with strategic elisions.

"Recognize the rhetoric? So much to do, so little time. Polish Social party, German Social Democratic, Spartacus. 'Where great things are . . . the wind about the ears . . . I'll be in the thick of it.' Fighting for, fighting against, fighting among themselves. Another rally gone badly. What's this?"

He eased to a full stop, cocked his head.

"Keep moving, comrade," Maud ordered mid-shove. Whatever fascinating tidbit his internal antennae had picked up, now wasn't the time to stop and meditate. To steal from the sleepers, they needed the sleepers asleep.

"Lots of time in prison for feeding wrens and magpies."

Disappointed by the faithless, defeated by the corrupted, knocked in the head, shot, pitched into a canal, Rosa, Red Rosa.

A saga of sudden death—what better inspiration for two Deserters on a break-in mission?

"'Get the bitch out, she's bleeding on my car!'/'Big mouth, big arse! It figures, eh?'"

The triumph of murdering bully boys, leaning over bridgeworks, watching the water below bubble and perc. Laughed all the way home, throughout the trial, their country laughing with them over Red Rosa's rough end.

> "Many corpses in a row
> and now Rosa's.
> Many corpses in a row
> and now Red Rosa's too."

—The usual caterwauling conclusion, but in this recitation Repeat threw in an admonitory codicil:

"Do not feel sorry for Red Rosa! Do not pity the dead!"

Regardless, Maud did feel sorry—for the legendary Red Rosa, for the Rosa they called their own, for herself, for Repeat, for their cave-bound comrades, for the sleepers they intended to rob, all dishonored by what they were about to attempt. The sleepers also counted as Valley defectors. In a well-fed universe, Deserters wouldn't stoop to the treachery of robbing simpaticos.

As they neared sleeper territory, the too-visible moon appeared to wink. A clear sky, no less. When they could have used its camouflage, benefited from it, what happened? Farting snow relinquished the stage to luminous clarity. She could even distinguish individual tree trunks. And then, among those distinctions, an un-tree-like glint.

Ducking behind a boulder, she snatched Repeat along.

"'To know something you had to go inside, feel, step outside, look—twice. That was knowledge,'" Repeat observed.

She saw no other flashes, but every instinct warned her that the woods held company. And then she realized who. No one else skulked among frozen trees past midnight.

Furious, she jerked up and Repeat jerked with her. They didn't have time for Seven and his farting games.

"Show yourself, Seven," she jeered. "Show that precious goatee so I can rip it off your farting face."

Big surprise. He didn't obey. A blowhard threat, in any case. They couldn't waste energy on vengeance either.

"Onward, Repeat."

"'You feel power most when it's . . .'"

. . . working against you.

She could fill in the finale of that quip too.

Get in, load up, get out—that's what they had to do. No touring of the premises, no loitering among the snoozers. No unnecessary gambles.

Same statue guards and stone-edged pond. Only the compound itself was brand new terrain. New and massive.

"We'll have to scout the perimeter first," she whispered, already sounding aggrieved, already feeling defeated. Despite the distance and time drain of that undertaking, they had no choice. They had to make the circle. Without a sense of the overall setup, they'd never find the larder. Best case scenario? They'd locate a ground-level window, get a handle on the sleepers' favorite alarm system—tech, primitive or human—and, if the rebel gods smiled on them, pinpoint the kitchen on their first reconnaissance loop.

Not even close.

The survey of the outside circle revealed only wall. Behind that impressive barricade some of the sleepers nestled in their beds. But did they all? A critical bit of (lacking) info.

Maybe sleeper cooks labored by night, napped by day. Maybe not all the food was kitchen-stored.

Stop coding trouble!

Sleepers ate, had to eat. And what they gobbled had to be stored somewhere.

So find it!

Iron gates closed off the widest entrances on the west and east. No visible locks, but hot-linked, probably. She brushed against the wall closest to her nose, testing.

Nothing happened.

"We'll go in over the wall."

Repeat bowed assent.

Grabbing hold of the nearest jutting stone, she scrambled to the top and, spotting no visible threat, signaled for Repeat to join her. As soon as he also straddled the wall, he cleared his throat and threw back his head. Swiftly and firmly she covered his mouth. No doubt the time warp beneath them inspired all sorts of rehash, but they hadn't come for entertainment; they'd come for sustenance.

On inside turf, they stayed close to the bumpy walls, crept forward. Stone at their feet, stone overhead and, to their right, stone boxing an open but strangely snow-free courtyard. A farting stone labyrinth.

"Remember where we started," she whispered, hopelessly disoriented herself.

Every pillar had an identical twin; every arch, a companion. In the mountains, she'd learned to spot bent branches, stomped brush, the dropped butt of a NicStick, but she hadn't scouted a building since they went after the suit. Even then, the Deserters hadn't worked from reality. Since security would have reported any non-classified on a walk-about, they relied on a woefully inadequate grid derived from outdated PRIME schematics. If Repeat hadn't remembered to destroy the censor block on the way in, their infamous ranks would have been arrested before rounding the first corner.

Corners. She'd forgotten how deeply she despised those architectural stalwarts. The sleepers' cocoon presented a maze of obscure nooks and crannies.

Yet another complication.

Inching to the right, she mistook her own lurking shadow for someone else's, suppressed a shriek.

"'But I don't want to go among mad people,'" Repeat

barked.

"It's okay. It's nothing," she murmured, no more reassured than he.

Nose in the air, she sniffed hard for a whiff of leftover dinner, some scent to bulldog. But the only thing she inhaled was the stench of her own yeasty armpits. Repeat went rigid behind her, but it took another two, three, seconds before she registered why: footsteps, unmistakably footsteps, belonging to persons plural.

"'The present is always under attack from the past and future simultaneously.'"

"Shhh. Shhh."

In the middle of a disaster, she scarcely needed to fabricate worst, so she invented best: late-night snackers en route to the elusive kitchen, two sleepers deaf enough for them to tail.

But why would sleepers moan?

The shuffling stopped, resumed.

Fart!

On Valley runs, they went prepared to beat off rival scavengers, but a sleeper raid should have been a dream heist, an auto-slide—in *theory*.

Fart!

This was what happened with you fell for the rhetoric, swallowed whole the hype.

Sucker!

Quite obviously not everyone in the snooze castle accommodatingly snoozed.

The hubbub grew louder; the whoever in motion drew nearer.

In a brawl with multiple sleepers, she and Repeat would have to try to knock out the lot before any one of them screamed. But could they? Arm flung across Repeat's thumping chest, she dripped sweat. In the dead of winter, she dripped sweat.

Oddly the delegation slowed, slowed further, slowed to a teeth-gnashingly retarded pace. Moans gave way to indecipherable, semi-strangled words. And then: no words, no shuffling. Nothing.

She stretched to sneak a peek.

Barely distinguishable: two figures, each dressed in flowing robes, the lead robe flimsier. The follower seemed to be clutching a scratch pad. After each moan, he marked it. The lead robe darted sideways, slammed hard into a stone column, hopped wide and darted on, companion in hot pursuit.

Fart!

Roaming sleepers. How many others had passed on their dream potions? How many others traipsed the place at night?

At the first semi-promising door, she pulled a pry from her fellow burglar's inherited tool belt. More sanguine than she, Repeat opted to depress the latch. Without resistance, the door swung on its hinges. Monstrously suspicious of that ease-in, she proceeded, weapon raised.

They weren't jumped—or rewarded, surrounded by bed frames, motley sex toys and chewed teddy bears, but no food.

"'Happiness is a longing for repetition,'" Repeat opined, picking through the bear pile, comparing scruffy ears.

"Happiness is a farting kitchen," she snapped. "A simple farting kitchen."

A series of unlocked, undefended doors—and each and every one led to inedible sleeper junk.

Think, think!

A monastery in the age of virtual. Would sleeper monks demand a second-floor snack bar?

Near the stairwell, she paused to sniff again. Her nose had picked up something . . . pungent. However ripe, teddy bears didn't smell that high. The odor came from a smaller storage vault, down a side corridor. She took a deeper breath to verify. On a food hunt, her nose had never failed her and didn't mislead her now. Inside that space: a veritable wall of cheese.

While Repeat stuffed their satchels with dairy, she lit a flamer to search for something, anything, rank or freeze-dried, to supplement that cache. Instead of more food, she uncovered linens—thin, but doubled or tripled, they'd repulse a bit of the cold. The box of oven mitts she seized greedily. The Deserters hadn't scored gloves—real or counterfeit—in many a raid.

In the far corner, behind a batch of empty crates, stood a grimy desk topped by an even grimier early-mode E-screen. Weirdly placed, but apparently functional. Beneath the dust, a faint blueness glowed. In sleeper storage, that hookup looked utterly innocuous, almost inviting. She edged closer, fascinated by so retro a model. What was an E-screen, any E-screen after all, but a slate, a message board? Hardly wicked. Not even contagious.

Impulsively, she extended a callused finger. The moment her flesh made contact, the screen went black. Cursing, she leapt back, her mistake already uncorrectable. Overhead, something boomed.

With one hand she shoved Repeat, the other grabbed as much as it could on the fly. Half of that last-second loot tumbled out of her pockets, white and yellow rectangles plunking on stone as they streaked past a courtyard now emblazoned with lights, no shadows left to hide them.

It would come down to speed. Who ran faster: rested patrollers or woozy Deserters. And all because she couldn't resist the farting lure of a farting E-screen.

She thought they ran toward where they started, but that path dead-ended at another, higher wall—an obstruction they'd have to scale to escape. She linked her fingers, cupped Repeat's foot, hoisted. Midway up he missed a handhold, landed back beside her. They couldn't both get away. It wasn't possible. There wasn't time.

In one arc of motion she stripped the sack from his shoulders and tossed it high and wide, then tossed her own bag. With only his own weight to manage, Repeat shimmied faster. At the top, he glanced back.

"Return to camp. I'll stall them here."

He didn't quote, but he didn't move either.

"Go!" she said.

"Bu . . . t . . . t . . . Ma . . . a . . . aud," he pleaded, his face a warp of indecision.

"GO NOW!" she screamed, since not screaming no longer equaled immunity.

She heard the drop on the other side, the scramble to collect table linens, oven mitts and gummy cheese. On the count of ten, so that no one, not even the sleep dazed, would mistake her position, she again lit a flamer and held it under her chin. If she could have wedged that light source behind her eyes, she would have done so to lead them to her, and only her, her skull transformed into a beaming old-style jack-o'-lantern.

A jack-o'-lantern awaiting capture by an army of ghosts.

11

She hadn't come from The Valley; she'd been abandoned on the steps of The Retreat. She didn't count as a standard Recovered—not even that. Within a tribe of refugees, she still didn't fit. Almost worse than the revelation itself was its needless postponement. She could have known—always. The information was there, available for call-up. Night after night, misidentified and misinformed, she'd crawled into bed, turned out the lights, dream-searched for a mother PRIME had already ID-ed and located: Rosa J, once holed up in these mountains—much closer than a Valley cube, truly within range of a daughter's open window. Deserters knew how to sneak-about, thrived on it—hadn't PRIME said as much? But Rosa J couldn't be bothered with even the nuisance of salutations. Family got in a Deserter's way.

Was Rosa J alive? Dead? Buried beneath a pile of snow-ringed mud? Did it matter? If a mother never wanted you, did it make any difference whether or not she continued to exist?

Luce bit her lip, refused to cry. *Kinders* cried. She wasn't a child anymore. Not a Recovered, not a child. Not what she had thought she was, not what she seemed. Not. Not. Not.

When Parish and Connie burst into her room, she winced at the sight of their unity, the pair of them bonded by a classification she no longer shared.

"Luce! Are you processing?" Connie screeched, shaking her. "The nods captured a thief! And not just any a thief, a De-ser-ter thief."

To drive home the reference, Connie raised her eyebrows.

She disentangled herself, stepped back. "What kind of deserter?"

Parish snickered. "Yeah, Con. A deserter from what? Snow?"

"When they brought her into Deprivation, she was wearing a coat with *lizards* on it!" Connie squealed.

She, Luce heard.

"Not lizards, *birds*," Parish corrected. "*Painted* birds. And quit squealing. You'll summon the nods."

But Parish was elevated too. She kept stroking her bald patches.

"They caught her near the food lockers, stealing cheese. Her eyes were dilated. She could barely stand up. When she saw the patrol coming, she staggered toward them like a walking corpse. But *not* a corpse," Connie emphasized, spraying spit. "Alive!"

"Definitely alive," Parish confirmed. "And currently stashed in Deprivation's isolation ward, under round-the-clock observation."

"The Deprivation super's ecstatic, natch," Connie revealed. "A subject who hasn't slept eight hours straight in decades within pinching range—it's like manna from heaven!"

"And *my* super is furious," Parish elaborated. "He says prolonged deprivation counts as a chronic, so it's a Disorders aberration, but the Deprivation techs wouldn't concede. They already had her annotated."

"Who does she look like?"

Both Parish and Connie balked.

"What do you mean 'who'?"

If the captured Deserter resembled her, wouldn't one of them say so? Wouldn't her friends key her now?

"What color is her hair?"

"Red, isn't it?" Parish asked Connie.

"I never heard red!"

Was it red or wasn't it? The room sped up, spinning Luce with it. What if her mother wasn't dead? What if she dreamed just down the hallway?

"Are you . . . able? You're looking a little . . . locked."

"Luce's isn't locked, she's fine!" Connie shouted. "Now quash while I spill the rest. The prisoner speaks some kind of primitive language. Like a genuine wilderness woman."

Parish rolled her eyes. "First of all, she isn't a prisoner; second of all, she just says 'fart' a lot. And what's this 'wilderness woman' theory? She's probably a Valley reject—the same as that other dreamer crone."

"She's NOT from The Valley!" Connie insisted.

"And you know this—how?"

"Common sense. There were two Deserters left. One buried her chum, got desperate and tried to raid us."

"*Dead chums*? Since when were we discussing dead chums?"

Connie scratched her nose, momentarily discreet—but how long would that reticence last?

"It's a Connie theory," Luce blurted. "Another whacked-out Connie theory."

"Have you been Archiving again? Tell the truth."

"I've dropped in a few times, so what?"

"Are you viral?" Parish roared. "You can't just 'drop in'! You've got to have a plan, a system. If they catch you, you'll be warded in Deprivation. Forever!"

Connie's sulky pout flip-flopped into a huge, lopsided grin.

"Brilliant! From Deprivation I'll have full access!"

"Between the nods and supervisors, you won't get near the thief."

"Parish's right. Deprivation will be stocked with observers."

Connie laughed at both of them, flitted toward the door.

"Such a GOOD bunch of Recovereds!"

"That's not what I meant and you know it," Parish said.

Connie paid no attention; Connie was juiced. "Be obedient, follow the rules. Be my guest. I couldn't give snot what you lamers do. I'm getting within thief range."

"Snot to you too, Con!" Parish snarled, cherry-red between freckles.

Luce stood apart, threw her support to neither side, too focused on her own calculations to bother with their spat. A newly discovered talent: calculation. Probably she had a flair for remorse-free deception and deviousness as well, both guaranteed by birthright, further gifts of the blood. Without question, crafty Connie would weasel her way in to see the thief— so be it, so what? Connie wouldn't get there first, now that she competed with a certified rebel's child.

12

In Rosa's dream, the dreamer recognized her own beady eyes, grackle-black. Trying to soar above the sleeper's compound, she and her wings got no help from wind.

"'Which way I fly is Hell; Myself am hell,'" her bird brain twittered.

Flapping proved useless. She still dipped, dropped and smashed into a lineup of sentry statues that recognized her sorry self, despite the bird getup, tipped off by the ragged beat of her treacherous heart.

"'The heart is the toughest part of the body,'" Repeat used to say, a compliment that didn't commander-apply. Like the rest of her miserable self, her heart was weak, a failure as an organ and as a sentiment. She had ditched her only child.

In the dream, after her bird-self crashed, she sank human, into the mud of a sleeper pond. Mud rose past her knees, her elbows, packed her nose, her ears, and still she heard the cry.

Dead for real, she'd still hear that reproof.

Get used to it, Rosa. This tape loop is forever, the dream-song promised.

Vibrations. Voices. She opened her eyes to a net of snow-heavy branches, evaded their clutches, wiggled free.

"Where's the lieutenant? ANSWER ME!" she yelled—maybe yelled. "I'm the COMMANDER! Stop laughing!"

Were they laughing—or plotting?

"MAUD!"

"Maud's not here, commander."

She tried to place the face.

"TELL LIEUTENANT MAUD TO REPORT TO ME IMMEDIATELY!"

"They went on a raid, Maud and Repeat. Repeat brought back cheese and some . . . wrappings."

"Who's talking? Who are you?"

"Cook, commander. It's Cook."

Sallow cheeks. Harmonic voice. Cook. Yes.

"Get Maud for me. Tell her we need to talk."

"She wants Maud," someone said.

Hadn't she been demanding exactly that? Hadn't she made that CLEAR?

On a slow, slow journey, she traveled toward Repeat. The others were confusing mushes, hazy proxies, difficult to pin down, but the soul of Repeat, transparent as glass, gleamed like a beacon. Long before the invention of Commander Rosa, Repeat had practiced anarchy, declaring and redeclaring from a cave's gut:

"'I begin to doubt beautiful words.'"

I begin to doubt.

Repeat would snitch on Maud.

Sweet as a penitent, she approached, petitioned that savant.

In riddles, he responded.

Had they all gone deaf? She was asking for Maud!

She fisted a tree trunk, gashed it with her teeth.

"Commander, stop!"

Stop? *STOP?* Had they forgotten the rebel creed/screed? Stopping was anti-progress. Stopping was *bourgeois.*

She tasted blood but smelled soap—a scent out of time. She knocked away the wad patting her face.

"Where did this come from?"

"From the sleepers, commander. It's all they had time to

steal."

Gibberish. Gibberish. Maud wouldn't go to the sleepers. Maud would never raid the sleepers, not even in revolt.

"They took what they could. Some old-style tablecloths and these."

Again and again she ran the image, but her brain refused ID.

"Oven mitts, commander. For gloves."

Oven mitts? In snow?

"MAUD!" she squalled toward the ridge top, as oven mitts circled round. "I'LL FIND YOU MAUDIE! AND WHEN I DO . . ."

"'We who sleep with anger laid beside us like a knife . . .'" she heard and finally decoded: the sphinx's riddle, the piteous truth.

Maud despised her too. Despite years of togetherness, because of years of togetherness, Maudie had learned to hate her too.

III

1

As a young child Maud slept soundly, as only the very young can sleep, secure in the delusion of a changeless world. The moment she closed her eyes, she fell into the sinkhole of dream and remained there, snug and content, until morning streamed in. Always she left her cozy little bed feeling supremely confident of return. No separation anxiety, not then. No reason for angst in the rest department—not yet.

There were no beds per se at Take Care, but mattress rolls covered part of the play floor. Pooped, she and her peers could curl up, close their eyes and nap as often and for as long as they wished. No guardian/keeper warned them they'd have to wean themselves of the nap habit by Second Tier. Her parents hadn't warned her either. At night, they leaned over her bed with their raccoon eyes, wished her sweet dreams and returned to their desks. A rude surprise, Second Tier. Whoever got tired and cranky midday received a new diskette rather than a pillow. "You'll like this. This will keep you awake," the keepers said, pointing toward the E-screen. Some of her peers still fell asleep regardless, but not her: from one Tier to the next, she'd lost the knack of instant dream. When the keepers reported a drop in "spunk," her mother scanned her with a body meter, puzzled by the normal readout. Her father asked leading questions, none of which she knew how to answer in a way that would satisfy. She wasn't hurt; she wasn't sick; she was beset by a new sensation: free-floating dread. Little by little she came to realize her parents suffered the same malady. Their raccoon-eye rings grew steadily darker; they rested less than she.

Her parents hailed from the "straddler" generation—a demographic chunk that came of age prior to ALL ACCESS/ALL THE TIME. Necessity demanded they retool: adjust to Corporate control of food, drugs, housing, Zip-Alls, childcare; accept the concept and practice of working more, sleeping less. Get with the program, citizens. And make it quick.

By Second Tier, chubbette Maud was with the program cheek to jowl.

Old habits, even in new circumstances, die hard.

Soft pillow, softer bed cloths, dim lights, unlimited heat in a sleepers' den—she should have been snoring. Instead, whenever she closed her eyes, she continuously relived the botch: dropped cheese, Repeat's bony buns clearing the wall, her own broad rear as decoy, the flamer under her chin, capture—every part of that sequence rife with anxiety and despair.

What if Repeat hadn't made it back?

Once the sleeper army found her, she'd kicked, cursed and spat like a wilder to give her accomplice more time to scat. Her captors had kept a respectful distance throughout that performance; they'd also taken her pyrotechnics in stride. When she stopped hissing, she'd been escorted, courteously, to this room and left, thus far, unmolested.

Disarming treatment—but geared to soothe or unhinge?

No monitors perceivable to the naked eye broke the pattern of walls and ceiling. The only obviously odd contraption was a metal arm that overhung the bed, dangling a limp, flesh-colored cap that neither hummed nor flashed. If designed to attach to a body, it hadn't yet been attached to hers. But to leave that dangling threat beside her all night had been clever. Very clever.

A knock grazed the door. Dry-mouthed, she sat up. This morning's jailer looked like an old-style nun.

"Don't be afraid."

"Who says I'm afraid?"

The jailer nun pointed at the clutched pillow.

Fear/readiness. A matter of opinion. If wires or needles hid beneath that ballooning robe, she wanted an extra shield.

"Are you hungry? Would you like something to eat?"

Again she checked the walls, looking for peepholes. Surely this farce had been arranged to amuse a larger audience? Since the jailer nun's question was too absurd to answer, Lieutenant Maud studied in silence the spy who shared her casting call. Why would anyone dress in that garb? If all sleepers dressed this bulky, conceivably, she could have escaped along with Repeat. The weight had to slow them down; it couldn't speed them up. Then she remembered the moaner's duds. Flimsy, almost diaphanous. Did weight of dress reflect rank? Were sleepers ruled by costume?

The jailer nun stood placidly, hands crossed at the waist. But her eyes were ultra-bright, exceedingly clear and mega alert. How to give the slip to orbs so well-equipped to track?

"Perhaps you're not hungry yet? Perhaps you'd rather wait?"

Maud stifled a scream of laughter. A Deserter, not hungry YET? How long did it take to build up an appetite, a quarter century?

All very curious: this "at your service" posture. To test its limits, she said:

"Oh I'm hungry. Ravenous, in fact."

"Very well. What can I bring you?"

"What are you offering?"

"Anything you'd like."

"*Anything* I'd *like?*"

She smirked, the jailer nun nodded.

"I order it; you deliver it."

"As soon as the kitchen prepares it."

Kitchen. The very word made her flinch.

"Are you . . . in pain?"

What kind of twisted interrogation was this? A jailer asking a cheese thief if she's hungry, pimping an unlimited menu, feigning concern about a facial tic? It was bizarre. So bizarre Maud responded in kind.

"Where is this kitchen you're talking about?"

Without the slightest hesitation, the other pointed downward, at a diagonal. "On the first level, near Assembly Hall."

Since when did jailers answer questions on demand? Since when did they give away locational secrets without pay-off bribes?

Don't confuse a dumb wardrobe with dumbness, she cautioned herself. Candor could also serve to entrap.

"This 'anything I'd like' meal—my first and last, correct?"

A convincing show of bafflement.

"We hope you will share many meals with us at The Retreat."

Baffled herself and loath to show it, Maud scowled. If they truly didn't intend to hand her over to the PROs, did that mean they *sympathized* with the Deserters? Harbored other Valley Antis? Was the dream business an elaborate front? A sham to fool Corporate?

Uneasily she shifted on the bed.

"We have wonderful egg maroons and breads. But the chef can prepare a heartier meal if you prefer."

"Hearty," she answered automatically. "Make it hearty."

"There are fresh pulls in the closet. And behind the far

door bathing facilities, if you care to bathe."

Irked by the reference, butt-naked, she stood, hoping the spectacle of her filthy mass displayed in all its mottled glory would disconcert. A leaf floated from her hair nest to the floor, but the jailer nun neither blanched nor gawked, simply patted the grimy bed print.

"And don't angst about the soiled cloths. They'll be changed."

"Do that. I can't abide dirt."

Again the other solemnly nodded. Didn't it figure? Squeaky clean and utterly humorless.

An escalating banshee-like shriek interrupted their peculiar tête-à-tête. The walls were thick—just not quite thick enough to muffle a shriek.

"I tried! I tried! I tried!" a female voice wailed.

"Oh dear. I'm sorry you had to hear that."

"I'll bet you are," Maud agreed, showing teeth, instinctively squaring her feet.

Otherwise focused, the jailer nun sighed.

"Lathinia was so distressed when we found her. We had hoped to see improvement by now, but if she continues to disturb you—"

"Who the fart *wouldn't* be disturbed by that yowling?"

"If she continues to disturb you," the jailer nun repeated, "we'll transfer her to another ward. In the meantime, please make yourself comfortable while the dietitians prepare your meal."

Someone here has definitely gone insane, Maud thought. *Quite likely: me.*

Then she remembered the hidden camera(s). Maybe sleepers specialized in flexible script. Maybe they sat around, watching, as clueless Antis squirmed. Maybe *that's* what made them guffaw.

Supposedly alone, she shimmied her naked backside in every direction, a little fart-you to her hidden audience, before embarking on a more methodical spyglass search. Inch by inch, up, down and sideways she hunted but no hole could she find, pinprick or larger, in the main room. The bath facility was smaller but crammed with gadgets readily convertible to peeping instruments. Humidity adjuster. Floor warmer. Crescent-shaped aroma-dial. Mint-scented flusher. She probed and prodded the insides and outsides of those luxuries, ransacked an entire shelf of body salves and soothers, and still detected no lens, whole or cracked.

Cautiously she stepped into the bath stall and turned the tap. Water spurted from the overhead nozzle and bounced off her chest. Warm water, not hot—so sleepers must not scald Antis on principle/on the sly. For the first few moments, standing in that hydro flow, she pretended her surveillance rout-out continued, but soon she didn't care if the whole compound had a bird's-eye view of her caked eyelashes and yellow teeth. It felt too good beneath that blast. She'd forgotten the exquisite pleasures of waterworks. Forgotten, but speedily recalled.

Mountain muck poured off her in rivulets; her gritty hide liquefied and swirled down the drain. For the first time in many a cycle, she saw her bent and callused toes. Beneath the grime, her flesh felt tender, bloomed pink. Bigger and bigger patches of skin appeared, as she leaned forward, deeper into the spray, allowing it to unkink her neck, massage her shoulders, tickle her butt crack. Eventually the water dripping off her dripped crystal clear, shockingly pristine. She was clean— another forgotten pleasure. Standing on the floor warmer, gazing into the reflector, she saw the particularities of a body

Sleep

she'd long ignored. Hair actually auburn. Pubic thatch to match. The Maud in the mirror looked bonny, civilized—and alarmingly vulnerable. Part of the bulk that had defined and served her so well for 15 cycles had, in less than 15 old-style tick-tocks, washed away.

To regain some of that bulk, she upended the closet's offerings, scrounging for her blue-birded duster but, in concert with dirt, her Deserter duds had also disappeared. Naked or sleeperwear—those were the options. Since her nakedness seemed to disorient only herself, she dressed in something floppy. Not the jailer nun's outfit exactly, but equally roomy. She wasn't fond of clothes that swung; they made for a provoking combination of impeded, clumsy and accessible. There for the snatching.

The cloths had been changed, the bed remade. Whoever slipped in to perform that service had slipped out again, as inconspicuous as lint. As she circled the room, the only noise she heard she caused: an annoying, ankle-level swish.

The window view provided another angle of the snow bereft courtyard. Neither the window cover nor the window itself was bolted. Too far to leap, in any case. Even if she escaped the compound with a broken leg, dragging a fractured tibia, she'd never make it back to camp.

Several compartments surrounding the dry courtyard she recognized from last night's attempt at plunder. If the jailer nun's description turned out to be correct and not a ruse, the kitchen had been directly at their backs all along. She and Repeat had come that close, only to fail themselves and their starving comrades.

Another knock, another robe, this one carrying a piled-high tray. Guiltily she felt her mouth fill with saliva. As a prisoner, she ate gourmet while her fellow Deserters dry swallowed cheese. Disdaining the utensil clip, she dug at the tray with her hands, shoveling in as much as her mouth could hold, chewing solely to keep from choking. Her shrunken stomach might have protested, but her mouth could have decimated five trays' worth—easy.

"Is there anything else we can get for you?"

As ungratefully as possible, she growled refusal. Not quite as unflappable as her forerunner, the second jailer fled without properly closing the door, allowing the glutton to eavesdrop.

"The chef was concerned. It's a lot to digest on an empty stomach."

"She ordered hearty. The supervisor said oblige."

Hail to Herr Supervisor! Whoever the fart he (or she) was.

The next visitor didn't knock nor was he outfitted in drapery. He wore a fossil of a lab coat, bleached to an immaculate white. Was this the "give her what she wants" supervisor? Doubtful. He didn't emanate power; he reeked servility.

He offered his hand, old-style. She could have used that hand to sponge off her own greasy digits but instead left it hanging, untouched, in the air between them. Why playact civil? The farting sleepers were her captors, not her pals. While she picked her teeth, the hand remained outstretched, an extension that, all in all, lasted much longer than she'd expected.

"I'm head technician here in Deprivation."

Squeaky voice. No vibrato. No tension, either.

She snorted twice. "Into irony, are you?"

He leaned forward expectantly, eyes bright. "Pardon?"

So much for irony. She rephrased plain.

"You call this DEPRIVATION? I call it EXCESS."

The pasty face beamed. "Amazing! Humor doesn't usually rebound so quickly."

When she barked displeasure at that comment, to HER amazement, he quick-stepped back and covered his heart. What the fart did he have to be afraid of? This was his prison, his enforcers. She didn't have shoes yet, much less a breakout plan. Still, as long as he seemed cowed . . .

"Where are my clothes? My REAL clothes?"

An assistant swiftly produced a pile of laundered and neatly folded rags.

"The nods mended as best they could, but some of the . . . decorations . . . seem to have faded," he apologized.

"The nods?"

He nodded. "You've met several already. One brought you early meal???"

"The robe that brought me breakfast?"

He half covered his mouth, spoke confidentially. "We don't use that feeding descriptor here. Because of the implications of the second syllable—if you take my meaning."

She did not. Regardless, she hammered on.

"But you're no nod."

"No. As I mentioned, I work in Deprivation."

"But you *didn't* mention what you're supposed to be *deprived* of."

For a moment he seemed to be weighing whether that remark represented another example of her "amazing humor." To help him decide, she spat a nasty wad past his ear. In a flash, one of his minions, cloth in hand, scrubbed the insult clean.

"Sleep, of course," he said.

"Sleep what?"

"Sleep deprivation."

"Sleep deprivation in sleeperville. That's rich."

"Also accurate," said he.

But she'd heard enough on the topic. Idiotic or no, it was

off point.

"So now what? I get shifted over to Incarceration?"

"There is no Incarceration."

"Just Deprivation."

"Deprivation, Disorders, Dreams and a few other labs with attached wards. We hope you'll visit them all."

"You hope?!?" she exploded. "Since when do prisoners decide what to visit?"

A lumpy vein began to throb near the peak of his forehead. The nodders on either side cringed as he fixed one after another with a penetrating glare. Turning back to her, he said: "Did someone *imply* you were obligated to remain?"

"What kind of invert is this? You caught me stealing food!"

"You were hungry."

"So I'm not being detained for stealing?"

"You're not being detained at all," he insisted, "but we'd be very grateful if you stayed."

The nodders, in apparent agreement, nodded vigorously.

"Because of your unusual"—he groped for the word—"*background*, you'd be invaluable to our research. As our guest, I can assure you, you'd be treated to every amenity."

She glared at each singly, wide-glared the collective, expecting the revelation of a PRIME-size bluff. But they returned belligerence with frankly hopeful expressions, as if she were a messiah, not a thief—and fart it, she fell under the influence of that ludicrous optimism. If Mr. Deprivation wasn't a completely duplicitous fiend, if for some unfathomable reason he honored the terms he seemed to be offering, she might yet get out of this snoozeria with a tank load of supplies.

"We could start after mid-meal . . . if you aren't too tired."

"Quit stalling, Deprivation man," she overruled. "We start now."

2

"I was thinking I'd try for a job in Deprivation," Luce said, more to the floor than to her supervisor. "Not that I dislike it here. I just thought a change might be . . . instructive," she finished lamely.

"Exciting too."

When she looked up, he chuckled. "Deprivation's definitely the place to be these days."

"You don't mind?"

"Not at all."

"Gratitude," she said uncertainly, loitering. She would have liked him to mind a little.

Armed with her supervisor's apparent blessing, she entered the Deprivation Lab. A senior nod presided at the check-in desk.

"Salutations." She forced a solicitous smile. "I've been told you need additional assistance."

A bit of a fib, but did it convince?

Distracted by the bustle behind her, the check-in nod glanced over her shoulder. Near the isolation section, technicians and nods scrambled about, consulting in rapid whispers, uncommonly excited, almost super-charged.

"Apologies. What were you voicing, dear?"

A stack of papers, bumped by an elbow, cascaded to the floor nearby. During retrieval, two nods nearly collided.

Terrifically difficult as it was to fix her gaze and keep it fixed amid the ruckus, Luce had to enchant the check-in nod. Via truth or lies, she had to create a favorable-plus impression.

"I have an excellent record. No lates or infractions. My supervisor said he would be happy to vouch for my"—she blushed—"integrity."

"At any other time, we'd love to have you, dear. But as you can see, we've recently had a rash of volunteers. Even the researchers are signing up for night shifts."

Knocking on her supervisor's door a second time, she felt intensely foolish.

"No luck, eh?"

"Jammed," she said forlornly.

"There'll be dropouts, guaranteed," he assured, chipper as ever. "Check back in a few days."

He assumed she was merely bored, she realized, prey to the usual teenager enthusiasm for thrills and intrigue. He had no idea that, for her, the quest was personal. In the wake of Parish and Connie's visit, for a very short while, she'd let herself fuse thief and mother, even rehearsed what she'd say when they re-met—a night dream transformed into daydream. But if the thief were her mother, someone in Deprivation would have noticed the resemblance, been aggrieved to learn "their Luce" was indeed an Anti's spawn and glided by to console— of that sequence, she felt absolutely certain. Since that hadn't happened, she assumed the thief to be an associate of Rosa J's, an intimate who knew what PRIME excised, someone who might be persuaded to share the details of what the commander had done and why.

"What's the hurry?" her supervisor teased. "'All things come,' et cetera."

Not strictly true, that maxim. Connie's nod-trainee robe wouldn't *come* to her; she had to find—and snitch—it.

She considered waiting until midnight, when Connie

would probably be Archiving, but that meant waiting through final meal *and* Assembly *and* hours of non-sleep—which she couldn't bear to do. Both body and brain demanded a quicker response. As soon as her shift ended, she began cruising Connie's corridor, listening, scoping, hovering at her door.

"Con?" she called and heard wonderful nothing.

There it bunched: in the very back of the closet, definitely worse for wear. Bulky, heavy. No wonder Connie had flubbed her training. Connie loathed slow-downs of any sort.

At final meal, Luce seized the chance to cross-examine Parish alone.

"Any news? About the thief?"

Aping casual. Making herself chew, swallow.

"Rumor has it she's a lot bossier than a transfer. Hungrier, too. Whenever she's awake, she eats. Enormous quantities—rich stuff, including revvers. The dietitians had to research a recipe yesterday; they'd forgotten how to cook her request."

"How long will the technicians keep her in Deprivation?"

"As long as she'll stay. They want to study everything about her."

"But has she agreed? To stay?"

Parish shrugged. "Since when do you care? You pretended you weren't interested in the thief—before."

"I'm interested, just not obsessed. Like Connie."

"But you're acting a little Connie-like," Parish noted. "A little shrill, a little jumpy. Maybe you should take a nap."

To finagle a Deprivation entry, fool the real nods and corner a thief, she'd need to sleep less, not more.

"And maybe you should try mothering someone else," she hissed, sounding not at all like the Luce either knew.

3

"After you."

When the deal-making head techer stepped aside, creating a clear passageway to the door and beyond, Maud sprinted, primarily to see if he or any of his lackeys would tackle her from behind. None did. In a docile pack they followed her into a room that made the one she'd left seem positively primitive. A solid wall of instrumentation, several E-screens, and row after row of microphoned seats.

Clearly she served as zoo exhibit of the day.

"I think you'll be most comfortable here," the head techer said, pointing toward a particularly plush seat, positioned on a slightly raised platform. By the time her ass stopped sinking, her knees were level with her chest.

She brazenly confronted her audience who mimicked discretion. Not a single sleeper unabashedly stared, pointed or chortled with amazement. Late arrivals performed a peculiar face/palm salute crossing the threshold. Unfortunate, that. Such hand jive revealed the inmates themselves were tagged and coded, and if the sleepers were, a thief in their midst would be double-tracked, wouldn't she?

In the distance she heard—or thought she heard—the die-out of another banshee wail. Gravely, a line of white coats filed in and took the remaining front-row seats, all of them cradling scratch. The sleepers had a fetish for scratch—but why? E-screens seemed plentiful enough—plentiful enough to deploy them as alarm systems in cheese lockers. Which meant either esthetics or nostalgia lay at the core of their paper worship. Sentiment being the easier of the two to exploit, Lieutenant Maud cast her vote for nostalgia. Deserter charity could conceivably be pitched as a campaign to lift the fallen. Anything was worth a try.

Loathsomely full, she belched and watched a few of the white coats record the episode. She opened her mouth to mock, then stifled the impulse. Until she knew exactly what the sleepers wanted of her and what she could filch in return, the best strategy was silence. In that decision, she wasn't alone. As soon as the head techer joined her on the platform, silence ruled. Moments passed; then clots of moments. No one spoke; no one stirred. Facing that sea of suspended animation, she reactively rocked on her padded butt. Humans shouldn't be capable of that kind of quiescence solo, much less in a crowd.

If this had been constructed as a game of patience, she lost, they won. The white coats were wasting time Deserters didn't have.

"What's the farting hold up?" she bellowed.

Side-stepping quickly, the techer detached her clearly unnecessary microphone.

"We thought you were resting."

Resting from what? Rest? Did that joke pass for sleeper wit? No smile creased the techer's lips.

"You're willing to proceed?"

Scowling, she slumped backwards. "As willing as I'll ever be."

"Very well. We'd like to begin, if we may, with a few questions about your daily habits."

A front-row sitter raised his hand. "If you were to estimate the number of incidents of irritability . . ."

Another sly jab? Again, her quizzer's expression gave no hint. But he did crane forward, as if her every word were worth its weight in microchips.

"Try again."

"Apologies. Rephrase. Did you notice an increase in irritability the less you slept?"

"I'm irritable now and all I've done in your bungalow is sleep—and eat."

"Have you exceeded twenty-four hours without rest?" a second white coat asked.

"Forty-eight?" guessed another.

And yet another: "Seventy-six?"

All the while she smirked. "Months or hours?"

Visibly horrified, a nodder rushed over with a cup of soothing tea.

"Got anything substantial to go with this?" she inquired and abracadabra: an impressive tray of snacks appeared as well. Not a bad ratio: one answer, one restorative feed.

"Could you describe any other symptoms you noticed after staying awake for such an extended period of time?"

"I noticed I was farting TIRED!"

Hostility roused the group no more than coy evasions. She waited; they waited. She looked at them, they at her, her stomach digesting tasty, apparently nonpoisonous pastries. She wasn't chained; nobody yanked off her toenails one by one. And yet it had to be a hoax, this seemingly benign examination, the preliminary to a much nastier session scheduled for another overheated room, a different kind of wired chair. The sleepers lived in the mountains, not in isolation—that much she'd learned by fondling one of their E-screens. Ludicrous to presume they were unaware of, or indifferent to, an Anti List and the names that appeared thereon. Eventually they'd pose an Anti question. Had to.

As the sugar kicked in, she bounced a bit on her chair,

composing snider and snider answers to their leisurely queries.

Eating habits?

—On a feast and famine cycle, eating "habits" didn't apply.

Visual acuity?

—On a winter mountain, what was there to see? Snow, snow and more snow.

Coordination difficulties?

—After a twelve-hour hike, pitch and twirl *were* the norm.

Hallucinations?

At that probe, she balked. For Deserters at the mercy of wind, rain, hail, hunger, dysentery and despair, life continuously teetered on the hallucinatory. Reality checked in and out of its own accord.

"Pass."

No one objected.

"If it isn't too discomfiting, could you explain how you managed to survive on so little?"

Sleep, they meant. Not food or shelter or faith. She could have pontificated endlessly about the blind faith that kept alive Deserters who, by any calculation, should have been struck from contention long ago. But her audience seemed as uninterested in rebel fate as in rebel atrocities or, for that matter, Valley politics. Their investigations fixated solely on the machinations of sleep. If a resurrected Charlotte Corday sat before them, paring knife in hand, they'd probably wonder, to the exclusion of all else, how many hours the killer slept the night before gutting Marat.

An exhausting monomania, theirs. The interrogated yawned, her chin dipped, her head dipped.

"Once more, please," the head techer directed.

"I heard him. He wants to know how we managed," she replied groggily. "Some of you must have come from The Valley. The body adjusts."

Murmurs of disbelief, or maybe, maybe dissension?

Most immune systems couldn't take the stress, reacted as if hit by invading bacteria, crashed. The majority of animals subjected to prolonged deprivation keeled over, died.

Yeah, yeah. Statistically the Deserters had proved themselves more resilient than caged rats. She wished that conclusion came as a surprise.

"With your permission, we'd like to run some tests."

At once she snapped to, lurched from the chair's all-encompassing embrace. Now she coded: lull the thief into a stupor with food and heat, then pounce.

"What kind of tests?"

"Blood pressure, heart rate, attention deficit—nothing arduous."

Savagely she poked at air. "Anyone comes near me with a spiker . . ."

The entire league of white coats shuddered, but not, it seemed, because of her threat.

"We want to study your composition, visitor, not alter it."

"And I'm to believe that on the basis of what?"

"Well . . . our word."

"Your *word*?"

"Or a . . . contract?" someone else shyly proposed.

Did they actually imagine she'd find WORDS on SRATCH a more inviolable treaty? Where had they dug up this nonsense? A PRIME file on chivalry? In any case, they already had her under round-the-clock surveillance—which rendered their latest gambit pure word play. Triple talk. Syllable gags.

"Would you prefer a contract? Because we certainly can draw up a contract. We wouldn't want you to feel at all uncomfortable with the procedure."

That theme again: discomfort. The sleepers' bugaboo. If she'd learned anything from the morning rigmarole, she'd learned that sleepers shunned discomfort like a mutant germ.

"I'll take your tests," she gambled, "if the eyeballing stops."

Everyone in the audience looked instantly at their laps, as if she'd objected to stares, not electronics.

"You'd rather not be filmed during testing?" the head techer ventured.

"Testing, eating, sleeping, pissing." She pointed to the room behind her. "Observation makes me uneasy."

"We can't film sleep, even if we wished to do so. It's not allowed. Founder regulation."

A what?

No one bothered to clarify. Just as well, she didn't remotely care.

"And rest assured: we film strictly for study purposes."

"No filming anywhere, of any kind," she nixed.

He turned toward his colleagues, who acquiesced.

Score one for a sleep-drunk lieutenant, she thought.

"I also want a debugger."

Incessantly watched and listened to as "visitor," "guest," or prisoner, she'd never be able to escape.

Imitating vexed, the head techer again canvassed.

"Do we have a debugger on-site? Can we get one? Maybe from a recent transfer?"

She ignored the nattering, belched again, languidly leaned back. She'd made clear the conditions of her "cooperation"; now it was up to them to deliver. No debugger, no tests.

The temperature so warm, the cushion so deep, their voices, even in crisis mode, so flawlessly monotonal, she felt herself slipping away, seduced yet again by her enemy, a.k.a. the sleeper god.

"'Sleeping all, sleeping sleep . . .'"

A remembered Repeat night-night as she drifted offline, off-guard.

4

When Lieutenant Maud woke, night still blacked out the window across from the bed, the interior darkness banished by one twist of the light key at her side. As easy and simple as that. Presto, bingo.

"Nodder!" she yelled.

So what if she woke the rest of the sleeping hive?

Swinishly sated, she had still dreamed of a mammoth pile of delectables—wines and stews and tender meats, pungent sauces and aromatic breads—that feast spread atop a table with legs as sturdy as her own, thick as stumps. A dog parked himself beside her, his eyes tracking the chicken leg in her hand. A professional beggar, he understood the art of tenacity. Without letup, he stared, whined, flashed his tongue and pawed at her arm. Eventually she shared a few morsels, worn down by that persistent appeal, but she did so grudgingly, with malice in her heart.

And so failed the test.

Selfish that dream script branded: a despicable, selfish scrooge who begrudged a mutt table scraps, who thrived while her comrades struggled, weakened.

Kicking the door, she shrieked. "What do I have to do to get some ASSISTANCE in here?"

After 48-hours of lockup in a sleeper zone, she felt as alert as her nodder jailers, aware of every air mote, every puff of her own flatulence.

"Yes? Yes? How can we assist, visitor?"

"I need a guide."

Like toads on toadstools they blinked almost in sync.

"Apologies. We don't quite comprehend. A guide???"

"A walk-about guide. To show me the place."

"The compound and grounds, you mean?"

"Just the compound."

"And when would you like to schedule that activity?"

"I don't want to SCHEDULE it, I want to DO it. Now."

"Before early meal? Usually you prefer—"

"To eat like a horse, snore like a locust and slow rot in bed. I know. Don't remind me."

"Actually, your snoring levels are quite moderate. They rarely crest above the low-medium range."

Not so her fully awake protest. Other anxious nodders arrived. Now she spoke to a bevy of robes.

"Has there been an accident? Are you experiencing discomfort, visitor?"

"I want to go on a walk-about," she repeated, speaking slowly, enunciating distinctly and vibrating threat. "The first time I asked, I asked nice."

The original wash of nods vanished and a new pair eddied in, took charge.

"I'm Fara. This is Rupert. We'll be your escorts."

"Good try."

"Pardon?"

Did they imagine their name-share would prompt a similar response from her?

"Where would you like to begin?"

"Kitchen," she blurted.

"Certainly."

Without further question or comment, the three were on their way, travelling downward, at a diagonal, precisely the direction Day One nodder had indicated.

"Explore, if you'd like," the so-called Fara invited.

Surrounded by every kind of foodstuff, perishable and non-, she suppressed the urge to grab and gulp. If only she and Repeat had found this overflowing bunker. Cans and cartons, bins and barrels, the chopped, the salted, the baked and ready-to-be. She turned away, motioned to continue. For all its chocs and syrups, the place left a bitter taste.

Rupert suggested they meander toward something called "Assembly Hall."

"What's that? Where you people assemble to sleep?"

Her interest wasn't entirely feigned. If all sleepers dozed in one place on a regular schedule, her getaway plans needn't be complex, only well-timed.

"You CAN sleep there," Rupert clarified, "although we don't actually assemble to sleep. The Assembly Hall functions as a meeting room for residents. As such, it serves a vital role in our community life."

The "vital role" of that airy temple didn't further sink her spirits, but its contents did. Yet another sanctum loaded with snatchable loot. Beneath the vaulted ceiling lay great heaping wads of pads, pillows and blankets, unguarded and unused. Who needed extra layers in a hothouse anyway?

She pointed. "Real or props?"

Fara looked askance, but answered, apparently her turn to answer. "They're real, but residents don't necessarily use them for warmth or cover. Some hold onto the folds while falling into dream."

Real blankets used as props, Maud translated. Who'd miss an armful? No one.

Back in the hallway, by calculated mistake, she bumped hard against several exit doors that instantly opened. No alarms. Was it possible the sleepers only cared who broke in, not who broke out? Was she inventing complications? Could she brazenly request a stash of food and wraps, curtsey, then trot off?

"This way," directed Rupert, heading toward a different set of stairs than the ones they'd descended. "Our other laboratories are located in this section of the compound."

Once they reached the second floor, something besides her own booming voice broke the mausoleum-like quiet. Judging by the sound preview, a clomping herd headed their way.

"Who's coming? The sleeper brigade?"

Ha, ha.

She barely had time to yuk at her own feeble joke before it exploded in her face. The thundering mass did resemble a militia, but not one composed of sleepers. Spilling around a corner, gathering force and speed along the corridor's straightaway, a battalion of shaved heads and Zip-Alls charged straight toward her.

No cubbyhole within bounding distance, she lipped the wall, trapped in a horrible déjà vu.

"Visitor, are you stable?"

A dozen possible informers brushed her elbow. Her current hair and floppy duds were alterations, not a full-scale revamp. She wasn't unrecognizable—not even slightly, not to the knowing eye.

"Indiscriminate snacking can upset the equilibrium," Rupert intoned.

With great difficulty she kept her mouth shut until every shaved head had pounded elsewhere. But when the last of those images from a past life vanished, so did her restraint.

"What the fart was THAT?!?"

"The tour group?" Fara chirped. "Valleyites considering transfer."

Valleyites "touring" the sleeper village? Considering a "transfer"? *Since when*? In the old days, her days, Corporate lambasted the sleeper cult as slackers; even the chat lines mocked their laze.

Then again: Valleyites continuously rampaging through the corridors might serve as a nifty distraction.

"When and how many tours?"

"One a day, usually. Lately, several."

"For the precise number, we'd need to check with Welcome," Fara elaborated. "Is that a priority for you, visitor? Knowing the exact number?"

Before Maud could reply, her jangled nerves got another tweak. Travelling the same path as the stampeding tour group: another creature, her progress severely compromised by a rash of hesitations, half-turns and full-out stops. Not the same ethereal, white-clad specter who'd interrupted Deserter foraging, but definitely the same species. A sleepwalker, Maud realized now.

"Please do not petition the cassandra. Questions might wake her."

But who'd want to quiz a walker?

"Visitors tend to be inquisitive, and cassandras predict the future."

High-wire mysticism, baseless mucky muck. Hard to believe the sleeper cult ever called The Valley's wired gully home. Among this crew, Maud felt ragingly rational—and she an Anti.

"To your immediate left is the Dream Lab . . ."

The facility's glass entrance revealed a low-lit parlor with old-style posters.

". . .where dream drafters offer assistance."

Another nutty sleeper classification to clog her brain when

it needed to be storing layouts, work schedules, pockets of sleeper negligence, loopholes to slip through. She stopped, pressed her temples.

"Apologies," Fara said. "We didn't mean to overload."

"Overload what?" she asked crossly.

"You, visitor. With ceaseless activity and input."

Sleeper logic, sleeper jargon—absolutely farting priceless. But she used both to beg off and recompute in solitude.

"I am tired. I need to rest."

"Of course."

Instantaneously her escorts reversed direction, returned her to her quarters in silence, nodded goodbye.

Not a total loss, the morning walk-about, although not as productive as she'd hoped. But for what exactly had she hoped? A neon arrow pointing to Deserter gift bags, already stuffed and ready for transport?

Her eyelids drooped, weak of will, of strength. Fantastical foodstuffs hovered, awaiting sleep's permission to commandeer her brain, tempt and tantalize her dreaming glands. Her resistance was half-hearted, semi-bogus. If nothing else, a Deserter could recognize a losing battle, confronted with same.

Dream insulation muffled the approach. What she heard, assumed she heard, was the entry of a standard nodder, albeit a nodder moving at a rapid clip.

"Visitor, please, I need to speak with you."

Once again her eyelids betrayed her: rising when they should have stayed put. Dwarfed but not concealed by nodderwear, crowding the bed, an amazing phantom: the commander's duplicate.

Even if she'd been fully cogent, the resemblance would have startled. Coming out of dream, she thought she remained in the clutches of dream, invention making mock of the real.

But Rosa's child was shockingly, eerily real, a near-flawless replication of her mother. The same dark, determined eyes. The same set jaw. The same thin lips. A cheek mole, for PRIME sake. Rosa's cheek mole.

"You don't know me . . ." began Rosa's twin, sincerely, sublimely ignorant—or an excellent thespian.

Cornered on a sleeper bed, Maud labored at a distinct disadvantage. Whatever the intent of this interview, she needed to put distance between herself and the force field that was Rosa's daughter, stake out a wider space in which to maneuver. She got from between bed cloth, as far as the windowsill, before realizing she'd gone as far as she could go. To occupy her hands, she picked up the debugger, fidgeted with it. Too bad it *hadn't* exposed a surveillance cam nested in these walls. Under current circumstances, even an unseen audience might have improved her performance, inspired her to fashion more artful lies.

". . . but I hope you will help me."

"Help you what?"

"Answer some important questions—important, at least, for me."

Her mother had been that earnest once. They all had been.

"You want answers from a thief?"

"Information, I mean," the other stammered, "relating to The Valley."

"Why not quiz one of The Valleyite toursists? No shortage of *them* around."

"*Please.*" Rosa's twin glanced worriedly behind her. "Let me explain. My name is Luce, and—"

"*Luce!* What the fart kind of name is 'Luce'?!"

A flush of color. "It's not my original name. The nods chose it."

"Did they now?" Maud burped a laugh.

"Aren't you going to ask me what I was called . . . before?"

"No."

"Because you already know?"

Because you didn't have a name before the nodders deigned to assign one, Maud could have said. *You were only "the kid," Rosa's inopportune kid.*

"Do you? Know?"

Rescue came in the form of company. A swell of voices in the outer room, the beginnings of a nodder convention. One yelp and a genuine member of that clan would discover the impostor who, sin of sleeper sins, had disrupted a thief's sacred rest. In the long run, a rat-out would probably spare both of them grief, but Maud couldn't bring herself to snitch on Rosa's flesh and blood—not even to keep that relative in ignorance.

With a flick of her wrist she indicated a hiding spot behind the door, then set about manufacturing a credible smokescreen. Since the nodders were familiar with visitor ornery, she simply upped it a notch. Mega-decibel obscenities. The thief in storming, stomping mode.

"How the fart can I rest with this racket going on?"

A chagrined choral of apologies. But apologies didn't suffice; she had to clear the room.

"I can't SLEEP"—that magic word—" with all this chattering and milling about! I need absolute SILENCE. I need PRIVACY!"

A few more scathing expletives accomplished that goal, the nodders scattering like swiped-at flies.

Rosa's twin and her dark eyes, radiating mistrust, edged back into view.

"I've done you a favor, now do one for me. Tell me how you slipped past the entrance check."

"The I-dent? I'm legal."

"So why the robe?"

"To fool the other nods—from the side view, anyway."

"Stole it, did you?"

"*Borrowed* it. From a friend."

Before sassing back, the kid gnawed her lip. Confrontation didn't come as easily to her as to her mother. The sleepers obviously hadn't taught combat as first response.

"So you're a rule-breaker."

"Sometimes it's necessary to break the rules."

"Is it?"

"You should know. You've broken plenty."

"Have I?"

Again Rosa's twin gnawed her lip, harder this time. With a bit more goading she might yet be provoked into a full-blown temper tantrum, worthy of a tempestuous commander.

"Rules you probably broke with my mother."

Maud refused to balk—or flinch. "Who the fart's your mother?"

"Her name is Rosa. Rosa J."

A crumpled printout emerged from beneath the robe's folds.

She snorted—strictly for effect—twisting for a better angle. She'd never actually seen an Anti List onscreen or on scratch. The desire to lay hands on that official warrant was too keen to resist. For all their miserable failures, the Deserters had been important enough to rate inclusion on the Anti List. Most of the names—including her own—were accurately coded; their crimes, too, had been logged correctly, without exaggeration. Not a single instance of sensationalizing the evidence or the facts; an indictment whose tone never strayed from the dispassionate.

Rosa's twin reached over and pointed at a face composed of dots: the commander's face before fifteen Deserter winters had sharpened those cheekbones into boomerangs. Did that nodder robe hide another sheet of fatter dots, revealing a lieutenant's face? Was Rosa's twin that cunning?

"Believe everything you read?"

"I believe this."

"Anyone can print a list."

"It's valid."

"Corporate skews files. Even sleepers must know that."

A rash tirade. By defaming The Valley apparatus, she practically invited the question: "And murder? Do they misreport murder too?" What fine, twisty evasion would she concoct in response to that? "Depends on your definition"?

Hardly.

The Deserters were killers, guilty as charged, guilty en masse. The weapon that downed the two guards could have been hers or Rosa's. That it belonged, in actuality, to neither absolved neither. If the positioning had been different, if they had been the first to intuit the threat, she and Rosa, she or Rosa, would have pulled the trigger too.

"Are you saying this isn't my mother?"

She'd been thinking too much, listening too little. Maybe Rosa's daughter only wished to confirm her mother's identity, not her mother's crime-by-default. Regardless, an informer had to tread carefully. Anything admitted—or withheld—packed serious repercussions. She couldn't credibly deny the resemblance, no one less than blind could. The kid had the printout and already knew her mother's name. Very likely she also knew—or strongly suspected—that the captured thief doubled as her mother's lieutenant. Other than those obvious givens, how much should be confirmed? How much would Rosa want her daughter told? How much did Rosa's daughter truly want to hear? The kid had been raised by overload-phobics; her tolerance for the unpleasant couldn't be very high, might be zilch. The Deserters' history presented as one long continuum of unpleasant, unfortunate facts, as did the personal history of Commander Rosa. Could the commander's daughter cope with—forget *accept*—that kind of bad news deluge?

"We found a grave, my friend and I, not far from here. A mile, maybe a little farther, east."

"The mountains are littered with graves," Maud hedged.

"But this was a new grave. With a twig marker."

—So the kid knew about Four's grave too.

"Is it my mother's?"

The printout slipped from her fingers, fluttered, rocked like a fragile cradle on the warm, polished floor.

Since opening her eyes to Rosa's twin, a part of her had been prepping to serve as (false) witness; to bend the facts and mold the tale to suit a sleeper's fantasies; to gloss, sanctify, even mythologize the lost mother, as necessary. A mother alive set up expectations, unrealistic hopes for a parent/child reunion, replete with love and understanding. She appreciated the dangers of that info feed, but the alternative made the pulse ring in her ears. Even through silence, she couldn't, wouldn't, corroborate the commander's unverified end.

It had begun to snow again, tiny, insidious flakes that spotted the previously spotless courtyard. Behind her, Rosa's daughter grew restless, the nodder robe swishing like an old-style broom. By now, in truth, Rosa, Repeat, all the Deserters, might long be lifeless, covered in a sheath of crystalline white.

But as yet that conclusion was fearful speculation, not proven fact.

As yet.

"Your mother's not dead," she declared, not for loyalty's sake or Rosa's sake, not even for the kid—for the simple selfish comfort of having someone else trust in that statement along with her.

"Your mother, Rosa J, is alive."

5

"Are you listening? Did you *hear* me?" the visitor demanded.

Stooping to retrieve the printout, Luce felt the room jackknife around her. Head, arms, bones, flesh—all of it—felt shatterable as glass.

"You're not going to retch, are you?"

"I don't think so," she said and swallowed hard.

"Isn't that what you wanted me to say? That your mother's alive?"

"I just didn't expect . . ."

But she must have hoped? In some deeply secret part of herself, hoped for a reprieve, hoped exactly for the answer she'd received? Her mother wasn't dead. Was not. Rosa J lived.

"Maybe you didn't want to know," the thief said with sudden coldness.

To steady herself, to protest, she reached out. "Oh no, no. I wanted to know. I *needed* to know."

"Did you?" the other mocked, shaking off the grip. "I wonder."

She tried to refocus on the wobbly page of dots. She'd been foolish to bypass visuals on all the Deserters, especially Maud D. Very, very foolish.

She looked up. "You're . . . ?"

"Not in here," the other nixed. "In here I'm the visitor. Or the thief."

"Was my mother with you when you broke in?"

"No."

"And the grave?"

"Someone else's."

"Then Rosa's safe? My mother's safe?"

"I said she was alive, didn't I?"

"Alive—*where*?"

"You'd better leave now."

"But—"

"Don't be a dumber. The second-shift nodders are on their way. Get out while you can."

And then her mother's comrade savagely shoved.

6

Rosa's double on a research jag presented trouble and opportunity all in one package. Maud had ejected the kid to protect her nod cover, yes, but also to scheme.

Both factions went into their next confab with clearer agendas and better-defined goals. Maud herself took pains to appear formidable; the kid, for her part, attempted the same, speaking brusquely, parading a bravado courage she couldn't possibly possess. This go-around, Rosa's double not only looked like the commander, she behaved like her mother—an impersonation all to Maud's advantage. She'd honed her skills negotiating with the original.

"You knew my mother in The Valley?"

"You've done the background."

"And you were with her in the mountains, when I was born?"

"Stands to reason."

"Did she consider keeping me?"

"Some free advice. Before asking a question, consider the consequences."

"Did she?"

"Did you sort what I just said?"

"Did Rosa J consider keeping me? Yes or no!"

"Keeping you wasn't an option."

"But did she ever *want* to keep me?"

A little tremor there. A bit of a whine.

"I can't say what the commander wanted. Just what she did."

"Left me with the nods."

"We were on the run. We weren't set up for an infant."

"A baby was inconvenient."

With one lunge Maud was close enough to slap that insolent mouth and almost did. To hear Rosa blamed for perhaps her most generous act—giving this Luce a chance, a life—galled her to the core.

"You've got some farting nerve. Living in cushy sleeperville and complaining about it."

"I'm not complaining. I'm trying to understand."

"No you're not. You're searching for someone to blame. Yesterday you were thrilled to have a mother. Today she's a pox on your psyche. You should be farting grateful you aren't chained to an E-screen, watching maggots multiply."

"Is . . . is that why you wanted to change The Valley? Because of the work?"

She scowled, backed off. "No one changes The Valley."

"But you tried? With my mother? Because you thought trying was important?"

The between-the-lines appeal also chimed in loud and clear: *More important than raising a kid?*

A puerile thing yet, Rosa's daughter. But did she deserve a lecture on the perils of misplaced commitment and humiliating defeat? Hang tight to the rickety bandwagon of World-Wide Improvement, young comrade, because once you lose your grip, there's nothing left but farting freefall.

"I asked you a question."

"You ask a lot of questions," Maud fenced, sensing the opening she'd been waiting for. "Problem is, you're asking the wrong person."

Gratifyingly, for the Deserters' cause, Rosa's doppelgänger paled.

"What do you mean?"

"The person you should be quizzing is the commander. Rosa."

To voice the next request, Rosa's twin had to start twice and even then the words were scarcely audible.

"Could that happen?"

"I could make it happen. By taking you to her."

"You'd take me to my mother? You'd do that?"

"Depends." She waited another beat, two. Cruel, wasn't it, to keep the kid in suspense? "I can't play wilderness scout in a sleeper compound. You get me out, I get you to Rosa."

7

Getting the visitor out wasn't the only stipulation, merely the first. Maud also demanded supplies: food and clothing, as much as the two could shuttle. The slightest hesitation on Luce's part contorted Maud's lips, turned a blue-eyed stare into a steely glare.

"Downloading second thoughts?"

"No," she insisted—a version of truth.

Even if—a major *if*—she managed to fulfill Maud's extravagant demands, including hoodwinking supervisors, supervisor assistants and any number of nods, would an Anti honor her promise? Would she really lead a stranger to the Deserters or discard her as excess baggage as soon as they'd cleared East Gate?

"Remember: the clothes have to be heavy. None of that flimsy, airy, cassandra stuff. The mountains aren't temperature-controlled like this farting place. People freeze in the farting mountains and stay farting frozen until farting spring."

She ignored, had learned to ignore, the gratuitous cursing and cranky temper, but the subtext alarmed her. "You said Rosa was alive."

"Last time I saw her."

"Stop trying to scare me. Because you can't. Scare me," she said as her gut shimmied.

"Glad to hear it," Maud snapped. "Now, can we get back to discussing supplies? You'll have to do the collecting. I'm watched too closely."

"But."

"No buts."

"What if—"

"No what ifs! Just get it done. I've already spent too many hours in fantasy land."

"You're asking a lot."

"Can't handle it?"

"I didn't say that," she said. "It just won't be smooth."

"Are you after sympathy or your mother's location?"

Maud couldn't or wouldn't understand the risks she so meticulously detailed. The nods knew the eating and dressing habits of every resident. When they tidied rooms in the morning, they straightened closets, collected pulls for the laundry. Any resident who tried to hoard food under the guise of night snacks got reported, subjected to a physical examination, signed up for one or several "Is Anything Troubling You?" sessions.

"Find a way," Maud said, unimpressed. "And find it fast."

To stockpile instantly the amount in demand required help—but whose? The more people involved, the greater the chance of discovery. Without meaning to, Connie might gab from pure spillover excitement. Parish was the only fellow Recovered whose discretion Luce implicitly trusted. But Maud's list couldn't be covered with only Parish's assistance; they'd need Connie to collude and connive too.

"It's not something I can organize overnight," she told Maud. "There's so much to do—and plan."

"Then start doing. Start planning," Maud replied, haughty, relentless, ruthless—everything PRIME proclaimed a Deserter to be.

Everything her mother might also turn out to be, when and if Rosa J were ever found.

8

Because the courtyard was generally nod-free near twilight, Luce asked Parish and Connie to convene there.

Connie arrived first, rubbing her palms and stamping her feet. "Why here? It's freezing!"

"Because it's safer."

"Oooo—I like the twist of that."

Parish arrived annoyed. "What's with the coded message? Even the narcos woke up long enough to wonder what all the whispering was about."

An inauspicious start. If the narcos labeled Luce's behavior strange, who wouldn't?

"Could it be Miss By-The-PRIME is contemplating a seditious act?" Connie teased.

"Are both of you absolutely focused?" she asked, pulling at her sleeves. "Because I'd prefer to voice this only once."

"We're here, we're prepped. Now spew. I'm icing," Connie summed.

"I've made a discovery."

"Have you been Archiving without me?" Connie accused.

"No. The information came from PRIME."

"What kind of information?" Parish asked, boring in.

"Information about my mother." To keep up her nerve, to keep talking, she fairly chattered. "I know who she is."

A hush settled, weighted by awe, maybe envy. The nipping cold was forgotten, inconsequential. A Recovered had identified her mother—something they all dreamed, but nothing any of them expected to accomplish. In the abstract, in the longed-for stage, sharing the news was pure joy, but caught in the moment she felt torn, apologetic, once again separated from her nominal kind. De facto, a daughter with a known mother no longer shared the same sense of loss.

"Who?" Parish asked.

"A Deserter."

Connie gasped. "A real live outlaw? *Our* PRIME revealed that?"

"Not entirely. I talked to the thief."

"You talked to the thief! How'd you get in? Why didn't you take me with you? Stop! Was that *you?* I thought a nod had tidied! I thought a *nod* had recycled my trainee robe! But *you*. . ."

Parish cut off the jag. "The thief knows your mother?"

"I can't *believe* you got in before me, *without* me! I can't believe I didn't try that ruse-gag myself!"

"Zip, Connie," Parish ordered. "Let Luce talk."

She tried again. "I had to speak to her. I thought she knew my mother. I thought she might confirm the grave we found was hers."

Connie blanched. "That was your mother's grave?"

"No, no. A Deserter's grave, but not hers."

"I don't process," Parish said. "You found some grave and assumed it was your mother's?"

Luce produced the printout. Both Connie and Parish stared at it, then at her.

Connie squealed, then smushed her mouth. All scanned for nods in the murky light. "Apologies. This is so MEGA!"

"The thief . . . the visitor . . . knows where Rosa is. She says she'll take me to her."

"When?" Parish whispered.

"As soon as I collect the supplies she wants. Lots of food,

clothing too."

Parish nodded; Connie danced in place, bit into her hand; a little squeal escaped regardless.

"I'm asking for your help, but I understand if you don't want to give it."

"Are you viral? Of course we'll help!"

Parish nodded again.

Only she trembled.

What if she found her mother only to get rejected all over again? A Recovered's primal fear: separation wasn't a mistake; it wasn't a mix-up; it wasn't an oversight; it wasn't a temporary state of heart and mind. Rejected once, a Recovered could still fantasize about reconciliation. Rejected twice, she'd have to accept the worst: her mother meant to give her away, keep her away—permanently.

Connie's nose was bright pink, Parish's cheeks chapped from cold.

"No pressure, no penalty," she said, her last shaky attempt at fair play, at having the decency not to trade on friendship, on the universal Recovered longing to recover the lost.

"Just loads of fun!" Connie yelped.

"I'll get the food," Parish volunteered. "A resident working kitchen owes me a favor."

Luce explained that she already had a blanket supply, stashed along with Connie's trainee robe—the robe Connie would need to don again.

"For mayhem?"

"For messaging. I think it's better if I keep my distance from the visitor until . . . departure."

"I agree," Parish said. "Steer clear of Deprivation. Connie can ferry the final instructions."

But would she? The plan would soon depend on Connie's

not crashing, on Connie doing what and only what she'd been told to do.

"Will you commit to that, Con? To act as go-between? No inventions or improv?" Parish interrogated.

Connie held up two pink thumbs.

"Rodger-dodger! Alley-oop! Aye, Aye, el capitán!"

A *yes*—Luce hoped—in Connie-speak.

9

Wonder of wonders, Connie performed flawlessly.

"Tell the visitor to sleep—or pretend to sleep—this afternoon. After curfew, she has to request a drafter. Me. Specifically. It's better to meet in the lab, but if she can't manage that, her room will do."

Connie closed her eyes, moved her lips, memorizing. "Sleep in the afternoon. Request you. In the lab. Gotcha."

"She shouldn't insist on the lab, just request it."

"Request you. Request lab. Don't insist," Connie revised. "Is that all?"

"That's all." An all that covered everything, meant everything, to the declarer.

"All righty, then. Later, gator," Connie yipped and took off, scurrying at first, but just as quickly slowing down to a speed any nod would sanction.

In prep for the long night ahead, at final meal, Luce ate voraciously but without appetite. Every bite swelled in her mouth. Outside the cafeteria, in the echo-y hallway, Parish stopped fingering her tightly tucked bandanna to reach out, enfold, squeeze.

"Good fortune. I wish I could go with you."

Luce held onto Parish and Parish's hug longer than she'd intended.

"Me too."

She would have felt safer with Parish along, more in control.

"Don't angst about Connie. Just focus on the event."

Focus on the event, she repeated for inspiration, lying in bed, waiting to be summoned. What if Maud thought the plan was inane and refused to comply? In the Connie-conveyed message, she'd forgotten to include assurances that she had the supplies. Maybe Maud wouldn't budge unless and until she reviewed the stockpile.

But then came a tap, tap, tapping.

"Apologies for the disturbance, dear," the nod said, looking less sorry than imposed upon in the streaked light.

Luce made a grand show of rubbing her eyes.

"The visitor has requested a dream drafter."

"Now?"

She had to question the timing, to seem perplexed. Residents reported dreams on schedule, during daylight.

"I'm afraid so, dear."

"I'll need to change pulls."

"Don't rush. The visitor will be waiting in the lab."

"Not in Deprivation?" She tried to make even her blink seem innocently confused.

"Another request," the nod reported with a sigh.

Cautiously she stepped into the night-lit hallway, although caution, as yet, wasn't required. She was still on a legitimate mission, pacifying the prickly visitor. Two nods clucked in sympathy when she appeared at the Dream Lab entrance.

"I'm supposed to . . ." she started to explain.

"We know, dear. Enter."

Maud, alone in the waiting room, looked up. "The dream drafter finally shows."

Disconcerted by that wisecrack, she hesitated.

Come on, come on, Maud signed impatiently.

Speaking loudly for the nods' benefit, she prompted: "I

understand you requested a session?"

"That's why I'm here, drafter gal."

Nonetheless, when the door to the workstation closed, Maud's smirk turned grim. In the dreamer's chair, she leaned over and finger-wrote on the desktop: **Wired?**

While logging on, a requirement, Luce explained what she always explained to skeptics: The Founders had only the highest respect for dreams and dream exploration. The by-laws unequivocally guaranteed private, uninterrupted dream sessions.

Nevertheless, Maud blocked her hand. "No E-screen."

"It's the usual procedure. We need to follow the *usual procedure*," she emphasized.

Obstinately Maud shook her head, snatched a blank Morpheus pad from a side shelf, sailed it into the drafter's lap and shouted at the walls: "No computing! The visitor distrusts microchips."

Where it was recorded, on a Morpheus pad or an E-screen, even *if* it was recorded, probably didn't signify. She'd suggested the dream session as a precaution at best, an alibi at worst. But this tampering with the plan, this unreasonable, bullish defiance, alarmed. They hadn't left the compound, and already they profoundly disagreed.

"This *truly* isn't necessary."

"It's necessary for *me*," Maud snorted.

Laboriously, resentfully, she wrote at the top of the bent scratch: **Visitor Requests Morpheus Record.**

"Whenever you're ready to start."

"Long or short version?"

"Whichever you prefer."

"Whenever, whichever," Maud sarcastically mimicked.

Many residents began hesitantly, wary of reactivating a

dream. Maud too procrastinated. "You know what I mean by black dark?"

Luce nodded; she always nodded in the drafting chair.

"If you fisted it, you'd get resistance—that dense."

Again she nodded, habit kicking in. She had no idea whether Maud's recall was genuine or fake, but she went through the motions, misgivings multiplying like mold the nearer she came to accompanying a shifty thief, an accused killer, into the wilderness.

"My job was lookout. Just me and the blackness getting chummy. . . .Y

ou're not writing this down."

"I'm listening. That's what I'm supposed to do."

She was also thinking: about darkness, about entering it with Maud. She wasn't accustomed to darkness. Day and night, however dimly, The Retreat stayed lit. Even on her ramble with Connie, bright moonlight accented the ground and trees. No closer than a dream description, Maud's dense blackness unsettled.

"I wasn't a kid in the dream, but I thought like a kid. Running ghost and goblin files in my mind, scanning a million dark closets. *Crash the program. Vacate the menu*, I told myself. *It's only night. You'll live through it. You have before.* But I hadn't lived through night in dream, see. A dream can feel exactly like forever, like you'll never wake up."

Again she mechanically nodded, although Maud had ceased to notice. The visitor might have been reciting to herself. Her eyes had dilated slightly; she gripped the arms of her chair. Beads of perspiration dotted her forehead.

"At first, strange shapes cavorted. Then the darkness developed a voice. Buzzy, with secrets. 'Arrogant bastard,' I called out. 'You and your farting games.' I raised my gun, fired randomly. After that it wasn't a visual; it wasn't a noise; it was pressure with a message: 'Take some down. Catch a snooze. No sentry remains one hundred percent vigilant. Relax. All is well. All is well.' I tried spouting counter-prop. 'Anything can happen when you're asleep. Sleep pulls the wool over your eyes.' 'Sleep opens a disorderly house.' But the defense was useless. My eyes were lulled; my brain was lulled. I plunged so far down I lost all memory of up. A farting lookout fast asleep."

By the time Maud finished, the color had drained from her face; there was a tremor in her knees. The Deserter confederate looked haunted, a different being altogether.

Mesmerized by the transformation, the drafter also sat motionless, as tensely watchful as a voyeur. Residents who reported similar dreams usually finished with an attack by a specific fiend, some monster crouched in the shadows, biding its time until the climax. Luce had never heard a dream that equated sleep with treachery.

"You blamed yourself for falling asleep?"

At once Maud reverted to her former petulant self. "A lookout watches; she doesn't sleep!" She wiped her mouth with her sleeve, jumped up. "Are we finished here—yes or no?"

"I have to include a classification."

"So do it."

Besieged, Luce penned, then scribbled through. "Besieged" sounded too much like a breakout clue.

Come on, come on, Maud signaled.

Impossible to determine, she revised and left it, reluctantly, at that.

"You're upset," she told the dreamer, had practiced saying, long before.

"Not me," Maud denied, lock-jawed.

"Yes. This experience has DISTURBED you."

What the fart? Maud mouthed.

She also resorted to mime: *SO disturbed you need to go for a walk. Need ME to go with you.*

Without further delay Maud strode into the hallway and screamed as much at the two waiting nods.

"At this hour?"

"No controversy," she assured, catching up. "I don't mind."

"Are you certain, Luce? It's very late."

"We're starting a sleep strike," Maud ragged. "Maybe you two should join in. Deflate some of that puff."

"Please don't alarm. I'll be fine," she reassured: the nods—or herself?

"To take a walk, I'll need more CLOTHES," Maud complained pointedly.

"You'll need an extra wrap too, Luce," one of the nods providentially advised, providing the excuse she needed to stop by her room. "We'll escort the visitor to East Gate and meet your there."

"Don't tarry, drafter girl," Maud warned. "Or I'll take that walk without you."

In the nod-less hallway, she ran. From previous experiments, she'd discovered she could layer three sets of pulls if the bottom two were cotton, the top wool. To compensate for the thinness of her slip-ons, she wore an extra pair of toe warmers. Already her skin itched.

Beneath the bed, she found a fresh stack of pulls, stuffed there in the interim by Parish; those she frantically pinned inside her therma-cloak before waddling forth. She felt like a mummy, but the reflector showed only plump: plump and prepared for a temperature plunge.

10

Maud and escorts were waiting for her at the entrance gate, the nods wearing expressions of forbearance sorely taxed, Maud scowling and pacing.

When she joined them, Maud turned, and with a syrupy sweetness that fooled no one, dismissed the other two.

"Night, night. Sleep tight."

The nods seemed delighted by the very thought.

"Remember, Luce. You mustn't overtire *yourself* either."

Part commiseration, part warning, that farewell.

As soon as the nods departed, Maud grabbed, shook and ranted: "Have you forgotten our agreement? I can't stroll without FOOD. I'll STARVE."

"Nobody's going to starve."

"No food, no guide," Maud threatened.

"It's taken care of. Just walk," she said, wrenching free.

Floodlights still illuminated the grounds. Two newish transfers circled the pond aimlessly, not yet lulled to sleep. Neither paid undue attention to the visitor or the drafter, no doubt presuming any nighttime stroller shared the same malady as themselves: recalcitrant wakefulness. For their obvious indifference, Luce felt immensely grateful. Constantly deflecting suspicion turned out to be hard work, harder than she'd expected. Already she felt frazzled and the night's ordeal had barely begun.

"Where's the loot?" Maud demanded.

"Follow, please."

As they approached the third meditation bench, they encountered another, less easily duped stroller: a senior nod.

Abruptly she sat, snatching Maud down with her.

"Where's the farting FOOD?"

"Is that you, Luce?"

"Salutations."

"Salutations, Luce, visitor. Out so late?"

"We've just finished a drafting session. The visitor thought a walk would help her decompress."

"A walk?"

"A walk with frequent rests," Luce clarified, rubbing the bench beneath her.

"Unsoothingly late for a drafting session, isn't it?"

Maud glared. "I'm a late sleeper."

The nod ambled on.

"If you can't walk more than 500 yards without a rest stop, quit now. Because you'll never make it to camp."

"Patience, please."

No other company in sight, she reached behind the bench and pulled out a sack.

"That's it?"

"It's the first."

"How many—total?"

"Stop yelling!"

"I'm not a sleeper," Maud groused. "I'm expected to yell."

At the next designated clump of bushes, they found a second sack of supplies, plus a little something extra.

Infuriated, she swiped at Connie: "No one told you to guard the food!"

"Oh well," Connie replied, hopping.

"Friend or foe?" Maud demanded.

"Friend—supposedly."

Thereafter ignoring Connie, Maud rummaged among the

provisions. "This isn't enough."

"There's more, up the path," Connie chirped.

"Would you just LEAVE? They're probably already searching for you!"

"Nobody's searching for me."

"You don't *know* that!"

"Enough arguing. Forward," Maud ordered.

At the next switchback, Luce checked over her shoulder, then snapped her arm in the direction of The Retreat as if reprimanding a disobedient dog. Still hopping, Connie waved.

"Quit huffing about your friend," Maud said. "If anything, she'll serve as diversion. Nodders to the rescue and all that."

"I'm not huffing!"

But she was: huffing and stomping too.

Maud snickered, jabbed her in the ribs.

"It's not funny."

"I think it is."

"But it isn't! Connie vowed she'd be careful, *stay* careful."

Connie understood what it was like to want something so badly you feared the very want would jinx you. Every Recovered did.

"Don't be so hard on your comrade. Life's pretty dull in sleeperville."

She jerked wide, sped up to get beyond the range of those jabby fingers.

"And don't start fast if you can't sustain fast. We've got a farting haul ahead of us."

At the trailhead, they detoured slightly from the standard, well-marked course. Parish had proposed concealing the last of the supplies behind an outcrop of rocks near their lookout post. Safer to stash the largest bundle there, Parish judged and Luce agreed.

"This isn't an exit route," Maud carped.

"Will you *lax?*"

"Said the stomper."

Two full satchels, camouflaged by debris. Besides food and an extra beamer, Parish had somehow finagled the clutch of flamers Maud insisted upon.

"Elevated now?" Luce crowed, proud of Parish's amazing resourcefulness.

"We'll need to repack, redistribute the weight. Otherwise I'll be leading a cripple," Maud said as gruffly as ever, but clearly pleased.

"I can handle my share."

"And will. But since I'm three times your size, I carry three times the weight."

"Don't make allowances for me."

Maud actually laughed. "However we divide this stuff, it's going to be a press. You'll still get to play martyr."

"I didn't say I wanted to be a martyr."

"No one ever does—aloud," Maud said and laughed a different, odder laugh.

Not once during the redistribution process did Maud turn toward the smear of Valley lights. Only her own gaze drifted toward that seductive glow.

"I come up here sometimes," she admitted. "With Parish. Just to look."

The packing continued without pause.

"Not that you can see much. From this height. Through the haze."

Since before she could walk Luce had been taught not to solicit too much too soon, schooled in precaution: contemplate, digest, sort, re-sort, let lie. But to overload implied learning too much, and thus far she'd learned practically nothing.

"Why didn't you hide out in The Valley? Why come here?"

Unlike Valley lights, tonight's moon barely glimmered, as if bored by radiance. She couldn't see Maud's eyes but heard the growl.

"I agreed to take you to Rosa. Not teach Valley."

"I just wonder what it was like living there."

"Wonder something else. And strap this to your back."

"Did you meet my mother as a child?"

"No."

"Were you friends a long time before you deserted?"

"Long enough."

"That's not an answer."

"It's my answer," Maud said. "If it doesn't suit, wait and ask someone else. And walk pitched forward, not upright. It'll go easier."

From that point on, Maud led. Quickly, too quickly, Luce lost familiarity with the surroundings. Where there was no clear trail, Maud bushwhacked, hacking at vines and branches that snapped and popped under the attack.

"Don't use your beamer on sleeper grounds. As a last resort, only, once we're on the ridge."

"But," she said.

"Don't argue with me! Bobbing lights are trackable."

Trackable by whom? No one from The Retreat wandered this deeply into the mountains and Valleyites lived even farther away. But Maud gave her no chance to inquire, covering the inclines as swiftly as she crossed the few flat stretches, perceiving and negotiating night's passageways with a sure-footed confidence that contradicted the bias her dream message revealed. How could Rosa's lieutenant loathe a darkness she so easily breached?

Trying not to lag, Luce hunched her shoulders, scrambled low, fought through brambles that stabbed at her arms and cheeks. Already her thigh muscles quivered. If her mother could trek this slant a thousand times over, surely she, Rosa J's daughter, could manage once?

"That grave—we're above it now?" she called in spurts.

Maud didn't turn around.

"You—never—said—who . . ."

"So?"

"Tell me."

"If you were curious, you should have checked."

She stumbled on a rock, on something. "I don't understand."

Maud glanced over her shoulder. "You understand."

"No. I don't."

"Jumped in, dug it up. Understand now?"

The ground that should have stayed solid beneath her feet rippled.

"Don't look so squeamish. It's been done. Lots of times."

Done by Maud? By Rosa J?

"The dead don't feel the cold. Only the living," Maud proclaimed and marched on.

"I don't believe you," she called out feebly. "You're just trying to shock me."

Her partner whirled full around then, for a while walked backwards.

"Girlie, if I wanted to shock you, I could do a fart of a lot better than grave robbing stories. I could describe Terminateds drinking their own piss and slicing out kidneys, just to get a donor's night off the farting streets."

"Stop! I don't want to hear anymore," she pled, close to weeping.

Unmoved, Maud sneered. "Then stop quizzing me and concentrate on hiking. I told you it's going to be a long haul. Longer if you dawdle."

For the next rough and rugged mile, perversely determined to out-tough the tough, she did move faster—clumsy, awkward, graceless motion but it kept her behind Maud's rockfall. Little by little the desire to compete sputtered. She ached with stupid weariness. The dream search for her mother never ventured beyond the statue-ringed pond and meditation benches; it hadn't trained her to venture this far. Back at The Retreat, all but the most recent transfers would be snug in their beds, hooked to night caps, dreaming. She could have been among them, dreaming too.

She must have dozed off, walking. The last visual she remembered was a line of overburdened, snow-weary evergreens.

A hand snatched at her.

"Hey! Stay awake. Hey!"

But her legs folded anyway. From the vantage of a frozen cushion of white, she heard bumps, scrapes, curses. The snow at her ear had a heartbeat.

"Open your mouth."

She recognized the taste: choc, sweet and thick.

"Don't just suck, chew. And swallow! I can't have you zoning out again."

"I thought we were there already," she woozily reported. "Except the mountain was The Valley, and we were on the streets. Just you and me. The only people."

Maud grunted and pulled her to her feet. "You're going to have to walk on your own. I can't carry you too."

"I can walk," she said, staggering, resolving to stay awake, or at least ambulatory, an imitation cassandra drifting through the ivory wilderness.

As the pitch grew steeper, to lever herself forward, she clutched at any available solid: attached branches, rock faces, icy roots. The scrambling caused a tiny avalanche of dirty snow. If she fell, she too would roll and bounce, maybe as far as the faraway Valley. Above the tree line, not even trees sheltered. What lay ahead and at their backs was the same terrible, windy emptiness.

"We've got to traverse it," Maud announced at the base of a jagged cliff. "Watch where I put my hands. Keep your weight over your feet. *Don't* hug the rock."

She did as she was told, creeping forward in minute increments, looking neither up nor down.

"A couple of feet more. That's it. Keep going. Here. Grab here. You're doing fine. You're doing fine."

After that scary interlude, according to Maud, the route was supposed to get easier, but it didn't get easier, not exactly. The slightly wider path continued to climb.

"Are we close?"

"Very."

Near the top of the ridge, Maud stopped, lit a flamer, then dropped to the ground, scratching and sniffing.

"Is this where they were? Is this where they're supposed to be?"

"It's where I left them," Maud muttered, face tense, flamer twirling.

A desolate, desolate spot, a million hours, a million miles from heat, ready light or comfort—or so it felt to a renegade sleeper. Luce couldn't imagine deliberately seeking out this place, calling it home. Even the surrounding silence felt old and layered and private, a thing utterly unto itself, withholding welcome, distrustful of interlopers.

"They should have stayed here. The other caves are higher. Too high."

"You don't mean farther up? Farther than *this*?"

Luce heard the hysteria in her voice, felt it shudder through her ribcage. How could anyone higher stay alive?

"Rosa must have gotten confused," Maud said, as if thinking aloud. "Or she just took off, and they followed."

"Where? Do you know *where*?"

Maud wasn't listening; she peered toward the ridge top, stamped her feet in the hard snow. "We're going to have to move faster. A lot faster. As fast as you can."

And so again they stumble/ran, in circles, it seemed, until Maud's internal compass located a small opening in a wall of rock.

"Stay here unless I call for you," she ordered and disappeared inside the hole, carrying a lit flamer.

To keep warm Luce slapped her hands, kicked. Never had she felt more forsaken.

"Rosa! Repeat!"

Disobediently she edged closer and closer to the mouth of the cave, listening to the echo of those unanswered appeals. From a crouch she charted shadows cast by flamer light, watched as those same shadows faded. Between the open patch of feral behind and the cave's dank, narrow walls, she had a choice of two terrors.

"Maud, I'm coming in too," she yelled, steeling herself for contact with the putrid slime of the cave's floor. But when something squirmed beneath her palm, she couldn't stop herself, she screamed.

The flamer doubled back, and still she screamed.

"Listen to me, listen to me. If you're Rosa's daughter, start acting like it! We don't have time for crack-ups. Your mother's in trouble. They all are."

In her hand Maud held a shred of plaid material. Outside the cave, she wordlessly pocketed it and again took the lead.

It didn't seem possible to keep hiking, to hike faster, but now they hiked at a pace that made no allowances for timorousness or exhaustion. Luce kept up because she had to keep up, convinced she'd be left to the elements if she faltered: Maud no longer seemed aware that anyone travelled with her or shared her mission as the sky turned from black to gray, prelude to a filmy dawn. Something wild and near flapped its wings, the only soundtrack beyond their hustling. Two sets of footprints and only two, one pair cramped and pigeon-toed, the other widely spaced. With every step they scored the snow. Idiotically Luce began to count the tracks as they made them, left them, hurried on, as if counting would reveal and deliver their unknown destination. She followed Maud mechanically now, without interference or questions, relying on the power of inertia to keep her going. The specifics of her body and her load had blurred into a dull numbness; she was simply a weight zooming through space, a crude, ungoverned lump of matter that moved, and would move, until Maud called a halt.

Slamming into Maud's broad shoulders, she lost her balance, tumbled backward and landed on her rump. When she tried to get up, her feet slid out from under her and she fell again, face forward. Only then did she process the lumpy circle of shapes rising with the morning mist, one of those apparitions weaving toward them with arms outstretched. He seemed to be waving off calamity.

"'Some must watch while some must sleep,'" she thought he said.

"It's me, Repeat, it's me," Maud replied, tearing at her sack. "I've got food, clothes." Gathering him into her arms, she poured milk down his throat as if he were a kitten, or an infant. "Don't just stand there, Luce! Help me! Distribute the wraps! Start a fire!"

Stupefied by that convocation of spirits, she couldn't oblige. She could scarcely breathe. Maud was the one who saved them: igniting the ground with flamers, wrapping those skeletons with blankets, forcing choc into pair after pair of filthy, scarred hands, shouting again and again into that gallery of crusted, vacant eyes: "Where's the commander? Where's Rosa? Repeat, *where is Rosa?*"

Shivering, recoiling from that bedlam, she backed farther and farther away, colliding with nubby snow. She felt as if she'd entered a dream, a miasma of indescribable pain and suffering, injury and neglect. And then her own pulse seemed to sense its echo: a weaker beat, drawing her like a distress signal toward an outlying cluster of slick rock.

On that hard bed, at a distance from the rest, one final, ragged bundle curled upon itself like an animal seeking warmth.

Closing in, she felt every muscle, including her heart, relax as if at last she'd reached the end of a grueling marathon. With shaky fingers, she eased aside the shredded silver collar, a futile buffer against mountain wind.

Exactly as she hoped, exactly as she feared, the face beneath the cloth caricatured her own. Sallow, haggard, the unmistakable face of her mother. In the flesh.

In the flesh—but dying.

IV

1

Even after months of living in the same compound with her mother, there were mornings when Luce woke in her Retreat bed and believed she'd found Rosa only in dream. Regardless how hard she concentrated on reviving the exact details and sequence of her journey to and from camp, her quest and Maud's rescue remained stubbornly fractured, a jumbled mishmash of sight and sound. What she remembered, she remembered hazily: the novelty of her own exhaustion, her mother's sunken face, the bleached halo of dawn—bits and bytes of memory that, like dream, blurred the boundaries between what was and seemed to be.

On first sight, at that campsite at the end of the world, the Deserters had unnerved her. But once Maud warmed their joints and filled their stomachs, once their brains processed Maud's sidekick, the commander's twin, she unnerved them. The one Maud called Cook circled, pointed, then pinched. Hard.

"She's real," Maud informed. "And if you keep pinching, eventually she'll pinch back."

All were frostbitten, malnourished, scarcely coherent. The thinnest one, Repeat, lurched and reeled, calling out prophecies, cassandra-style.

"'Look at my life. Look at the life around me. Where is this beauty that I am supposed to miss? Joy? I have none. He who was living is now dead. We who were living are now dying, in the decayed hole of mountain, in the faint moonlight.'"

She couldn't recall every pronouncement—there had been so many—but she remembered the doomsday slant that unified the lot. She remembered feeling as if The Retreat were light years distant, no haven she'd ever reach again. She remembered believing they would all perish before the next darkness covered them.

Maud, and only Maud, refused to accept that fate. Continuously she nursed those barely breathing skeletons, feeding, warming, consoling, inspiring. Through sheer force of will she got all but Rosa on their feet and functioning within or despite of delirium. Maud/angel of mercy veered so sharply from Maud/captured thief, Maud/sneering trail guide, the recast so altogether different from the many Mauds that came before, Luce's own sense of isolation intensified. Even among Deserters, she counted as the alien outcast.

"We're going back," Maud announced one nameless hour, checking Rosa's pulse. "Your mother, we'll transport. Luce, you'll heft the back end."

She'd assumed Maud aimed for The Valley, a destination no more insuperable than anywhere else. The woman beside her, the person she couldn't yet call "mother," seemed incapable of surviving any kind of transfer anywhere. A failure of imagination on her part, as it happened. She also failed as a carrier, tripping, jarring Rosa and wounding her own knees. The thinnest one, Repeat, had to take her place, chanting as he lugged.

"'Take time to be holy, the world rushes on . . .'"

That the ravaged Deserters arrived with beating hearts amazed the residents, the nods and the vast majority of technicians. Her supervisor took the longer view.

"They started Valley. Obviously they're adapters."

At The Retreat, they adapted yet again, delighted with

the very sleep/feed/rest routine recent transfers found so odious. As the Deserters' liaison, Maud vocalized the group's demands and controlled access to its individuals, as fiercely protective as an old-text mother hen. She exhorted, extorted and got. Long after the snow began to melt and the waterfalls began to thunder, she insisted on maximal heat within their quarters.

"We haven't been hot in years," Maud justified. "It's a craving."

Eager to examine such extraordinary exemplars of SSD survivors, the technicians pleaded for immediate interviews, however brief.

Maud refused.

"They'll get chatty in time. For now, let them be."

Repeat, the one exception, began chatty, remained chatty. He also revived fastest—without gaining kilos. Concerned dietitians made it their mission to concoct magnificent high-caloric snacks to pad his bones. They even consulted Cook to gain insight into the mysteries of Repeat's queer metabolism.

"He doesn't like wood rat," Cook reported. "And now that I ponder it, he isn't overly fond of berry mush either."

"Oh dear! We *did* use berries in the berry bread," one of the kitchen staff confessed. "He didn't communicate his dislike of fruit."

Maud had to explain, and re-explain, Cook's joke. She also had to vouch for Repeat's vigorous health.

"Detach! He's thriving!"

"But he's so terribly thin."

"If he ate all day every day, he'd still be a pole," Maud insisted.

Unconvinced, the dietitians went back to pouring over their cookbooks, old-style and E-screen refined.

Healthy enough to wander around the compound, Repeat wandered endlessly and without restriction. No one denied him access anywhere. He trailed cassandras and their scribes, accompanied nods on daily rounds, sat in on assimilation sessions, peered over the shoulders of technicians and soon recited from a whole new category of fact and fancy.

"'Sleep to forget all but the essential. Nathaniel Kleitman, hero. Sleep/*sleps*/*schlafen*: what foxes do in caves, what rodents do in nests, what guinea fowl do in trees'"—and on and on and on.

At such outbursts, Maud squawked with delight.

"Aren't you afraid he'll overload?" Luce once asked, concerned herself for his welfare.

"The man's been on replay for fifteen cycles. How can he possibly overload?"

Although Connie didn't share Repeat's overload immunity, she happily risked the repercussions of an in-depth Anti snoop. A week after the Deserters settled in at The Retreat, everything PRIME recorded about the clique, Connie knew also.

"Your mother's genuinely famous, you know."

That, yes, Luce did know. As Rosa's recognized daughter, she'd become something of a demi-celebrity herself. Recovereds who weren't genuinely her friends began dropping by her room to chat; rarely did she pass a nod who didn't pat her head. The technicians, too, showered her with inordinate attention. After years of being treated as no more or less than a typical Recovered, suddenly she excited their interest.

"Compositionally, you represent a healthy version of your mother's extraordinary genes," she heard time and again.

Nonetheless, just now, she wasn't especially keen to contribute to sleep research, nor did she want to discuss her dream narratives, past or present, with every technician or assistant technician who sidled up to her at Assembly or in the cafeteria line.

"Any new patterns since finding your mother? Any variations in length, theme, crisis points?" they probed. "Are you quite certain?"

Even her own supervisor, intrigued by the co-dreaming possibilities of rebel and child, asked to review her file.

"But I've never dreamed of kidnapping," she swore.

"The connection needn't be so blatant," he said. "The link might be as subtle as a chill."

It was odd, being approached by people she'd known all her life as if she were a stranger, as if she were someone new.

During a routine night cap check, a nod who used to oversee the *kinder* wing lingered near the foot of her bed.

"Does my system need repair?"

The nod shook her head, indulgently smiled.

"I simply wanted to restate how elevated we are for you and your mother—since the rescue."

"We?" she repeated.

"Those of us who lived in The Valley when the Deserters violated Corporate. We were all so impressed by their attempt."

"The risk or the defiance?"

"Both."

"Did you consider them heroes?"

The nod tittered. "Let's say we considered them anomalies. Very interesting anomalies."

"But if you knew about my mother, why didn't you recognize me?"

"The hackers only posted her name, not a visual."

Deceitful or ill-informed, one nod still computed as one

nod. Other nods, technicians, even supervisors might have known about her Anti origins and refrained from sharing the news—out of kindness, meanness or a combination of the two. As an Anti's child, she could no longer assume goodness motivated the majority or the minority.

For stealing from Retreat larders, she, Parish and Connie were required to admit at a special Assembly Hall gather.

Before the moderator officially summoned her to the platform, Connie rushed onstage, flailing her arms, eager to confess.

"Yes, it's true. I was in on this crazy scheme from the get-go. Me and Parish and Luce. Desperadoes to the bitter end."

Parish rolled her eyes. The recording nod wasn't recording, Luce noticed.

"So I hunkered down in the bushes," Connie shared and demonstrated, riveted by her own moment-by-moment accounting. "And I said to myself: 'Chum, this is it. Now or never time. You've made your bed. You've cast your lot.'"

"We've heard enough, dear," the moderator finally interrupted. "We have all the information we need."

"But there's more! A lot more!" Connie argued.

"Maybe some other time, dear."

Parish delivered her brief remarks in such a clipped, no-nonsense manner she might have been sharing a meal menu.

"I offered to collect the food, and did. A friend needed help, and I gave it. A Recovered will always search out a parent, regardless of rules and regulations."

As instigator, Luce confessed last. "It was my conception," she acknowledged. "I asked for assistance. I approached Parish and Connie."

Although truly sorry she'd gotten her friends in trouble and alarmed the nods, she didn't regret her own actions. Given

Sleep

the chance to reconstruct that slice of the past, she would have changed nothing because Parish's explanation was also her own. To find her mother, she had to lie and steal and did.

But even that minimal, rote apology was cut short by Maud, charging the podium, screeching and shaking her fist.

"You can't punish a kid for visiting her mother!"

From the back of the Assembly Hall, the Deserter contingent agreed. Claps, whistles, Cook's bright white kitchen-staff hat flagging in support.

Startling and wonderful, the Deserter defense, but totally unnecessary. The residents weren't a vindictive group. They listened politely to the charges, the Recovereds' statements, Maud's bluster, and in the end passed the lightest of sentences: a week's probation for the ringleader, shorter probations for Parish and Connie, none of those reprimands carrying an isolation clause.

She could and did continue to sit vigil by her mother's bed.

Bathed, medicated, a feeder in her arm, Rosa remained in the infirmary. Her eyelids twitched, her heart raced, her toes curled and uncurled, but the eyes beneath those twitchy lids stayed blind to outside venues. The med technicians insisted the shut-out was neither organic in origin nor irreversible. A case of mental resistance, they diagnosed. When Rosa J felt ready to respond, she would. In the meantime, she slept. Recuperatively speaking, that inclination was all to the good.

On the off-chance that strategy changed without warning, however, Luce planned in advance. Once Rosa J felt well enough to wake and ramble, they'd tour the compound, including all the public and private cubbies of Luce's world—bedroom, drafting desk, Valley lookout post. Between excursions, they'd relax in the sunny courtyard and discuss a wide range of topics. Nothing would be forbidden. Bit by bit they'd find out more about each other: likes and dislikes, similarities and differences. Bit by bit they'd bond.

The majority of Recovereds couldn't understand why she wasn't satisfied simply to have Rosa J in residence, even if the commander did continuously sleep. No other Recovered had ever found her mother, much less a mother with followers.

"Besides, the thief is sort of like your mother too," a trainee in Deprivation pointed out. "I mean, she's always shouting advice."

But not about The Valley—or life there. Without exception, the Deserters shared a "good riddance" attitude toward their former residence.

"You've never considered going back?"

"To stay?" Maud snorted. "Never."

"But it was your home."

"Under duress."

"And even now, after all this time, you aren't the least bit curious?"

"Whatever's going on down there, I don't know and I don't care."

Don't know. Don't care. It didn't mesh with the typical anarchist credo, and Luce said so.

"Spoken like the young spore you are."

"I'm not that young."

"Young as they come," Maud dismissed.

More willing to reminisce while he created, Luce trailed Cook around the kitchen, serving as his roving taster.

"More butter or more cream?"

Whatever she answered, he added extra doses of both ingredients as soon as the other cooks turned their heads. "As camp cook, I didn't get to stir much. Too few ingredients. It's a very satisfying activity, stirring. I didn't realize how much I missed it."

—Stirring, he missed, but not The Valley. The Valley he missed not a whit.

Occasionally Parish or Connie sat with her as she watched her mother sleep, kept her company while she waited for the opportunity to ask if Rosa J hated The Valley too—that and other questions, so many, many others.

"Is that the way you'll look—advanced?" Connie inquired.

Would she? The woman who dreamed next to them had skin that seemed more carapace than flesh. Rough, buckled, craggy. Thus far unresponsive to the oils and emollients the nods assiduously applied.

"The days are getting warmer, brighter," she reported to her sleeping mother.

Outside The Retreat's walls, birch trees budded; leaves, big and tiny, began to overlap. The courtyard turned green, bees swarmed, the walking trails sprouted touch-me-nots, trillium, bluets, weeds; wandering vines curled into thickets of rhododendron and laurel; redbud branches hung heavy, lined with blossoms primed to explode. Honeysuckle turned spring into a scent as well as a vision.

And still her mother slept.

"Winter's over," she whispered into Rosa's ear. "You can wake up now."

Maud said: "Give your mother some leeway, kid. She hasn't had a good sleep in 20 cycles. She'll wake up eventually and when she does you'll be here. She's not going anywhere and neither are you."

Parish was less sanguine. "And what happens when she

does wake? She'll probably think you intend to punish her. For abandoning you."

"And what's wrong with that?" Connie charged. "I'd love to punish my mother, wouldn't you?"

2

As Luce entered the cafeteria, Connie blindsided her from the right.

"Where have you been? I checked your room and everything!"

"In the infirmary," she warily replied. "Why?"

Connie beamed. "You know that skinny Deserter? The repeat guy?"

She didn't say "yes." *Know* had become a complicated proposition as of late, packing a PRIME-size load of conflict.

"When I found him in the courtyard this morning, talking to himself or the sky or whatever, he was alone. No nods or anyone else around. Can you believe it?"

With Connie, always, you had to factor in buildup; it couldn't be bypassed.

"So, quick as a bat, I interrogated him! Can you guess about what?"

"I'm not really in a guessing mood, Con."

"Okay, okay, I'll spill anyway."

She had no doubt Connie would do exactly that.

"I said: 'Hey there, Mr. Repeat, resident to resident, what's the REAL Deserter story?' No maneuvering, nothing subtle, just straight-out TELL ME. TELL ME NOW."

"And?"

"And THIS."

Handing over the micro-tape, Connie imitated a drum roll.

"Wise-cracker of me to record it. You'd never accept it from my lips. Beyond skewed."

But Luce did accept the tape from Connie, gingerly, as if it might detonate.

"Attend! You almost dropped it! Don't you *want* it?"

How to explain? In her new lexicon, *want* had become as fraught a term as *know*. She'd quizzed the Deserters about The Valley, but not the Deserter story, longing to hear Rosa's version first.

"You're waiting on your *mother*? The mother who trashed you? The woman who might still be sleeping this time next spring?"

Alone with the tape in her room, she paced, trying to sort through a jumble of desires. Repeat's account would be Repeat's account: one that might contradict her mother's, foul an explanation, a vindication, she'd been forever desperate to hear. But for once Connie's take was sensible. Why continue to wait on the mother she'd been waiting on all her life? Her opportunities might be more limited than she'd imagined. Her options might be Repeat's version or none at all.

Twice, straight through, she listened as it had been recorded. The third time she recalibrated, filtering out Connie's yips, Repeat's noisy breathing.

"Come on. The *real* Deserter story," Connie urged and, in his way, Repeat obliged.

"*One should be careful into whose head one gets.*"

"*The truth, my friend, is always incredible; it becomes believable only when diluted with lies.*"

Full strength, dilution. State your preference. Speak up, speak up, we haven't got all century.

Or have we?

"Cold is good," Commander Rosa says. "Cold keeps you awake."

Don't like the policy? Welcome to leave.

Bye bye, comrades, bye bye.

PRIME, PROs, the underground—we've left those already. Seven of us. No, eight. No, twelve. No, seventeen.

Our claim to fame? We made a man soil his pants.

Oh, those were the days.

Are we agreed, comrades, on the heroic act of insurrection? The storming of the corridors of technological presumption?

Details to cherish:

Soft hands, still soapy.

(Yes.)

In the very act of re-zipping his fly.

(Yes, yes.)

A blood bath in the corridor, but did he notice?

(No, no, a thousand nos!)

Only begged for his own life, the bastard. Begged and pleaded and got it back, got a farting hero's welcome while his kidnappers fled to exile, ennui.

"One can perhaps be a hero without understanding what is happening."

But can one remain sane?

("Hear that?"

"It's nothing."

"Listen!"

"It's nothing."

"It's never nothing," says Commander Rosa.)

Move, keep moving, continue the march back to dust, to hell: "a limit situation." And take heart, my comrades, take heart: "War is the most ancient of religions and it will be the last."

Eventually she gave up, quit straining to decipher a version that would always remain a muddle, its narrator disinclined to tell it straight.

Leaning back on the pillow, she closed her eyes, disappointed but not entirely surprised. She could still, she supposed, resort to auto-suggest. In theory, finding her mother in actuality should have freed up some dream space, allowed the possibility of other quests. In theory, if she willed it, she could broaden her search to cover more than a Deserter commander.

"Deserters plural," she chose as her hypnotic prompt, repeating that phrase until it slurred.

What at first she interpreted as bright light turned into the whiteness of all-surround snow. No visible prints ahead or behind, including her own. Each time she stepped, her previous step dissolved as if it never was, never had been. In the white cosmos, whenever she paused, there was no noise. Whenever she stopped breathing, there was no life. A fixed and frozen set and then: something new. A thaw.

Snow melt. Ice drip. A steady runoff trickle that floated her closer and closer to the surface of dream, urging a trip to the flusher. Neither entirely awake nor fully asleep, she stumbled in the direction of the communal washroom, untied the bottom half of her resting pulls and squatted. To keep the grogginess from catapulting her forward or backward she held on to the flusher's lid, leaned a shoulder against the partition, and pissed an endless stream. Pissed and dozed and pissed some more, trying to image her body back in bed, dispense with the necessity of the arduous journey in reverse. No success. So she gave the reins to memory, let blind instinct be her guide.

A mistake.

Almost instantaneously she slammed against something that grabbed.

New terror mixed with old as she collapsed to the floor, scrambling madly backward on her hands and knees. But what she saw when she dared look was no cassandra per se, just a being who could have passed for a walker: flesh suitably pale, his gift the gift of prophecy. All he lacked was a diaphanous shroud.

Repeat, she processed, immensely relieved. *Only Repeat.* No one who wished her harm. Simply the cause of another accidental collision in another nighttime hallway. Tomorrow, a bruise, at most, would commemorate impact.

From the floor, she smiled weakly.

"For a mini-moment, you spooked me," she said.

Rocking back on his heels, he whistled, expelled a great gush of air as did she, falsely assured her trauma had ended.

Recited for an audience of one, the tale he chose to share was brief, pitiless and excruciatingly blunt. Not a tape, not a garbled sequence she could pretend to misunderstand. Firsthand, not secondhand, advice.

"A real mother is just a habit of thought to her children."

In the sleep palace, one daughter disagrees. She searches in snow, in PRIME, in dreams—hungry for filler. She wants Commander Rosa to reveal the past: that mystery, that death.

"What do you want from me?" the commander demands. "A tale? A wish? 'A parlor trick to make the world disappear?'"

But at story's end, it was the storyteller himself who vanished, weaving his way elsewhere as she cowered in one of the world's forgotten corners, sobbing into her knees.

3

Around Parish, Luce didn't have to pretend. Angry, sad, angry and sad, she could act the way she felt. In Parish's room, she felt sheltered—from everyone.

Regularly now, behind closed doors, Parish aired her sleek, virtually hair-free scalp. Only a few sprigs of bangs remained. Today the bandanna looped around her neck.

"In case a nod happens by."

"Positive plan," she endorsed.

None of Parish's plans qualified as "negative." Her calculations always incorporated the expected and the unexpected, left little to chance.

Since Parish flopped onto the floor mat, she flopped too.

"How about you? What's positive with you?"

When she shook her head, Parish grunted. It sounded remarkably like a Maud grunt.

"What about Connie's tape?"

"I couldn't really decipher it."

"Could Connie?"

Luce shrugged, picked at her knee, several times swallowed down what felt like a rock in her throat.

"But I heard another tale. Last night. Directly from Repeat."

"And?"

"He thinks I'm asking too much of Rosa."

"Of your own *mother*!?! What does he know?"

"He knows Rosa."

Parish reached out. For a moment they held hands glumly,

then Parish gave a shout.

"I've got just the thing to elevate you!"

From its hiding place beneath the mat came a wide sheet of scratch. A schematic of The Valley in all its labyrinthine glory.

"Mega, isn't it?"

"Did a narco give you this?"

"Better." Lovingly Parish smoothed the map's folds and crumpled edges. "But you never heard me say so."

Together they traced an elaborate web of thick, black lines that met, split off, re-intersected.

"And that's not all," Parish said, pushing aside the closet drape.

Behind the row of pulls hung a replica of The Valley uniform: sleek, tapered and shiny.

"Absolutely official Zip-Alls. Step in!"

"Could I?"

"*I* do, every night after lights out. They're really clingy. But efficient."

Indeed. With one zip Luce was in; with another, out.

"Ultra-mega!"

"Anytime you're in the mood for a fashion change," Parish invited and both giggled.

Hugging good night, they giggled still. Giggling helped. So did the hug.

When Luce entered her mother's chambers, Maud glanced up from the food tray but continued to stuff and chew.

"Utensil clips aren't really designed to handle serious meat," she garbled. "But feel free to congratulate me on my attempt to eat civilized."

Maud still routinely shunned the easy-digest menu to the detriment of neither her digestion nor her sleep. But the gorging had "broadened her beam," as she put it. Since the nods found Maud near the food lockers, her mother's lieutenant had grown fatter by a third.

"Try this. You look like you could use a protein jolt."

"Gratitude, no," she said, settling parallel to her mother's shins.

"If anything changes, I'll come for you. No need for both of us to stay round the clocker."

When she didn't instantly respond, Maud leaned in, inspecting.

"What's this? The chatterer's gone mute?"

"It's just . . . hard sometimes. Waiting."

Hard, but the established norm: Rosa existing, holding court, in a state of suspension, breathing but silent, keeping her distance, remaining as inaccessible as she'd ever been, a cipher who'd once lived in the mountains and now passed her days and nights sleeping in The Retreat's infirmary.

But she shouldn't have proclaimed that hardship.

Maud's brow bunched; with a Deserter's rough manners, she shoved aside her tray and freed her hands to drive home her pique with jabs.

"Plenty of food, plenty of sleep, plenty of clothes, plenty of friends. A *severe* trial, I'd say."

"That's not what I meant."

"No?"

"No!"

Maud sucked her teeth. "Charming."

"What?"

"This tendency to RETRACT when someone SCREAMS at you. Where's your farting BACKBONE?"

"Cease, Maud."

"A first-class whiner, kid, that's what you're turning into.

And a cowardly one at that."

"I'm not whining. I made an observation. Can't I voice an observation? It's my life too."

Apropos of nothing, Rosa's arm jerked to the side, suspending her feeder, and snatched at the air above her head. A med technician scurried in, shushed their squabbling and scanned for signs of wakening.

"Dream spasm," he eventually declared and returned to his exterior monitor.

The break in the argument seemed to have snuffed it. Fine by Luce. She'd never yet won an argument with Maud.

"Cheer up, kid. The longer she sleeps, the less likely she'll wake grouchy."

"Is she usually grouchy?"

"Wouldn't you be? Living in farting snow?"

"In The Valley—was she grouchy then too?"

"No time for grouchy in The Valley."

Maud returned to slurping and crunching. Luce's own stomach began to heave.

"Connie taped Repeat," she blurted.

When Maud hooted, food sprayed on Rosa's bed cloth.

"Doing what? Telling his new Founder story?"

"The Deserters' story, actually."

Again Maud hooted—with less eject, but Luce moved her chair anyway. Maud wasn't finished devouring.

"Couldn't understand a word of it, am I right? A bit of a challenge, Repeat's stories, until you get used to the style."

"I've also talked to . . . the others."

"And?"

"And I know about your dagger fingernails. And Repeat's stutter. And Valley E-screen comedians. The terrible jokes they told."

"All true." Maud licked both thumbs. "So who'd want to live in a place famous for dreadful comedians?"

She felt her face go hot.

"Now you're teasing me."

"You need teasing, night and day and then some. Go back to bed. Eat a meal. Draft a few dreams. Whatever. I'll stay with your mother. And I promise, if she opens her eyes, you'll be the second to know."

On her way out, passing the technician's monitor, she turned for one final Rosa check. Via that boxed screen she watched huff-and-puff Maud plump Rosa's bed pillows, smooth the rumpled covers, retuck the kicked bed cloths—each of those tender ministrations more suited to a nurse than an Anti.

"So what if your mother turns out to be a killer?" Parish had speculated weeks ago. "In the bigger scheme, she's just your mother. Nifty to meet, maybe, but not *you*. What she did and all that, it's past tense. Not her future and definitely not *yours*."

Despite being a legitimate Recovered, Parish always tilted forward, not backward.

More and more, Luce admired that orientation, envied its courage.

4

Time seemed to move at slug-speed or a fraction thereof. Every day felt like ten, every night one hundred and ten.

Connie's Deserter passion subsided, bottomed out. On her current Archival sneak-ins, she binged on prison info, fascinated by chain gangs and homemade shivs. From ripped pulls she fashioned a pair of leg shackles and wore them surreptitiously knotted around her ankles, camouflaged by her regular pulls. Parish had also developed a new enthusiasm: a recent transfer named Benedict.

"I cornered him at Transfer Orientation. He's a certified yakker," Parish reported. "There's *nothing* about The Valley he won't spill. For instance: Corporate guarantees an apartment to anyone who works off PRIME. Anyone. So you don't have to worry about finding a place to live. It's provided. Can you imagine? Your very own apartment!?!"

The new recruit also taught Parish Valley jokes.
"What's the worst sin you can commit in The Valley?"
Luce frowned, thinking.
"Sloth," Parish said. "What's the second worst?"
"I guess I'm not programmed for this."
Parish grinned. "Continued sloth."

In a twisted way, that *was* a giggle. But Parish seemed to find it funnier—maybe because she was in the chat loop and Luce wasn't. The gabber confided in Parish—Parish's discovery, Parish's contact, Parish's new friend.

Lately, Luce had been seeing a lot less of Parish, Connie too. When she bothered to show up at the Dream Lab, her supervisor, with no trace of a gulpy chuckle, excused her with a wave of his hand.

"Scat. Be with your mother. We can manage without you."

Apparently everyone could manage without her. And manage quite well.

Whiner, coward, Maud had accused. *Unlike your mother,* the implication. The only fault that blemished Rosa J's perfect heroine record: giving birth to a whining coward.

Dismissed from the Dream Lab, disinclined to return to the infirmary, she wandered the courtyard, exited via East Gate. Already the morning chill had turned toasty—the return of cotton pull weather. Outside the compound, the new season had broken open the landscape, thickened it. Not that long ago, the trek to the lookout post had seemed such a strenuous undertaking, a semi-bold adventure. Now the distance seemed negligible, the destination almost claustrophobically close to The Retreat and all who dwelled within. Even the stench of ragwort seemed radically diminished, a minor offense to the nostrils, compared to the foulness of a Deserter camp. As a receptor she'd obviously changed. But had anyone, besides herself, noticed?

Between crisscrossed blossoms, she recognized a swatch of Parish's back, sped up, started to call out before the greeting clogged in her throat. At their exclusive lookout post, a place they'd never invited Connie or any other Recovered, Parish sat huddled with someone else.

"Luce? Is that you?"

She couldn't, despite the inclination, crouch behind rhododendron forever.

"Salutations," she sheepishly offered, stepping forward, brushing at the petals caught in her hair, looking only at ground. Into that frame of vision walked Parish's slip-ons, joined by a newer, longer, un-scuffed pair.

"Mega coincidence! This is the exactly where you two should meet! Luce, this is Benedict. Benedict, Luce. She's hooked on Valley too."

Flushing, she glanced up to see a short man, shorter than Parish, with a cap of black hair and pointy beard.

"You're *Luce*?"—as if Parish had mispronounced her name.

"Yes. Luce," she confirmed, formally raising her palm and placing it briefly against his. "Soothing to meet you."

But it wasn't soothing. It was awkward and tense and queer.

She felt painfully embarrassed, inside and out.

"Amazing," he said.

"It *is* an amazing spot, isn't it?" Parish agreed, grinning toward The Valley. "Luce and I think this is the primo primo lookout. Don't we, Luce?"

Used to think; after today, that preference might shift.

"I have to return . . . to the infirmary."

Parish pivoted. "Don't leave yet! The infirmary can wait."

"Do you sleep in the infirmary too?"

Why had he added that word: "too"?

"*Luce* doesn't sleep in the infirmary. Just her mother. Her mother's a Deserter."

"And you're the commander's daughter."

No one had referred to Rosa as "the commander."

"Luce, look." Parish pointed. "See that little squiggle to the right? That's the quadrant listed on my chart. I'd totally miscalculated my location, but Benedict corrected me."

"Were you born in The Valley? Like Parish?"

She hesitated. "No."

Again Parish explained. "Luce was born in the mountains."

"But not at The Retreat," the inquisitor pressed, listening to Parish, watching her.

"The Deserters lived in the mountains too. In exile," Parish supplied.

The information didn't seem to surprise. Everyone else who heard that detail for the first time reacted with surprise.

"See that fork?" Once again, Parish peered and pointed Valley-ward. "If you veer to the left there, eventually you cross a path that leads directly to the streets. Isn't that accurate, Benedict?"

"More or less. The Valley isn't unreachable."

Parish clapped. "Hear that, Luce? *Not unreachable.*"

"Born in the mountain wilds but raised as a sleeper," Benedict said about her but not exactly to her. Then he burst out laughing.

Parish whirled around, suspicious at last.

"What's jolly about that?"

"You'd have to be a Valleyite to understand," he said.

Parish rubbed her naked crown dreamily, as if it were a talisman. "Then we'll just have to become Valleyites, won't we, Luce?"

5

Following mid-meal, she returned to the Dream Lab, determined to work a shift, needing to. Her supervisor should have needed her to do the same. Dream activity levels at The Retreat had spiked, the chief assistant divulged. For several weeks, a record number of night narratives had been pouring in, requiring the lab crew to labor throughout the afternoon to accommodate all session requests and log the collected data.

"At this rate, we'll fill two databases by cycle's end," the chief assistant said. "Then I can retire."

Luce didn't recognize that word: "retire."

"Old word, old concept. Basically it just means rest," he explained, fidgeting. "Anyhow, be forewarned: the next dreamer is a handful in more ways than one."

—Another confusing comment.

"She's already shuttled between here and The Valley a dozen times this season. Hates both locales, loves to gripe—which you'll discover as soon as she opens her trap. *Mouth*," he revised. "Apologies. I tend to forget your improbable youth."

Chances were she'd have disliked Transfer #734-A-10 without the prompt. Transfer #734-A-10 wasn't a woman who strived to be liked, or cordial.

"I'm in dream overdrive," the selfsame snarled, slamming against the E-screen console. "The second I doze off, I'm inundated with images. And don't think I don't know exactly why. It's because *they're* in residence. The non-traditionals. They're infecting my dream space, cluttering it."

Luce sat up straighter, stiffer.

"Are you referencing my mother?"

Transfer #734-A-10 harrumphed.

"Your mother and her *kind*. Deserters, Antis—call that element what you will. Any manner of change disrupts sleep patterns and plots. Your supervisor said so himself. And even if you are genetically linked, as a drafter you're obligated to confirm my thesis."

"Dream drafters can't confirm *or* deny."

"Nonsense. It's part of the job descript."

"It's *not* part of the descript."

"Oh? Is *arrogance*?"

"Shall we begin?" Luce countered sweetly.

As soon as #734-A-10 departed, with a single keystroke, she deleted not only the dream classification she'd so obligingly, obsequiously, entered but #734-A-10's entire dream chart as well.

"Ta ta" as Connie would say. "Toot-a-loo."

If caught, she'd lie. What was a lie, anyway? Just another chunk of what the truth couldn't be.

She was still trashing code when the next dreamer unceremoniously barged in. She recognized him first by his still too new and un-scuffed slip-ons. When she looked up, she looked again into a stare.

"Salutations."

"Nice cube."

He took a seat, stretched his legs in front of him.

Already deviant once this afternoon, she indulged a second rash impulse.

"So you know the Deserters?"

"Doesn't everyone?"

"Know them personally, I mean."

Instead of clarifying, he pumped her: "Parish says you saved your mother's life."

"It was Maud who saved everybody, not me."

Ever so slightly he hissed. "Ah! The amazing amazon Maud."

"Are you Maud's friend?"

"I wouldn't flag it friendship."

"But you're acquainted? From The Valley?"

"We've met," he sparred—supremely noncommittal.

"She's not quarantined, in case you'd like to visit."

"The lieutenant is preoccupied with the commander. She doesn't have time for old acquaintances."

"I could inquire, if you'd like. Facilitate a chat."

He ignored her offer, stroking the hair that extended his chin. "Quite the jolt, I'd imagine. Finding your mother after so many cycles."

She didn't contradict—why bother? Connecting with a lost parent qualified as a legitimately shocking event. The reaction didn't distinguish or brand her, by any manner or means.

The measured stroking continued. "It certainly buzzed me. The commander doesn't exactly broadcast maternal."

That line sounded rehearsed, but Luce, too, had been rehearsing.

"Why do you call Rosa 'commander'?"

"Isn't that what she calls herself? An Anti commander?"

"I have no idea what she calls herself. I've never heard her speak."

A disruption, a noisy one, interrupted their jockeying. Any disgruntled transfer might have instigated the mad banging, but the particularities of the accompanying nasal complaint strongly suggested the return of Transfer #734-A-10.

"I demand admittance!"

"Calm yourself, madam."

—Her supervisor's voice, minus the leavening chuckle.

"Who's the horn?" Benedict nonchalantly asked, glancing toward the door.

"Step aside, supervisor. "

"You will *not* interrupt a session."

"I most certainly will. A missing file trumps dream bilge. You've got an insurrection in your quadrant. That Anti brat trashed my contents."

"We will investigate the purported misplacement of your file. Until then—"

The door jerked open. Her supervisor valiantly grabbed hold of #734-A-10's vibra-belt, but couldn't control her trajectory. Just back from The Valley, she weighed at least fourteen stone. If Benedict hadn't lifted his foot and sent #734-A-10 sprawling, that considerable mass would have landed on its intended target: the dream drafter.

"Sincere apologies, Luce," her supervisor said once he, two assistants, Benedict and a waiting dreamer had combined forces and successfully wrestled #734-A-10 into the arms of a squadron of nods. "As of today, she is banned from the lab."

"Bloody lunatic," the chief assistant muttered, rubbing his collarbone.

The supervisor un-twisted his lab coat and finger-forked his mussed hair.

"Apologies to you, sir, also. Please proceed with your drafting session. You will not be disturbed again. You have my guarantee."

"Whatever the fart that's worth," Benedict said and laughed.

Luce would have liked to share his hilarity, but felt too

skewed to indulge. No one had ever tried to attack her before. Then again, she'd never deliberately deleted a dream file.

Reluctantly she rolled back to the E-screen and pressed re-start.

"Gratitude, Benedict."

"No need to gratitude me. She's a Valley plug. I should have kicked her when I had the chance."

"A plug? I don't compute."

"Be elevated you don't," he said.

They sat for a moment without speaking, she concentrating on calming, he—on what?

By degrees his sneer turned moodier, nastier.

"So: *my* turn to dream code?"

"Draft," she automatically corrected. "At The Retreat, we call it dream drafting."

"And I just . . . commence?"

"Whenever you wish."

Instantly he hunched forward, pressed his face into his cupped hands, spread his fingers, his expression hidden from her and the room.

"I'm on a street. An empty street, except for the devilish wind. It's an all-out battle just to stay upright."

Following that rushed beginning, a lengthy pause.

She made a hasty judgment. Primary content: wind war.

"A woman is coming toward me, also buffeted by the wind. I can't at first see her eyes, just her lips. We're about to pass each other when a gust slams us together, hard. I try to push away, but she's not helping. Instead, she crushes tighter against me, pressing my rod. Unzips what's left of my Zip-Alls. Exposes herself."

Behind the mask of fingers, he began to pant.

Copulation dreams were rare at The Retreat—or rarely reported to junior drafters. Embarrassed, she concentrated on the E-screen, its counter-hum.

"That's when I start shaking her, slapping her. Because I want those wild eyes to see me, focus on *me*. But she doesn't care who I am. *If* I am. Bitch leaves me dripping on the street."

A soft, nod-knock.

She coughed lightly. Benedict dropped his hands.

Behind the message nod, Repeat bobbed and weaved.

"Further apologies, but visitor Maud requests your presence in the infirmary, Luce. She insists that I convey her message as spoken: 'Tell the kid to get her skinny butt over here NOW.'"

"'The desires that connect beginnings and ends make of the middle a charged field of force,'" Repeat added as Benedict's chair travelled steadily backward, away from the E-screen, into the corner behind the door.

In her mad dash out, she almost clipped his elbow, almost toppled a monitor nod, snubbed a transfer and his query, but once within the vicinity of infirmary she abruptly stopped, stayed stopped.

Maud found her moored to the floor in the tech anteroom, holding her elbows, breathing through her mouth.

"*Finally.* "

"Cease, Maud."

"Cease what? When you go in, go light on the dramatics. Agreed?"

"Agreed."

Maud moved aside and still she hung back.

"What's this? You've been yakking at her for weeks. Now you don't know what to say?"

How to explain? With Rosa's eyes closed, there was still a

distance between them, a shield. Standing in front of a mother awake, she'd be utterly exposed.

With a sharp jerk, Maud flung her forward, inward.

"Commander, there's someone to see you. That relative I mentioned? She's here now. She's arrived."

Sleeper-slow, as if fighting brutal opposition, Rosa J turned in their direction.

"Luce," Maud introduced. "This is Luce."

The wan face receiving that information seemed neither impressed nor particularly intrigued. The reply, pushed through a throat adjusted to, accustomed to, silence, sounded like a nail scoring metal.

"I don't know any Luce."

"Look again, Rosa," Maud scolded.

Instead the commander shifted, re-closed her eyes.

"Rosa! This is your daughter!"

But the commander continued to twist away, clearly communicating her preference: better a blank wall than a daughter's face.

6

Rosa had accepted her death, welcomed the expiration. Then she woke, alive, breathing, her body stubbornly determined to breathe on and on.

Another disappointment for an ex-Commander. Another mission thwarted.

"Are you awake, Rosa? Rosa? You *are* awake! You can't bluff me."

Relentless Maud.

The feeder in her arm convinced her the PROs had made a pact with the gods of air and dirt and RAM: we'll revive, you punish.

"Usually your daughter's here, glued to your bedside. Counting every heartbeat," Maud vouched.

A vague but anxious presence, waiting, watching. She'd felt it, assumed it was Maud.

"Part of the time it was me. But when it wasn't me, it was her."

"It was you when I opened my eyes," she argued to postpone what she hoped forever to avoid: meeting a person she'd already monstrously failed.

White coats and gray robes circled in, reset monitors, straightened bed cloths, congratulated.

"Such lovely eyes! It's so wonderful to see them sparkle."

The clangy insistence sounded Valley, but the lilt threw her. Too optimistic, too gushily supportive.

Out of the side of her mouth, she demanded of Maud: "Am I in custody? Are you?"

"Up for a chuckle? We're here under house protection, not house arrest. The sleepers have offered the Deserters sanctuary—for as long as we care to sponge."

But how did "sanctuary" translate? What precisely did the sleepers demand/require/expect in turn?

Maud gave her no chance to ask.

"I've sent for Luce. I vowed I would."

She shook her head.

"That's what the sleepers named your daughter. Luce."

She shook her head again, kept shaking it as Maud disappeared, reappeared, nagged, bullied and shoved forward a being who resembled less a daughter than her own past self.

Except for the mole. Rosa's mole sat to the right of her nose. This Luce's mole sat left—like the first abandoner's.

Too much to endure, that merging of then and now.

"Congratulations, Rosa," Maud lashed upon return.

"Leave me alone."

"Mind gaming, tough testing your own daughter."

"Leave me alone."

"Not until you explain yourself."

"Explain what? You drag a sleeper kid in here . . ."

"Not a sleeper kid, *your* kid. She asked to see you. As soon as you deigned to open your eyes."

"So I could invite her to tea?"

Maud glared, circled the bed.

"To talk."

"Apparently she's already been talked to. By you."

"She wants to chat with her *mother*. The girl scaled three thousand feet to find you—and, believe me, sleepers aren't hardship-trained. Speak to her, Rosa. For your sake and hers."

She tried to make the noise bubbling in her throat sound like a snigger.

"I don't have a 'sake' left, Maudie, and neither do you. For a while we had frostbite. Now we don't even have that. We have THIS."

She kicked viciously at sleeper swaddling, tucked ever so tight.

Maud threw up her hands.

"Your daughter wants to know."

"Daughters want fairy tales."

"Then correct the fairy tale."

"She's a sleeper! She couldn't stomach Deserter dreck."

"Maybe, maybe not. But that's her problem, isn't it?"

She cut her eyes. Too casually, Maud leaned against the bed, arms folded.

"Doing the dare trick, Maudie?"

"Let's make it official, shall we? Lieutenant Maud dares Commander Rosa to spend an hour with her own flesh and blood."

Valley-fat, Valley-clean Maud. Pushing, shoving, demanding, commanding.

"Since when do *lieutenants* give orders?"

"File it, Rosa. I KNOW the story, remember? I KNOW the history."

"And which version would that be? The one where we're the good guys or the bad? The exalted or the doomed?"

"Every story has a warp. Luce isn't after definitive. She's looking for a version she can live with."

As if such a thing existed. As if grossly incompetent Commander Rosa could summon it, even if it did.

Tired of the conversation, tired of looking at the delegate Maud, she turned back toward the wall.

"That may dissuade the kid, but it won't gag me. I don't care where you stare, but you'd better listen."

"Advice from a sleeper convert wearing sleeper finery. A walking, talking ad-scam."

"I'm wearing what there is to wear."

"Enjoying it, too."

"What's the matter with you? You've got a bed and food and no E-screen. You've got a roof over your head and walls between you and winter. Your comrades are alive and for some reason the sleepers think we're miracles of science, worth defying an Anti List for. You've got a daughter who'd worship you if only you'd let her. Nobody's starving in farting snow . . ."

The blast of anger she'd counted on surfaced wet.

"I thought you'd abandoned us," she said when she could. "I thought you'd deserted the Deserters."

"It was either me or Repeat. We couldn't both clear the wall in time."

"A sleeper wall. The sleepers you agreed never to raid."

"You were dying, Rosa. We all were."

"Then we should have died. Let nature take its course."

"If so-called nature had taken its course, The Valley would have killed us long ago." Her hands jiggled, her lips quivered. She couldn't control either. "What's happening, Maudie?"

Her former comrade came, sat, wrapped her in a Maud-size hug.

"You're still tired. You haven't entirely recovered."

"A Recovered. That's what she's called here, did you know that? One of the white coats enlightened me when you ran after her."

"It's just a word. There are worse words."

"Sometimes, when we were hiking in circles, hiking just to be hiking, hiking nowhere, I'd think: *cold, hungry, insane and none of it worse than being a Saver save."*

"The situation's different here."

"Is it? Maybe every stray feels the same. No matter where she's raised."

"I don't believe that."

"Why would you? You weren't a stray. You had what the übertexts called a 'standard-issue family set.' Unique among Deserters."

Maud didn't challenge that snipe, but she got up, walked as far as sleeper glass.

"They keep their courtyard snow-free—just like Valley streets. A strange ritual for the wilderness, don't you think?"

Hardly could she shill for tradition—but Maud could.

"When you arranged to meet them, that last time, before we . . . left."

"Just ask, Rosa. Forgo the preface."

"Would you do it again, given the chance?"

Maud shrugged.

"I only saw my father. Maman didn't come. Too ashamed, too afraid, too angry, who knows? Once I was reclassified Anti, Corporate reneged on her promotion."

"But still you tried to see her."

"She was my mother. Maybe still is."

"Maudie?" Her voice had gone to pieces again. "If my parents turned out to be alive, do you think I'd want to see them too? Even though they're total strangers?"

Maud sighed—whether in sorrow or defeat, she couldn't decipher.

"It's a natural impulse, Rosa—or used to be, once upon a time."

7

Rolled toward a courtyard blasted with sunlight, Rosa wasn't ancient but looked it, felt it: bony-kneed, wheeler-bound, swaddled in lap cloth, exhausted by the upcoming inquisition even before she suffered it.

Craning her neck, she tried to see ahead, beyond the cavalcade of strolling robes.

"So where is she, if she's so eager?"

Maud pointed. "Up ahead. Lax."

The intervening years hadn't reshaped the scenery. Same stone benches, same spiraling path, same shimmery pond. Only her dream rendition distorted this setting, insisting the water plunged deeper, suggesting the danger, or promise, that running, someone could stumble, fall, splash, founder, drown.

"There she is," Maud proclaimed. "Exactly where she promised."

Luce/cut loose. Such a wicked sense of irony these cultists must possess.

In a sleeper infirmary, white as snow but warmer, Maud had praised: "You should have seen the kid, taking fall lines like a farting mountain goat." A kid used to clipped hedges, accustomed to pathways so smooth they scarcely jarred a wheeler's wheel.

"See her now?"

Had Rosa's own skin ever been that smooth? Her teeth that clean? Her eyes that clear? Had any reflector she stood before at fourteen, twelve or eight zinged back such well-being?

Never. She was a Valley creature, born and bred.

Abruptly Maud spun the wheeler, parked it, forcing its occupant to squint up at the duo above.

"Gratitude for coming," her daughter began, with such deference, in such a timid hush, Rosa tensed. Did the sleepers teach quiet talk? Punish kids for exuberance?

"Fresh air, sunshine. Precisely what the commander needs," Maud boomed.

"Are you . . . fully comfortable? "

Again Maud interceded. "Who wouldn't be? Out here with the birds, bees and breeze?"

"I just meant . . . if it's too bright or . . . otherwise . . . taxing . . ."

"She's staying put and so are you!" Maud vetoed, vanished. Maud, who should have stayed too, who'd spent time with this Luce. Knew her. Liked her.

Her daughter's hand strayed upward, brushed a cheek that instantly flushed. It had been a long time, a very long time, since Rosa had shared company with anyone capable of the subtleties of blush.

"What?"

"Yours is on the other cheek. I hadn't realized—"

"Can we shift to the shade?" she blurted.

The glare had begun to remind her of 24-Valley bright.

As if she were as fragile as an uncooked egg, her daughter rolled her gently, gently to a cooler spot.

"Is this . . . satisfactory? There's another arbor, up ahead. If you'd like to compare."

"This is fine," she said, aware of the word's peculiarity in her mouth, on her tongue. When last had she used the descriptor "fine"?

Beneath a canopy of whispery green, she twiddled with

the lap cloth, reluctant to launch into an apology that, started now, extended past sundown, would barely cover a tenth of her transgressions.

"It doesn't have to be *perfect*," Maud had coached. "You're having a conversation, not giving a lecture."

But if her admission/confession/conversation fell short of convincing—what then?

"I was a little rough—before. When you came to see me in the infirmary."

"I understand. It must be difficult to replay."

Such unexpected kindness, such undeserved good will. How should she respond? Choc-coat or speak candidly, crudely? Truly an elder, she'd have a glut of stories to choose from. As it was, she had only two: Pre-Anti and Post-. Her life wasn't an arc; it was a split. What could she share? A color wheel of blue E-screens, black bats, yellow flamer fire. Counsel from a spoiler, and a sham.

"Not difficult so much as pointless."

"Apologies. I don't mean to pressure you."

—As if pressure, that tripwire, hadn't always ruled a Valleyite/Deserter's existence. But how could a sleeper child hope to understand the insatiable demands of a tyrant E-screen, the endless struggle to catch up to and surpass a floating finish line?

"Maybe if you started by describing your life down there?"

A suggestion, not a demand.

"You first: Maud says you're some kind of drafter."

"A dream drafter, yes."

"Must keep you occupied here where the dreaming never stops."

"I have free units, too. For research."

"Sleep research?"

Another blush/flush. "That, and Valley research."

She shifted her gaze, counted statues: one through eight. Finished, she counted again. The other kept talking.

"But it's been frustrating, conducting research on modified PRIME. There are . . . gaps. Not all the reports make sense."

Why would The Valley make sense up here? It hardly made sense square in the middle of its networked belly.

"A lot of the details don't connect."

"And never will," she replied, suppressing a hiss.

"Did you always hate it?"

That earnestness Maud spoke of. A big bald breakout.

"For as long as I can remember."

She expected, tensed for, the next question: "And did your hate serve murder or did murder serve your hate?" It didn't come. Something had distracted her daughter, drawn her attention beyond the statues, toward another veil of green.

"A friend of yours?"

"No. Not a friend. I thought I recognized a recent transfer."

"Aren't there dozens of those out and about?"

"Out and about, but not spying."

Before she'd slept a million cycles and yearned to sleep a million more, that word would have electrified every strand and half-strand of hair on her skull. Now she slumped lower in the cushioned wheeler, blinking and yawning, blatant proof of at least one Valley credo: to give in to sleep was to give in to an uncontrollable longing. No amount was sufficient. No amount thoroughly satisfied. A little induced the desperate urge for more.

"Is there a problem?"

"I don't like being watched—that's all."

Then bypass The Valley, kid, she could have said. *ALL ACCESS/ALL THE TIME is a two-way contract.*

Could have, didn't, dozing.

"Were you bored, living in The Valley?"

Jerking awake, she heard herself laugh. The sky immediately joined in, cackling too.

"'Bored' doesn't compute in The Valley."

"That's what Maud says."

"What else does the lieutenant say?"

"That Valley workers 'ache for boredom' and the 'farting leisure' to hear themselves think."

"Sounds like a Maud rant."

"But what about workers who start opposite? People who have too much leisure? People who've already thought every thought in their heads in triplicate?"

"Spend a little time with her, you'll see," Maud had predicted. "Once you get past the sleeper veneer, she's as stubborn as you."

"Some thoughts are worth repeating," Rosa replied, half in jest, half to remind herself the young couldn't fathom the tedious repetitions ahead. If they did, they'd bail by twenty.

"You said before that you hated The Valley. Did my father hate it too?"

Father?

Did a single perky sperm rate the title? Fleeing the E-screen, fleeing bats, she'd run into something human, someone who responded. Two minutes, five, and the deed was done. A random incident in a far too ordered universe. If the seeder's face registered during the moment, no memory of it lingered. Nor were the specifics revived by the visual prompt at her side. Luce of the sleepers looked more like a clone than a merger.

"Your father was a stranger. I didn't know his name—or ask."

As glassy and vulnerable as a doe's, the eyes that took in that remark. But Maud claimed this Luce of the sleepers wanted to hear, ought to hear, the whole callous, sordid, absurdist tale of Rosa J, Deserter.

"I was a stay-awake maven. Do you know what that is? Has your Valley research turned up the joys of a stay-awake high? There were days, the vast majority of days, when I didn't recognize my own image, much less anyone else's. Until you popped out, I wasn't entirely convinced you existed."

"But I did exist. I *do*."

"Here. You wouldn't have lasted in a Deserters' camp."

"Are you saying you gave me away to *save* me?"

She grimaced, shook her head, infinitely ashamed of being credited with so noble a gesture.

Funny, sad, pathetic, really: an ex-commander willing to admit to drug dementia, indiscriminate sex, non-maternal instincts and a host of other foibles but wary of confessing her most consummate desire.

She took a ragged breath, close to weeping, closer to gagging. Even as a private thought, the sentiment now seemed ridiculously grandiose.

"We were trying to save the world, Maud and I and the rest of the Deserters. The whole farting world," she said and heard, in response, the whole farting planet guffaw.

8

In Luce's new dream script, her mother roamed the globe, plucking up countries and oceans, stuffing them under her arms, swaying with the burden of world care. She tried to steer clear of the dream frame, a single unimportant daughter, but her neediness was too immense. She couldn't help pestering the woman otherwise occupied, couldn't stop clinging to the crusader's silver tunic, wouldn't release the bed cloth even after she jerked awake, hair matted, dripping drool.

If she didn't ask now, she might never ask the one question whose answer truly mattered.

The infirmary's lone occupant was kicking, not clutching, bed cloth, throwing off its touch. From that irritant, Rosa turned toward her, the intruder in the doorway, recognition conveyed by a slowly curling lip.

From some deep, internal warning system, an urgent message: *better the back of a mother's head than a lip curl.*

"What? You haven't heard enough about my worthless life? You've come back for gorier details?"

This isn't about you, Luce couldn't quite manage to declare. *This is about me.*

"Have I guessed wrong?" Rosa hectored the silence. "Is this some sleeper rite of passage? Burst into your mother's room/stare/bond?"

She sucked air, low on oxygen, held to the back of the bedside chair.

"Why didn't you terminate? Why bother having me?"

"Ah, yes. The mega question," Rosa replied, as if amused.

But not looking amused. Looking fierce and vicious.

"I've been wondering the same myself. Here's my theory. See if you agree. We're part of a gargantuan cosmic joke spun thus: Mother has daughter. Mother deserts her. Daughter locates mother, imagines mother will be eternally grateful. Mother is anything but. Quite the punch line, no?"

Longing for, inventing, a parent, never once had Luce envisioned a being who despised her, someone whom she'd grow to hate in turn. An inconceivable emotion implacably true.

How long would she have kept on hitting what wouldn't strike back?

From behind, Maud grabbed and trapped the battering fists, flung her like an empty sack toward the wall, shielding the commander from further daughter abuse. Yelling, cursing, spitting Maud and Rosa, silent as stone, curled in a ball, cupping her ears.

"Get her out! Ger her the fart out!" Maud ordered the nods streaming in, robes billowing in every direction. As did everyone, the nods obeyed Deserter Maud, scooping up the assailant, stroking her hair, her face, chant-lying in perfect harmony:

"All will be well. All will be well. All will soon return to smooth."

9

She was treated with stoic patience—even after she refused to self-sign the admission scratch, repeatedly broke from their clutches. Again and again the nods returned her to her new bed in Observation, tucked the bed cloth, brewed a tea relaxant, held her hand and murmured until at last she fell into a mercifully dreamless sleep.

A different routine but a routine all the same eventually established itself. A schedule like any other.

Awarded special clearance, Luce's supervisor visited.

"Do you mind a few questions?" oh so delicately he asked.

How could she, who'd so long searched for answers, deny that request?

"This dream that upset you. Can you estimate how long it continued, after you unhooked the night cap?"

"Apologies," she said tearfully. "I'm not sure."

He patted her shoulder—kind, considerate, but obviously disappointed. At every turn she disappointed someone else.

Connie sneaked in to see her after lights out.

"Trust me," she said, casing the place with a filched beamer. "This is mega better than the Deprivation set-up. Over there, they only wake you for meals."

Parish also got in—how she didn't disclose.

"The rumors I've heard! Did you really bloody your mother?"

Luce turned to face the wall, her mother's avoidance tic.

"I don't remember any blood."

"Understand: I'm not criticizing. Maybe she needed

bloodying."

"Whatever she needs, it's not me," she said and teared up again.

"You got along without her before. You will again. You will, Luce."

And how exactly would she manage that? By resuming the orphan life? By acting as if she had no parent in theory or in practice, even with Rosa in residence? By accepting the loss of Maud as her ally, now that she'd alienated her too?

Maud hadn't visited—to forgive or rebuke.

"I won't be able to work at the Dream Lab because I can't be trusted to facilitate soothe. Fresh dreamers are vulnerable to upset. They scar easily. It's the first caution listed in the drafter manual: *don't agitate.*"

"Then you'll assist elsewhere," Parish said.

"Where? I don't have the skills to be a technician or the patience to be a nod. What will I do here? Day after day, night after night?"

Parish glanced at the door, edged closer.

"There is another option."

When she leaned to whisper, Luce could smell the choc on her breath.

"You're . . ."

Parish nodded. "Everything's arranged."

"With Benedict?"

"I don't need an escort! How complicated can it be? You just follow the slope. Downward. Anyway," she said, "Benedict's gone. He left days ago."

"Then you're really . . .?"

"Primped and packed."

"But not tonight! You're not leaving tonight!"

"Tonight or tomorrow night—depending on your decision."

A nod entered with a dinner tray.

"Salutations, girls."

"Salutations," Parish said and cagily smiled. "And a restful evening to you."

"Gratitude, Parish. Luce, dear, how are *you* feeling?"

Amazement, panic, or both wiped blank her mind.

"Very well," Parish chimed in. "Luce is feeling very, very well."

The nod smiled, closed the door; Parish settled cozily on the end of the bed.

"You don't have to decide instantly. It's early yet."

She grabbed hold of Parish's pulls. "You won't just leave, will you? Before I decide?"

"Of course not. And just in case, I'll double-hoard choc-sticks between now and then."

When, in the fading twilight, the technician came to check her pulse, it raced—as if she were already in flight from The Retreat.

"The technician says you're very agitated, dear," consoled the follow-up nod.

She tried to will her face pale, her hands steady, cease visioning The Valley, desist from projecting herself poised on the rim of its light and speed.

"Perhaps you'd like a calmer?"

"I'd rather calm on my own."

"Certainly."

Auto-calming was by far the preferred remedy.

Without her vibra-belt, she couldn't be sure when final meal officially started or ended, but she estimated. As of now, Parish might be stashing choc-sticks, making the final preparations in her room—a space she'd never again inhabit. Would the scratch map come with them? Maybe they didn't need it? Maybe Parish had already memorized the locations of street corners and E-screen terminals. They wouldn't pack extra pulls because Benedict had sworn Corporate provided Zip-Alls. They'd be travelling lighter, faster, than she and Maud had travelled uphill in snow. If they couldn't locate Benedict immediately, Parish knew the coordinates of a backup destination: a kind of welcome center, she said. A Valley portal.

From the bed view, night pushed and shoved and conquered the sky, squeezing out every molecule of light.

The Valley was never full dark, Parish said Benedict said. Something somewhere always glowed.

"Speed-glowed," Parish elaborated.

High praise.

10

Rocked back in a chair outside Rosa's room, Maud cracked each knuckle twice, appreciating the ease of sentry duty in sleeper time versus dreamer time. First plus: in the reality of sleeperville, nodders and techers shared the responsibility of guarding a mother from her daughter. Second plus: she could order snacks.

The segregation—without exception—of Rosa and Luce had been her idea: a wise one, self-flattery aside. She'd browbeaten the sleepers until they'd conceded the point. Recent events supported the caution. Surprise visits led to outbursts, outbursts to fistfights. Both parties needed a cool-down interval. In due course, the kid's skill at translating Rosa rhetoric would improve. She'd learn Rosa's ways, and Rosa would learn hers. With a modicum of joint effort, they could still reach some sort of understanding if not an all-out truce. There was time and plenty of it. No rush in sleeperville.

No rush and a generosity spookily transcendent. Thus far she'd filched, lied and made a lying filcher out of one of their own, and yet the sleepers not only took her back, they took her advice, welcomed her mates, extended charity in lieu of retribution, tolerated the Deserters' eccentricities, accommodated her own flat-out refusal to coil a vibrating snake around her waist and various other rebellions, large and small. The only casualty? Rosa's purple lip. And that inflicted by a daughter, not a nodder, not a PRO.

"Ha-loo," she called at a stroll-by techer.

"Yes, visitor?"

"How's Luce recuperating?"

"Shall I check for you?"

"Don't bother. I'll roam."

If she didn't drop by soon for a friendly chat, the kid might assume she was nursing a grudge.

Repeat agreed to sub as guard, but preferred to stand on the chair rather than sit.

"'If a brother, expelled from the monastery through his own bad conduct, desires to return, he must first promise amendment of the fault for which he left it.'"

"Traitor squawk? A little late in the day for that kind of comment, isn't it?"

The squawker went mute.

"Back in a wink," she promised.

Outside the observation quarantine, she encountered Connie, spinning in circles.

"Were you whizzing like that in front of Luce? No wonder the kid stays agitated. You're worse than a screen prompt."

"I can't *find* Luce! She's not here or in her old room or the Dream Lab or the cafeteria or the Assembly Hall or the courtyard or anywhere else. And she needs to see something I . . . she needs to . . . come with me . . . somewhere."

"The nodders have probably taken her for a morning stroll. Settle! And quit clawing at your neck. You'll give yourself a rupture."

In a version of compliance, the wild child began to yank at her ears.

"This Luce must-see. How about you show me first? Then—*maybe*—we'll reveal together."

Whatever had set Connie spinning, it required a Deserter's vetting. Not every detail of Anti life had penetrated these monasterial walls and wouldn't, if a lieutenant could prevent the seepage.

"Sneak *you* into Archives? Before I even square it with Luce?"

"Would you rather I 'square it' with a nod? Recovered found archiving—third offense?"

"Snot!"

"Exactly—lead on."

However, on the excellent chance that Connie proved as schizy at hacking as message delivery, Maud took the precaution of swinging by the infirmary and crooking a finger at Repeat: a good sentry, a better hacker. The nodders could safeguard Rosa for a little while if the commander refused to safeguard herself.

In the airless Archival chamber, Maud and Connie shared an E-screen; Repeat swayed behind them.

"If you can't retrace the access route, Repeat will take over."

But Connie wasn't listening, otherwise engaged.

"'The dread account book is the mind itself. There is no such thing as forgetting.'"

Connie's fingers fumbled.

"Lax. Repeat's right, you haven't forgotten. Concentrate and retrieve."

Stunning but true, once sleeper Connie did lax into a rhythm, she deftly overrode a second-level security code and cracked Category 00 files, cruising the circuitry like a farting veteran.

"It's somewhere in this batch. I didn't notice the title, but I'll definitely recognize the frame."

A squeal of excitement, followed by a plea:

"*Please* don't tell Luce I scanned a second time."

Lieutenant Maud had no such scruples. She scanned. Intently. The initial cam shot featured an empty Valley street. The first figure to appear, a woman, swerved—but not from gusting Valley winds. Chemicaled, no question. From the opposite direction, another aimless figure shambled into focus, a shaggy Terminated from the look of him, neither character a videogenic star. Because of wind or a drug-spaz or both, the two collided, grappled, then fell in tandem against the entry bar of a tube link.

Maud reached across Connie, tapped "pause," then "resize." Rosa's magnified jaw, Rosa's frantic eyes. Indisputably Rosa. Two frames farther along, she tapped pause again. When Rosa's enlarged face and cunt twisted away, the commander left exposed her partner's glistening privates.

Fart!

Maud knew that stick too. And now she recognized the face as well: hairier, crazier, younger Seven. The bastard Seven.

"I'm not viral, am I?" Connie squeaked. "They're who I think they are, aren't they?

"That depends who you think they are," she replied in as flat-line a tone as she could muster.

"Luce's mom and that recent transfer, Benedict. That's who they look like to me."

She meant to point at the frozen screen, but struck it instead. "You've seen this man? Here? At The Retreat?"

"Haven't you?" Connie squeaked again.

"Get up," she ordered. "Get up, get up!"

Shoving Connie aside, she took over the keys herself. Ex-comrade Seven had followed them to The Retreat. He'd been here, shadowing them. Just as he had in the mountains. Watching. Spying. Reporting. Of course the farter was reporting. Why hadn't she realized?

"What did you call him? WHAT DID YOU CALL HIM???"

Sleep

"*I* didn't call him Benedict," Connie counter-screeched. "That's what he called himself."

Benedict. Of course. Too farting apt.

Behind her, Repeat began to chatter his distress. "'I have been ungratefully treated by a set of men who, void of principle, are governed entirely by the private interest.'"

As she entered and exited menu after menu, file after personal file, Connie tapped on her shoulder.

"How did you do that? Wait! Do that again!"

"'I am confident of satisfying the world that the charges against me are false, malicious and scandalous,'" Repeat brayed.

The Benedict personal stats were buried deep: informer deep. Labor as she might, she couldn't circumvent the final encrypt.

"Repeat, get us in."

If the man could stagger-virus PRIME, he could certainly bypass a PRO lock.

"'The first rule is simply this: live this life. Abandon attempts to achieve security. They are futile.'"

He typed in sync with his chatter.

"This is so . . . MEGA!" Connie cooed.

"There!" Maud shouted as the screen flashed Seven's profile.

Benedict Z. Terminated. Former occupation: Data weed. Last official residence: Apartment 1285DW. Contact point: Vicinity, North Sector (5) tube station. Successfully recruited: 08.07.63 A.M.C.

"Doctored?" she asked—the last possible slim-to-none chance of disproving what her gut already accepted.

"'To look for what is not told is the adventure.'"

Repeat-lex for nada.

Dick for brains a farting PRO! Recruited FOR that dick. Clearly under PRO orders to infiltrate a Deserters' camp, bang their commander, throw tantrums, stalk off, report. Between Seven and a string of well-timed up and down Decoratives, Corporate had been monitoring their rebel ranks as closely as they tracked glitch scanners in employee cubes. The PROs didn't *need* to eliminate the Deserters; they had them penned.

Every fat ounce of her heaved.

"Execute that sequence again, please?" Connie begged. "Because if I saw the maneuver twice, I'd remember."

"You're absolutely certain Luce hasn't seen this?"

Connie gawked. "You mean accessed it on her own? Luce isn't an Archives junkie. She wouldn't know how."

"Keep it that way," Maud grimly ordered.

"But will you demonstrate the final bypass? Just once more?" Connie whined, trailing them to the door. "I'm a speed-demon learner. Honest Injun, I am!"

11

Dressed in the gauzy gown of a sleeper, Rosa left her bed tomb, surreptitiously opened the door, expecting Maud's red head to be stationed beside it like a fuzzy alarm bell, but the guard chair stood empty, no red head or wide rear in the vicinity.

How convenient. Must be snack time.

Although the nods who pirouetted aside looked vaguely troubled by her up and about-ness, none objected. No sleeper would *dream* of instigating a quarrel. At most they suggested an "alternate course."

"May we supply you with anything, visitor Rosa? Are you having difficulty resting?"

Smiling taxed her swollen lip. Regardless she smiled and kept smiling as she explained the desire to "stretch her legs"—a phrase the Savers had taught her to deride. Physiologically, no one who sat at a desk needed a "stretch her legs" break, the Savers maintained. The request, and its practice, amounted to unconscionable shirking.

But, but, but: the sleepers readily bowed to that excuse and its feeble logic, inquired no further. Nothing sneaky required about giving the slip in sleeper land.

She meant to find Luce's room. See it, smell it. Not the site where her daughter now recuperated, her former quarters, the place where, in private, she'd dreamt of rescue by a mother savior.

A nod, make that a nodette, offered salutations in passing.

With the charm of a flea she requested directional assistance.

"I've been searching for quite a while," she coaxed.

"I'm not cleared to reveal."

"Don't angst. I can keep a secret. I'm very good at keeping secrets. We'll make this our secret, yours and mine. Which way?"

Reluctantly the other pointed.

A thoroughly utilitarian room, utterly devoid of charm or excess, as impersonal as any standard Valley apartment. Entering, she wondered if all sleepers' bedrooms looked this drab and plain or if plainness marked only the quarters of a Recovered—decor reflecting stigma.

A window, a closet, a dreamer's cap, a bed—neatly made up, all creases smoothed away. Beside the dreamer's cap lay a pad of scratch. She picked it up, scanning for something, anything, written in her daughter's hand. But the pages were blank, the pad unused or stripped of recorded entries. In the closet hung several copies of a sleeper's uniform, the hangers methodically aligned above three pairs of soleless slippers.

If her daughter walked in and found her, how would she begin? Was she even capable of clarifying what ought to be made as plain as this plain little room?

"You only believed you wanted your real mother because you imagined a perfect mother and called her real. You only assumed being raised by me would have been preferable because it wasn't your fate. You only yearned to hear about the past because the present had already shown you a blood relative unworthy of affection. And for all that I am truly sorry. If I could have spared you every disappointment, including the disappointment of myself, I would have. I would now. But I can't. The done won't undo."

She returned to the bed, wrinkling the covers, mussing

its neatness, waiting for the chance to deliver a speech that needed to be voiced but would, in the final accounting, alter nothing. The abandoned seek out the missing, obsess on fill-in, desperate for a storyline, a logical history, that progresses A to B. In a Saver ward she had pursued the same, fanatically tracking every parental reference, major, minor, traitorous and obscure—all in quest of an explanation that didn't, ultimately, exist.

As the door slowly opened, she held on to the bed, licked her puffy lip.

At the sight of her, Maud barked, but quickly adjusted. Maud always adjusted. Nothing startled Repeat because anything and everything that happened had happened before.

"Just as well you're here. Alone," Maud began enigmatically.

"I'm waiting for Luce."

"Before we discuss Luce, there's other news."

She hoped her scowl looked more impressive performed by a defective lip.

"No more 'news'."

"Yes, Rosa. This is information you need to process."

"'It is a truism: there are only two basic plots: one, somebody takes a trip; two, a stranger comes to town,'" Repeat hinted.

"Repeat invaded a PRO file—Seven's. His Valley tag is Benedict. He signed on with the PROs *before* he signed on with the Deserters."

Her purple lip blew out a laugh.

"A whiny PRO. Good cover."

Her merriment, she sensed, lacked company.

"Rosa. Look at me."

When she did, she faced rage as fresh as dandelions. Ole

trusty Maud, still able to bitch and bluster, defend the honor of dishonorable Deserters, ignore the comedic ironies of this latest factoid revelation.

"And he's been here, in sleeperville, hawking us too."

"Has he now? And where is the whiner currently holed up? In which cushy sleeper corner?"

Maud glanced at Repeat.

"We knew to hack into the PRO file because of a video, circa '20, old count. It came from a street cam. You were in it. So was Seven. And his prick. I'd guess the PROs used it as leverage."

So Corporate had a video of her fucking. They probably had a video of every employee fucking.

"And?"

Again Maud glanced at Repeat.

"Luce's friend recognized him—which probably means Luce met him too. Could be Seven arranged an introduction."

"To turn her into a Valley fink? Isn't that stretching a bit? Even for a Valley op?"

"Are you still *asleep*??? The Valley can exploit an Anti's daughter in a thousand ways!" Maud exploded. "This is bad schiss, Rosa! Very bad."

But was it bad—or entirely predictable? The daughter of a drone becomes an Anti; the daughter of an Anti chooses drone.

The keening at the door spilled inside. Another sleeper urchin.

Connie, Maud called that teensy sprite.

"She's not in Parish's room and neither is Parish! And now the nods are searching the compound, the grounds—everywhere."

"What's in your hand?" Maud accosted. "Relinquish!"

"I found it in Parish's room. It was . . . almost . . . hidden. Beneath the floor mat."

"Do you see this, Rosa? Do you see what it is? A map of the grid, north sectors five through nine."

From sleeper vantage, that trench must appear a gleaming showcase of spectacle, a glimpse into a neon-ed promised land. She could understand how her daughter, how anyone's daughter, would be drawn by the dazzle, the faux beauty of perpetual buzz.

"We have to find Benedict," Maud ordered—who?

"But he's not here either!" her new, young comrade squealed. "The nods said he'd left the compound a while ago."

"They've followed him to The Valley," Maud growled. "They followed that bastard to the farting Valley!"

"It might not have been his idea. Their descent," Rosa said and Maud looked at her with the same incredulity that followed commands to hike in snow.

"Of course it was Seven's idea! He *lured* them!"

She shook her head. Now Maud was fretting about stick; imagining Seven had designs on a kid—her kid, his desire warped by nostalgia. But Seven wasn't a pervert; he was a pawn. A desperate Terminated who'd made a tradeoff not wholly to his advantage. Didn't Maud remember? Terminateds did what they had to do to survive, including living in snow and eating wood rat. It wouldn't be Seven or any other person, PRO or Anti, who corrupted her daughter. The Valley itself would manage that feat entirely on its own.

"Give it up, Maudie."

"Rosa!"

"Give it up. She's gone."

V

Her PRIME supervisor was almost always complimentary. Graded online, she'd never yet fallen below Excel-minus.

Batch 86559?

"Completed," Luce voiced.

Batch 9Z1000?

"Completed."

Batch reflux?

<u>Nil</u>, she typed.

Sometimes she preferred to key rather than talk aloud alone.

Lately, she and Parish communicated, visited, mostly via screen. Sometimes she'd get a twinge, remembering their cafeteria and lookout chats, but since Parish could break into her script at will, it was almost as if they computed side by side.

The last time Parish co-opted visual, she'd been sporting visors.

All the cool beginners wore old-style shades, Parish informed, showing hers off in 3-D, funning with old-style model poses. Gnawed, degenerated, missing a stem, semi-melted—the condition didn't matter. Shades were mega, according to Parish. Parish kept current with all the latest updates—on PRIME and on the streets.

Fashionable, those shades, but useful too, in Valley glare. The lookout perspective hadn't prepared them for the extremity of light, outside or in. What the sun didn't provide, street amps did at every corner. Their work cubes were multi-beamed, fixtures recessed into the ceiling, walls and floor, controlled by a PRIME-coded central switch. On the journey down the mountain, as soon as she and Parish reached flat lands, they'd both started to squint. The last kilometer or so, they'd unfurled Parish's bandana and held it like a tent/shield over their heads.

They giggled, sometimes, about all the things their lookout view left out. About how clueless they'd been, coming in.

Benedict, no dreamer, no one ever mentioned the rankness of deadline sweat, how it was a scent you had to get used to, like a new keypad. The odor saturated Cubicle Row, but never rose to mountain heights.

"Not that we could have smelled it for the ragwort," Parish said.

Number two on the surprise list: begging as a practice and art form. It had been all very confusing at first: the stalking, the chase, the rapidity of the demands.

"Give it/give it/give it now."

Terminateds, they used to be called. Now Corporate ID-ed that cluster: Rejects.

The first street haggards she and Parish had encountered at the intersection of Jack and Kilby pursued them all the way to the welcome center. It was like a new game, tweaked with drama. They easily outdistanced the pack, thrilled to have reason to gallop that fast. Glad and giddy they'd tumbled into the welcome center and breezed through orientation, responding to the prompts of an awesome color bar as quickly as they'd dashed through Valley streets.

In the corner of her screen, a fidget.

"All is calm," she voiced, a lex slip.

The fidget took the shape of a bat, flapped its wings.

Sleep

Maud's little ha-ha.

"Verify," the bat squeaked.

<u>You just checked a session ago</u>, she typed. <u>Nothing has changed.</u>

"But it could," the Maud bat squeaked. "At any quark."

<u>I'm okay. I'm fine. Don't angst</u>, she typed, relying on stubborn script to enforce the message.

Equally stubborn, Maud refused to offline.

"Are you . . ."

So she blanked the screen.

REPEAT'S TALES OF REVOLUTION

COMRADE SAINT SIMONE

The aching head of Simone. A busy head on a shrinking body. No wonder it hurts.

But Saint Simone is into sacrifice, deprivation. Simone with her thick glasses, her cigarettes, her curly hair, her look of a starving cat. Simone the saint, the Jew, nestled now in her Catholic/Gnostic/Greek/Languedocian heaven.

What?

A message from heaven: Saint Simone objects. "If you separate the life from the work, you stress the pettiness."

Forgive us, Saint Simone. We begin again.

Frail, myopic Simone, filling pages and pages of notebooks in her sparsely furnished, barely heated apartment. Her parents fret, take her on sunny vacations, but always she returns to her cold room, always she returns to write of the discord between body and mind, proletariat and bourgeoisie. The smoke from her cigarettes curl around her head like a halo, like a martyr's crown of thorns. Late at night, our Simone, smoking, thinking, writing: "The world is necessity, not purpose." The world that must be experienced in all its hardships, not fled, not avoided by privilege of money, intellect, connections.

Teaching at Le Puy—a grand start? Teaching in a provincial lycée with the world in turmoil? Our Simone regrets. One must get closer to reality than a desk, than a stick of flaking chalk, than obedient, powerless children. So: off to the Renault factory of piece-rate earnings, our Simone so tired, so slow, so clumsy. In the full muck of reality, who has the energy for philosophy, for theoretics?

"True, the proletariat is much stronger than it was, but so is the bourgeoisie."

All the bourgeoisie except Simone. Nervous, anorectic Simone. "The real stumbling block of totalitarian regimes is not the spiritual need of men for freedom of thought; it is men's inability to stand the physical and nervous strain of a permanent state of excitement, except during a few years of their youth."

War, that permanent state of excitement/danger/challenge, arrives in any case, and our not-so-young-anymore Simone joins the anarchist militia, marches off to the bloody trenches of Spain. Weak but determined, dedicated but ungainly Simone gives her all, slices her foot, the body always betraying the mind's resolve, always falling short.

War after war after war, always another on the heels of the last, the deadliest poised to eradicate the myopic, philosophic Simones, polluters of a monster's holy land. In the country, on a farm, friends hide that clumsy, inept, imperfect body that now stands between Simone and spiritual perfection.

"By an extreme effort of concentration I was able to rise above the wretched flesh, to leave it to suffer by itself, heaped in a corner, to find a pure and perfect joy in the beauty of chanting words."

In the country, writing, praying, late into the night, our Simone labors to discover the perfect God, the perfect church, to sacrifice her frail, inept body to.

You remember the rest: intervention by the distraught bourgeois parents. Our Simone whisked to America, fighting her way back to London, eating as little as her fellow conquered countrywomen and failing fast, failing fast. In the sanitarium the medical whiteness is almost holy, is it not? But while the body accedes to medical science, the restless, questing mind of Simone floats steadily upward.

Thirty-four years of aesthetic contemplation and clumsy participation. Dead: our Saint Simone is dead. A life's arc that starts with privilege, middles with sacrifice, ends with sacrifice. If one lacks tormentors, one can always torment oneself. But, but, but, but, BUT: Does self-torment advance the revolution?

"Documents originate among the powerful ones, the conquerors. History, therefore, is nothing but a combination of the dispositions made by assassins with respect to their victims and themselves."

COMRADE SAINT CHARLOTTE

"Marat's head in exchange for two hundred thousand others," declares Charlotte of the timbered manor house, of the minor Norman gentry.

It seems a fair exchange.

The Jacobin swine have brought the Republic lower than low; killed her beloved Gombault, abbé extraordinaire. In her mind's eye she sees him still, bending over her dead mère, administering last rites.

Twelve July, she leaves a note for Papa, begging pardon for the impertinence of leaving for Paris without permission. But Paris beckons! Paris, thick with life, commerce, hysteria, political intrigue! Paris, where Marat, that sewer rat, soaks his scaly, flaking flesh in a tepid tub and spews bravado.

"Ten years more or less in the duration of my life do not concern me in the least: my only desire is to be able to say with my last breath I am happy that the patrie is saved!"

Careful what you wish for, Jean Paul.

"To pretend to please everyone is mad, but to pretend to please everyone in the time of revolution is treason."

Not to worry, Jean Paul. You have not pleased everyone. You have not pleased the woman exchanging her prissy white bonnet for the hat of a patriotic martyr—a sassy black one, beribboned in green. You have not pleased sweet Charlotte Corday of the timbered manor house, the minor Norman gentry, even now purchasing a five-inch kitchen knife, so handily concealed in the skirts of her dress.

As you sit soaking, working over old grievances—the snub of the Royal Academy of Science, the loss of your medical practice—sweet Charlotte is scheming to reach you and your filthy tub.

The heat of the day hangs in suspension over the city. Evening falls through that heat, bounces back. Restless Charlotte cannot eat, cannot sleep, obsessed with duty to her patrie. It is her noble cause; it is her theatre.

She gets as far as the top of the stairs before Marat's fiancée blocks her way.

Monsieur Marat is not receiving.

"But the Girondists are hatching plots in Caen! I have information!" Charlotte proclaims and like magic the closed door opens wide.

"Sit, sit," invites the soaking monster. "Tell me about these vile traitors."

Such tales our Charlotte tells, fondling the hidden knife! Names names. Invents names. Wallows in exaggeration because none will be remembered. The memory of Jean Paul Marat will die with him.

"In a few days," Marat declares, famous last words: "I will have them all guillotined."

Not so fast, Jean Paul. You who are so indifferent to ten

years of life approach the final stretch.

With a smug little smile, our Charlotte rises from her chair, the moment at hand. It is a little knife but ample. One thrust pops a hole below the clavicle and the tub bleeds red.

What? Is the man so rhetorically willing to die now screaming for help, screaming TREASON?

Our Charlotte ducks the flying chair but neglects to bite the hands that pin her breasts, proud to be caught, proud to be identified as the assassin of Marat.

At the trial: mass skepticism. This wee woman? Dreaming up such a master plot by her lonesome? It is an impossibilité.

"I have never lacked energy," our Charlotte reminds, offended to the core.

"And do you think you have killed all the Marats?" the court inquires.

"With this one dead, the others perhaps will be afraid," she answers.

And that is that.

Guillotined in the scarlet shirt of the assassin, Charlotte of the timbered manor house, of minor Norman gentry.

COMRADE SAINT JOAN

Saint Joan, the farmer's daughter.

You remember little Joan, who heard voices, the voices of St. Michael, St. Catherine, St. Margaret? A trio of saints, directing her beyond her father's fields, beyond the village, all the way to royal courts. Joan, the farmer's daughter, in line for sainthood herself, but not before a few missteps, not before some serious pain.

Saints alive! What's a daddy to do with a daughter who acts like a son? Joan can ride, Joan can run, Joan can drive a sword, given one. Joan can soldier as well as any man.

"Run off with the soldiers and I'll hunt you down and drown you myself," Daddy threatens, in his cups, overburdened by sorry livestock, blighted grain, a daughter too plain to attract a bachelor's offer.

Sit back, Daddy. Take a load off. It's out of your hands. The tide of history is headed for your village and your wide-faced, illiterate tomboy.

The dauphin in his curls is skeptical, and why not? A maid before him, dressed unmaidenly, the queer light of fanaticism in her eyes. Come to help him, says she. Come to restore him to a throne rightfully his.

(But wait: what's this? Another story about a woman on a divine mission? Can't a woman, just once, lust openly for me/mine power?)

Not our Joan: God's ambassador, dauphin's liege.

The dauphin considers her proposition, of course he does, covetous of me/mine power, suckled on it. A not unattractive proposition, he concludes, but why?

A) Because it's odd;

(Dauphins, bored with pomp and ceremony, are intrigued by oddity.)

B) Because the farm maid dresses as a man;

(Dauphins approve of cross-dressing.)

C) Because regaining the throne of France seems worth the niggling expense of arming one fanatic.

(Dauphins, being dauphins, cherish their cash.)

Vanity and greed fund Joan's divine mission, but so what? Vanity and greed have funded many a revolution.

Headed for combat, the virgin Joan permits no licentiousness, no loose talk or foul language among her troops. On the trail to glory, maid Joan holds those frustrated boys in check, and when at last they vent, at Orléans, at Patay, they win.

But enough triumph, suffering awaits. Her luck has to turn, has to, after the coronation at Rheims: otherwise our Joan will never make saint. A rough road, that road to sainthood. But down it she goes.

Captured by the enemy, soldier Joan becomes martyr. Abandoned by her troops, her country, her dauphin and most cruelly by the trio: Catherine, Michael and Margaret. The voices peter out, the microphones shut off. God may have a plan, but He's keeping it to himself. The Brits have a plan, and they're willing to share. Let the French clerics burn the bitch!

Ah.

In prison she accepts a bit of bread soaked in common wine, nothing more; prepares no defense in her head because it is her heart that leads her, her heart and her ears.

"You claim to have received direct inspiration from God?"

Oh yes, Joan says—for a while.

Then a worm of doubt wiggles its way into her prison cell, cozies up with the rats, the piss-soaked hay, the foul detritus of the caged. Long and hard our Joan prays for guidance, but her line to God and the saints crackles with static, the connection shorts, the signal disappears. Uninstructed, our Joan loses courage, conviction, zeal.

The clerics huddle, condemn: talks like a heretic, smells like a heretic, is a heretic. Worn down by worms, rats and static, our Joan agrees.

You blame her for wavering? She was a soldier, not a scholar. Her forte was action, not rhetoric. She was a follower, not a leader, at the mercy of an offline God. Don't get pissed with Joan. The clerics goofed too, issuing a sentence of life imprisonment. Didn't they realize? With or without God's blessing, a soldier must die in battle. Bravely.

It didn't take long. The heretic Joan recants, leaves the clerics in a pickle. If a heretic deserves life behind bars, an unrepentant heretic deserves . . . what?

Something . . . hotter. Something to singe the flesh right off the bone. So they decide, so it is done.

But.

Questions to consider apart from the sensationalism of shooting flames:

Did that second flare-up of courage carry our Joan through her last campaign? Or did that worm of doubt ride shotgun to the stake? And when that dry kindling began to snap, crackle and pop, when our Joan's toes turned the color of sun, did the saint-to-be look up or did she, in all her pained and wretched mortality, in woeful regret, look down?

VLADIMIR & EMMA: A Marching Ditty (with Echoes)

Emma left A-mer-i-ker
(Emma left A-mer-i-ker)
V.I. Lenin welcomed her
(V.I. Lenin welcomed her)
She had questions, doubts and fears
(She had questions, doubts and fears)
Then what the fart you doing here?
(Then what the fart you doing here?)

Len-in
(Len-in)
He's pissed
(He's pissed)
Len-in he's pissed—AT HER!

Are my comrades in the clink?
(Are my comrades in the clink?)
For saying that your methods stink?
(For saying that your methods stink?)
Anarchists in Russian jails!
(Anarchists in Russian jails!)
New Yorkers tell fantastic tales!
(New Yorkers tell fantastic tales!)

Len-in
(Len-in)
He's pissed
(He's pissed)
Len-in he's pissed—AT HER!

Tell you what my Emma dear
(Tell you what my Emma dear)
I know a way to get this clear
(I know a way to get this clear)
You go to the countryside
(You go to the countryside)
Talk to peasants far and wide
(Talk to peasants far and wide)

Uh-oh
(Uh-oh)
She did

(She did)
Uh-oh, she did—THEY SAID:

Fat cats, brutes and swindlers—whee!
(Fat cats, brutes and swindlers—whee!)
That's all a peasant ever sees
(That's all a peasant ever sees)
They promised us more bread and land
(They promised us more bread and land)
They promised us a helping hand
(They promised us a helping hand)

They lied
(They lied)
They're crooks
(They're crooks)
They lied, they're crooks—FART THEM!

Emma wept and Emma wailed
(Emma wept and Emma wailed)
This really is beyond the pale!
(This really is beyond the pale!)
What happened to our liberties?
(What happened to our liberties?)
This revolution's not for me
(This revolution's not for me)

Oh me
(Oh me)
Oh my
(Oh my)
Oh me, oh my—BOO HOO!

COMRADE SAINT ROSA

Red Rosa, Red Rosa.

What a worker that Rosa, another who died to save us. Rushing here, there and everywhere, organizing this, organizing that, addressing crowds who clapped, addressing crowds who jeered. Rosa, Red Rosa, plotting and scheming to save the huddled masses yearning to breathe free.

You recognize the rhetoric: from unshaped clay, Rosa the sculptor tries to sculpt unity, victory, progress.

But so much to do, so little time to do it! Establish the Polish Socialist party, spearhead the German Social Democratic party, inaugurate Marxist Spartacus.

"Where great things are in the making, where the wind roars about the ears, that's where I'll be: in the thick of it, but not the daily treadmill."

Oh the horrors of that daily treadmill! Eating, sleeping, rising, falling, nausea, fatigue, dependency, despondency. Avoid it, Rosa! Agitate, girl! Keep those hard eyes bright, that snappish mind snapping. Keep that fist raised high in the air! Storm those podiums! Sway those masses! Do your stuff!

"The world is so beautiful in spite of all the misery and would be even more beautiful if there were no half-wits and cowards in it."

Catch a whiff? A little petulance oozing forth? A bit of peevishness seeping through? Can you guess the curséd reason? In-fighting. Red Rosa is up to her neck in in-fighting. Every cause suffers the same. First there are the for and against. Then among the for, the for and the not-so-for: the for with qualifications, the hesitantly for, the somewhat for, the almost for. Gradations, distillations, the slide to rank apathy. It galls our Rosa, indeed it does. She is sick, SICK of namby-pamby cohorts, and quite soon she is relieved of them.

In her solitary prison cell, Red Rosa dreams of mass uprising, a tide of humanity pouring through the streets. She reads the natural sciences, feeds wrens and magpies.

"I teach them, my sole audience, the most revolutionary ideas and slogans, and then I let them fly away."

But once out, once the bird feeding falls to others, once she returns to the podium circuit, Red Rosa takes her quarrel public. The revolutionary leadership has failed, Red Rosa proclaims loud and clear. The revolutionary leadership is kaput. The leadership must be created anew.

And with that rallying cry, Red Rosa burns her bridges, plunges headfirst without a safety net. Pick your favorite doom analogy. All apply.

"Remember: to be human means throwing one's life on the scales of destiny."

Prophetic words.

Red Rosa's sad destiny?

Abduction and arrest by nationalistic bully boys. A brief stop at the Hotel Eden (cruel moniker). A rifle butt blow. Unconscious travel in a speeding car. A gunshot through the brain. The Landwehr Canal.

Red Rosa, once an orator, now food for carp.

The bully boys laugh, party, get cited for failing to report a corpse, for disposing of said corpse illegally.

But never mind, never mind.

"Many corpses in a row
and now Rosa's.
Many corpses in a row
and now Red Rosa's too."

COMRADE SAINT ANGELINE

Food for thought. Saint Angeline's rotten apples. Rotten to the core.

"Reject those rotten apples, however golden they appear," instructs Saint Angeline and the women of The Valley agree.

Her distracted technocrat husband off to lower case corporate; her sullen children off to school. And Saint Angeline left—with what?

Boredom, comrades, and a primitive keyboard.

Strictly to amuse—or always to agitate?—Saint Angeline spreads her fingers, begins to type:

<u>This is a story, merely a story, but one with premises worth pursuing</u>.

Into cyber, she routes that provocative teaser, sits back, smiles and waits, but not for long.

Oh no, not for long.

"Tell it! Tell it!" begs a network of bored wives and exasperated mothers. "How does it start? How does it middle? How does it end?" Requests no equally bored sister can refuse. And where, what, is the harm? Partial truths, imagined truths, fabrications, exaggerations, trafficking in the stuff of mystics and politicians, inventing on the fly, our Saint Angeline entertains the chatterers, grows fond of entertaining the chatterers, her network, her chorus, her army of collaborators.

No longer bored, not in the slightest, our Saint Angeline types:

<u>Consider these possibilities:</u>

<u>1) Eve was no myth</u>

<u>2) Eve passed on the apple</u>

3) Eve lived in a serpent-less, Adam-less, deity-less Eden
4) Eve really WAS the mother of us all.

And if, IF, these possibilities are likely, then ask yourselves:

1) What do Eve's daughters want NOW?
2) What should they demand NOW?

Has Saint Angeline any idea what she breeds?

Hmm.

Within hours, a story begun as cyber code spills onto the streets and reconfigures as graffiti. On walls, on curbs, the image of a rotten apple and beneath it a single imperious word: EVERYTHING!

A blight on the streets or a harmless jibe?

Hmm.

Homeward bound, confused children whimper and wonder; harassed, cranky technocrats grow crankier still. Where is LAW? Where is ORDER? But lower case corporate reserves judgment, intrigued by this message from the deepest interior, this succinct revelation of subconscious want.

EVERYTHING. Give us EVERYTHING.

Hmm.

Succumbing to the lure of fantasy, Saint Angeline and her chatter circle pay scant attention to corporate, their husbands or their children, too busy designing a seaside Eden where women will float belly up to the moon and soothe their own cranky souls. In their cyber dreams, Saint Angeline's circle envisions the War of the Great Divide and begins to plan accordingly.

But then a tipster, a traitor, some stay-at-home man or precocious child takes on the task, breaks the code and Saint Angeline disappears. Gone from one morning to the next. Gone without a trace but not alone. Poor Saint Angeline,

Sleep

yoked, even in exile, to her disgruntled husband and fretful child.

From chatterer to chatterer the shocking news spreads. Enraged housewives pour onto the streets, slinging apples, trampling apples, leaving the debris to rot and stink. What choice does lower case corporate have? Some force has to step in, seize control, hire a legion of PROs to wash down the streets, dismantle the apple trade, revoke the housewife exemption, ban the fruit but steal the slogan.

With just the merest tweaking, Eve's revenge becomes capital-C Corporate's.

Oh Saint Angeline! What did you enable? Not EVERYTHING, but its dwarf: ALL ACCESS/ALL THE TIME.

Kat Meads is the award-winning author of eight previous books and chapbooks of poetry and prose, including: *Quizzing the Dead* (2002), *Not Waving* (Livingston Press, 2001), *Stress in America* (2001), *Born Southern and Restless* (1996), and *Wayward Women* (1995). *Sleep* is her first novel.

She received a 2002-2003 California Artist Fellowship in fiction and a 2003 National Endowment for the Arts Fellowship in poetry. Other honors include the Chelsea Prize for Fiction, the Dorothy Chuchill Cappon Essay Award from New Letters, and the Judith Siegel Pearson Award for Drama from Wayne State University. Her short plays have been produced in New York, California and the Midwest. She holds an MFA in Creative Writing from the University of North Carolina—Greensboro and a BA in Psychology from the University of North Carolina—Chapel Hill.

A native of North Carolina, she currently lives in California.